A Matter of Time

Fergal Nally

Order this book online at www.trafford.com/08-0593
or email orders@trafford.com

Most Trafford titles are also available at major online book retailers.

Note for Librarians: A cataloguing record for this book is available from Library
and Archives Canada at www.collectionscanada.ca/amicus/index-e.html

Cover Design/Artwork: Fergal Nally
Courtesy of Combridge Fine Arts Ltd, Dublin 2 www.cfa.ie

Printed in Victoria, BC, Canada.

ISBN: 978-1-4251-7787-4

*We at Trafford believe that it is the responsibility of us all, as both individuals
and corporations, to make choices that are environmentally and socially sound.
You, in turn, are supporting this responsible conduct each time you purchase a
Trafford book, or make use of our publishing services. To find out how you are
helping, please visit www.trafford.com/responsiblepublishing.html*

*Our mission is to efficiently provide the world's finest, most comprehensive
book publishing service, enabling every author to experience success.
To find out how to publish your book, your way, and have it available
worldwide, visit us online at www.trafford.com/10510*

 www.trafford.com

North America & international
toll-free: 1 888 232 4444 (USA & Canada)
phone: 250 383 6864 ♦ fax: 250 383 6804 ♦ email: info@trafford.com

The United Kingdom & Europe
phone: +44 (0)1865 487 395 ♦ local rate: 0845 230 9601
facsimile: +44 (0)1865 481 507 ♦ email: info.uk@trafford.com

10 9 8 7 6 5 4 3 2

Also by Fergal Nally

Non Fiction

A History of Ashford Castle

A Manual of Oral Medicine

Fiction

A Matter of Conscience

Born in Dublin Fergal Nally is a doctor of medicine, M. D.
For many years he was Head of a clinical department in the
University of London and Consultant in several London hospitals.
Pain and cancer research formed a large part of his work and resulted
in many publications in the scientific and medical literatures.
He is also a Fellow of the Royal Society of Arts.

For Anne

PART ONE

1

Annette Nolan lay in the enveloping dusk--wondering lots of things. There was activity nearby, people whispering and hurried steps in the corridor. Outside, builders shouted as they finished for the day. She looked around the ward. Some patients were reading or dozing, others waiting for visitors.

Getting to the hospital that morning was hectic; packing, traffic and all the questions but the worst was saying goodbye to Patsie. She'd kissed and hugged him so much you'd think he knew. His liquid brown eyes and the way he raised his paw melted her heart. At the thought of it she cried and closed her eyes.

Dr. Nicholson came earlier and said nice things. She'd looked at him. Steadily. Not saying a word. Yet she desperately wanted to know--fear of the unknown was always the worst. Please could he tell her what was going on? Worn out and weary he looked. It must be all the hard work. She knew what tiredness was, the awful tiredness that brought her here. Dr. Sutton advised her parents that hospital investigations were necessary and he was such a good doctor. Everyone liked him and they were lucky to have him. Now she was trying to settle in and be good. Who knows? Perhaps she might even make friends with some of the children. Maybe not. And sister-in-charge was so cross. Despite that she looked forward to mum's visit. Dad couldn't make it because of an important meeting. She must understand that. And he didn't like hospitals anyway.

Still she wondered and wanted to know why.

At seven o'clock a yellow van drove into the car park. Slowly Ruth Nolan got out and locked the door with difficulty. She was nervous not knowing what was ahead. Dr. Sutton said something about Annette's blood and further tests were needed. She was admitted under the care of Professor Wainwright. Now Ruth had come to reassure her twelve-year old daughter even though she was frightened beyond measure.

Building work was going on in the hospital repairing damage caused by the dreadful fire. She found the main entrance and entered the lift to the fourth floor where the children's ward had been located. Yet she wasn't sure--signs were down to allow for redecoration. It was dark and confusing. Dust, debris and rubbish everywhere. How could they do this? A disgrace. A total disgrace. What next? She'd try and ignore it. There were more important things ahead.

The lift door opened and she stepped into a poorly lit corridor. She hesitated. The door closed behind leaving her in nearly complete darkness. Along the corridor a blaze of lights streamed out of a large glass door. She knocked. No reply. Knocked again hoping for an answer. It was really spooky up here. She was lost.

She knocked again, more loudly. Still no reply. Tried the handle. It was unlocked. She entered and closed the door. On the ceiling strong neon lights poured down. She walked past each bench transfixed. Along shelves mounted on every wall were specimen jars neatly arranged and labelled. Explanatory notes were easy to read; bone tuberculosis in a sixteen-year old female, heart of a twelve-year old male with rheumatic fever, brain tumour in a six-year old male. On and on it went. Gruesome injuries and diseases on display for all to see.

A chamber of horrors. All in young people. In disbelief she read the labels. Each specimen had a history of the patient, clinical findings and cause of death. As she walked she became more and more distressed. She ran from the room, made for the lift and pressed the descent button. After an eternity it responded and the ground floor arrived. Immediately she went to a temporary reception and asked where Annette Nolan could be found. Ward 3 A was the answer and please would she accept apologies for all the building work.

She slowly climbed multiple stairs to ward 3 A. Eventually she found the children's ward. Some parents had already arrived. She spotted Annette with a gloomy expression sitting in the corner bed near the window. She rushed over and the welcome was overwhelming.

'Is dad coming?'

'No Annette darling. He has an important meeting. Remember?'

'How's Patsie then?'

'He's fine and minding the place for us.'

Enough of this! Ruth just had to sit down and draw a breath. Her hands were shaking as she settled her coat across her knees.

The day's proceedings were discussed; what happened in the hospital, how nice the others were--except Sister Agnes. She was cross with everyone.

'Did the doctor come and see you Annette?'

Ruth felt a pulsating headache coming on.

'Yes. He's very nice. His name is Dr. Nicholson. Some tests have to be done but I'm not to worry about them. He promised to explain everything to me.'

'Oh dear.' She felt flustered. 'I hoped he'd explain things to us first.'

'He will mum. But remember I'm twelve-years old now.'

'Of course. And you're a brave girl.'

Annette was a brave girl. Always was. Probably made of sterner stuff than her mother. She knew what her mum said--exactly--and, often what was left unsaid. Her mother would give her good news with soothing words. As for bad news--that would be kept for dad to explain.

Ruth tried to change the conversation and found it difficult. News of the studio, more paintings planned by her dad. Still Ruth regretted her husband should have forgotten about his principles for twelve months with Mark O'Neil and set up his family in comfort. Who knows, they could plan a fine career for their only child once she recovered.

Suddenly Ruth's headache got worse and it became impossible to control. She trembled all over and burst into tears. Annette jumped out of bed and put her arms around her. 'It's all right mum. Don't cry. Please.'

'I can't help it darling.' She felt weak, unable to talk. Her eyes closed and tears fell freely. She groped for her daughter's hand, gripped it firmly and kissed it.

'Please Mrs. Nolan. None of this.' From the end of the bed a stern voice came. Sister Agnes stared at her. 'We can't have this.'

'You don't understand. I ... '

'I certainly do understand. You'll not only upset your daughter but also the others in the ward. We can't have this at all.'

'Please no. You don't understand,' she repeated and tried to stand up. 'I've had a most dreadful experience.'

This was embarrassing for Sister Agnes. She pulled the curtains around the bed and approached Ruth with a lowered voice.

'All right then Mrs. Nolan. We know what it's like to have a child in hospital but some decorum is called for under the circumstances.'

'You're right sister.' Ruth protested but didn't know how to proceed. 'Something else happened before I arrived in the ward.'

'Well?'

'I can't say. I must go now. I'll just say good-night to Annette and then be off.'

'All right Mrs. Nolan. Good-night to you.'

Ruth spoke quietly to her daughter until the bell rang for visitors to leave and then stood up. It was strange saying good-night to Annette for the first time. She kissed her on the cheek and rushed out without looking back. She couldn't bear it any longer.

Annette was in a state. She closed her eyes trying to let the silence act as a lullaby.

Ruth hurried down the corridor. Sister Agnes raised a hand with a rare smile.

'Mrs. Nolan. Could you spare a minute in my office?'

'Of course. I'm sorry for my behaviour just now.'

'Not at all. We all have problems and worries. Please come this way.'

They entered the office and sat down.

'Now Mrs. Nolan you said something dreadful happened before you arrived in the ward. You needn't answer this, but is it something we should know? Did it happen in the hospital?'

'Yes. It did but I can't … '

Sister was insistent. 'If it happened here then perhaps we should know about it.'

'Oh sister. It was terrible and I feel awful.' She began to cry again. 'You see on the way up to the ward I got lost and ended up in the pathology museum upstairs, I think. Those horrible diseases and injuries. I've never seen anything like it in my life.'

'I see. How unfortunate.'

'It was a nightmare.' Her voice trembled. 'To have them on open display and anyone could … '

'That's just a temporary arrangement,Mrs. Nolan. There have been major disruptions since the fire and departments had to be moved.'

'Yes but the idea of keeping a museum like that is horrendous. I can't believe it. It shouldn't be allowed.'

'You don't understand Mrs. Nolan. Medical science is dependent on … Mrs. Nolan. Please.'

Ruth stood up raising both hands in front of her.

'I don't want to know. Nothing more. I can't take it. I'm too upset.'

She rushed out of the room, along the corridor, down the stairs and into the car park. Sister Agnes lifted the telephone and dialled a number.

'Dr. Nicholson. Sister Agnes here. I think there is something you should know.'

2

Linda's death completely devastated John Nicholson even though before it happened there was an impending sense of mortality. Then the wonderful remission. Life started again and the normality it brought was something they thought could never be experienced again. Her willingness to undergo chemotherapy with an incompletely tested medicine pulled her through. The experts were dumbfounded. The result was a triumph for John and paved the way for the wider use of his work in cancer patients.

Then the shopping accident. Senseless and tragic. His beloved was gone within an hour of saying goodbye. Deep shock engulfed him. Daytime living was erratic and unpredictable. Numbness was a protective shield and most people left him alone. Yet, he didn't know if he wanted to hide away and be surrounded by inanimate distractions. Reading became a burden and meaningless; radio and television were pointless--sometimes an absurdity. He needed company--although not for long. He needed to be alone--yet not for long either. Life was a contradiction. Everything irritated, everything appalled. At times he was on the verge of breaking down and needed a hell of a lot of self-restraint.

In spite of medication advised by colleagues nights could be worse. But then, without it he couldn't sleep and mornings were exhausting. With it, he had some sleep--but disturbed. Dreams left him suspended in a twilight zone of imaginings and distorted childhood memories. It's strange what grief can do and how little control there is.

Sometimes before waking he longed to ask Linda about his dreams. Her body was not beside him and yet transiently he felt her weight and fragrance only to dissolve into memories. She might be in the next room or in the garden and they could talk. Reality told him it was not so and a sinking feeling like leaden weights pressed against his chest preventing him getting up.

These were natural feelings after the loss of a close one. Everyone said so. Eventually they would subside. It was a matter of time.

3

Tom Nolan sat at a long table with six colleagues. With a resolute expression he looked around and spoke in a slow voice.

'Gentlemen, thank you for coming tonight. It must be difficult for some. However you're aware our business is important. Also it's imperative we keep our venues private and not disclose our activities to anyone unless we agree on press statements. There are forces that would welcome an opportunity to obstruct and destroy our organisation. Our work must go on no matter what.'

He stopped and lifted a sheet of paper.

'Recently this document was sent by the organisation we're hoping to become affiliated. There're some fundamental principles in it, which are crucial to our work.'

He cleared his throat and again looked around. 'I'd like to read a short extract if I may. A full copy is available for each of you. It goes as follows:

… "We declare henceforth that all animals enjoy these inalienable rights: The right to freedom from fear, pain, and suffering--whether in the name of science or sport, fashion or food, exhibition or service …

… The right, if they are wild, to roam free, unharried by hunters, trappers and slaughterers ...

… If they are domestic, not to be abandoned in the city streets, by a country road, or in a cruel and inhumane pound …

… And finally the right, at the end, to a decent death--(whether they are endangered or not)--by club, by harpoon, cruel poison or mass extermination chamber …

… We have only one creed--to speak for those who can't …

…The Fund for Animals Inc."

For the next hour they discussed past successes and made plans for future strategies. Then six stern faced men left the room rented from the Plough Pub in north Dublin.

Ruth Nolan sat forlorn in the old yellow van in the hospital car park. A cold wind rushed through the window and she pulled her coat tightly around her. Her daughter's illness brought the fickleness of life into sharp focus. She felt threatened. If there was anything she could do to save her child, to bring her home safe and sound to the little house beside the harbour to walk along the seashore with Patsie--anything. She'd do it.

Yet Tom refused to come tonight. He'd an important meeting. Blast his meeting! And principles! They were more important than his family! More important than his own daughter's life! She had screamed at him before she left for St. Mary's.

'Will you come with me tonight?' She asked him.

'No. I can't. There's no way I can miss this meeting and I am chairman.'

'Well then, Tom,' she fumed before she left, 'now I see where your principles lie.'

The words hurt deeply. Annette had always been his pride and joy, they were good friends and he said he'd do anything for her. Now, he'd other priorities, other arrangements. And she was appalled.

As she prepared to leave the car park she noticed Dr. Nicholson climbing the steps to the main entrance of the hospital.

Later stepping out of the van the sound of surf on stones came up to meet her and, to the east, a full moon caused asterisks of light to bounce off the sea. They did little to quell the anger inside her.

4

John Nicholson headed for the radiology department. He wanted to spend the night before the funeral in Linda's room sorting papers and possessions. It could be a helpful distraction.

The sign on the door, <u>Dr. Linda Nicholson Consultant Radiologist,</u> made him crumple inside and the intense glare of the neon light emphasised the emptiness of the place. He went through the pile of papers on the desk; reports, minutes of meetings and correspondence; these could be dealt with by administration. In the bottom drawer of the filing cabinet was her briefcase. Inside were chequebooks, bank statements, private letters and a large A 4 diary. During the last months she spent ages writing but never said what was in it.

All she would say: 'Someday, alsking, darling, you can read it.'

Someday had arrived. He ran through the pages; hundreds were filled with beautiful scripted writing. There were various headings apparently unrelated. On the title page <u>Towards a Resolution </u>was written in block letters followed by <u>these ideas and thoughts are</u> <u>dedicated to my beloved husband, John, who saved my life in more</u> <u>ways that he could ever imagine.</u> <u>With my greatest love forever</u> <u>and ever. Linda.</u>

He placed his hand on the words as if touching them would, somehow, bring her closer. With lowered head he closed his eyes. Her voice told him to have strength and courage.

'Only a matter of time,' he said out loud, his words filling the room. He was unable to read anymore. The book fell to the floor. It remained open at some of the last entries. Slowly he picked it up. She was writing about music. How she loved music and this was reflected in her attitude to life. He read under the title <u>Resigned</u> <u>Sadness.</u>

… All my life I had been almost afraid of Mozart. His music was too perfect it almost terrified me. Yet someday I promised I would come to him and give in. In the meantime there was Schumann, Beethoven and glorious Chopin …

… In the last few months--now that my illness has become es-tablished--I felt that the time had come. And the miracle of the last four symphonies has possessed me …

… Dear John, if you ever read these scribbles please listen espe-cially to the slow movements of number 38, The Prague and num-ber 41, The Jupiter. And think of me …

… My attention was seized immediately. No unnecessary in-troductions. Even though there is an ineffable sadness, it is so mysterious and laden with unresolved tension. An achievement of the greatest mastery. It is music that is not only a celebration of existence it is also a yearning for a lost golden age. Some say it was written without a cause or purpose but as an appeal to eternity. Be that as it may it is unique. Nothing similar can be found anywhere…

… As you listen you will see that everything glows with a spontaneity and immediacy that is inevitable. Even though it is full of yearning and longing, somehow it always finds its way to resolution beyond measure …

… This is the greatest comfort and consolation--its magical resolution. I pray it will do the same for you Dear John. Listen and think. Mozart will speak to you for me. I promise! …

He put the book down and looked at his watch. Time to go. Tomorrow was an important day.

5

John Nicholson moved to the window as the bedroom curtains swayed in the breeze. Early morning traffic was increasing and clouds were racing to their destinations. Trees trembled as if some being was taking shelter in them; perhaps a sign of Linda's soul taking leave of home, hospital and surroundings.

He'd known her a few short years in Sweden; joyful times travelling in the Dalarna district where she was born. Then in Stockholm the work together in cancer research. The pattern of their lives was drawn out of untroubled happiness and went unrecognised until the return to Dublin--to major changes, problems and crises.

The diary in his hand was a revelation. What did it add up to? Everyone lives a hidden existence with secrets often going to the grave. Maybe she'd left some in her writings--things she dare not speak about. As he gazed at the moving trees he felt he was holding Linda's soul in his hands. Time to go to the funeral.

Father Ignatius kindly agreed to officiate. After all, being the chaplain to St. Mary's he was called to Linda's side when she asked. Her life was ebbing away and the request was answered swiftly. She'd asked to be accepted fully and extreme unction was given. John then arrived in the A & E department. That crash. So point- less tragic and unfair. She died peacefully with an amazing degree of acceptance.

A large crowd attended the requiem mass in St. Jude's the near- est parish church to St. Mary's. John sat with friends and colleagues in the first seat on the left. Bach's <u>Wein Ich Einmal Soll Scheiden</u> was played on the organ several times; its slow languishing melody was almost unbearable. When Father Ignatius appeared, robed in black, all stood. Making his way to the dais he gestured them to be seated. He spoke slowly.

'Sisters and brothers we've come together this day to help John celebrate the life of his dearly beloved wife Linda. She was tragi- cally taken from him in a senseless accident some days ago. There's no telling the reason. We cannot begin to question. Yet we will always want to know why.'

'An inquiring mind was always at the centre of Linda's life. She wanted to know more, to know why, searching and questioning. I've been told that her childhood was like a fairytale. Despite ill health, her mother Eve Lindstrom is with us today having trav- elled from Sweden. She told me Linda had a kind heart,always thinking of others. When her own husband, Jens, became ill Linda made untold sacrifices to make his final journey as comfortable as possible.'

Father Ignatius paused and looked at his notes.

'The same qualities became evident in her life as a doctor. Professor Isselherg, The Dean of the medical school, is also with us and his praise of Linda, both as a doctor and a human being, is amazing, particularly in her compassion for patients' suffering from advanced and terminal cancer. For this alone she deserves an everlasting reward.'

'Our celebration does not end here. John tells me her ability in music especially piano playing was extraordinary. Many words were used to describe her gifts and I'd become breathless if I were to repeat them today. Professor Wainwright was more concise when he summarized Linda's playing as full of grandeur and magnificence. A truly inspired performer.'

'So John I could go on with praise for Linda as a remarkable person. But I will not do so. Many of you here were her friends and knew her better than I did.'

'So let us kneel and remember a beautiful generous courageous gifted doctor and wife.'

'May she rest in peace.'

The rest of the ceremony was a blurred sequence of invocations and responses with sublime choral music. The priest had listened to John's wishes. When the formal ceremony was over a queue formed to pay respects to Eve Lindstrom and John. Brief words were exchanged, hands shaken with hugs and kisses from those who dared.

Gustav and Rachel Isselherg appeared from the crowd; both gave John a long hug and handshake.

'We had to come when we heard the news,' Gustav said and Rachel nodded. 'It's so unfair. Where's the justice? You have our deepest sympathy. Please come and see us if you feel up to it. We'll be in the Shelbourne for a week or there's always an open door for you in Stockholm.'

John nodded and smiled.

'Thanks for coming. It means so much to us.' He gestured towards

Eve Lindstrom. 'I can't promise but I'd love to come and see you.'

'Yes. Please do.' A hand appeared from behind Rachel and grabbed his firmly. It was Karita Isselherg.

'Karita. You came too?' He was amazed.

'Don't be surprised,' she smiled shyly. 'I had to come. Please try and visit us.'

'I'll try. I can't say more than that.'

'Of course John.' Rachel patted him on the shoulder and indicated to Gustav they should move on. Others were waiting.

As the cortege drove through the entrance to Glasnevin Cemetery a host of crows took flight and scattered from the tall evergreens. Light rain added a welcome to the new visitor. The hearse passed rows of headstones until it came to rest near a freshly prepared grave at the base of a gentle hill. Linda had told John she wished to be buried in a place near to where he lived. At present he lived in Dublin and hoped to remain there provided circumstances allowed.

As final preparations took place he spoke a few silent words to her.

'Here I stand,Linda. Saying goodbye is so hard. Your life brought light now darkness remains. You gave love and joy, only emptiness is left. My grief is total and I feel alone. No better friend there was for me. Safe journey onwards, my love, and arrive securely in your new home. Rest in happiness and peace.'

As the coffin was lowered into earth he bowed his head. Tears rolled down but no attempt was made to remove them. At the back of the mourners a tall blonde women stood watching. She was alone and spoke to no one and apparently was not recognised by anyone. Ruth Nolan blessed herself and walked away as the crowd dispersed.

As John closed the curtains that evening darkness rose and clung to the silent trees, which stood like weird statues pointing up to a clear sky where all light was gone.

In the lee shore of day the smouldering embers of words from friends kindled a mixture of consolation and confusion; he felt sick with the strong drug of suffering and abandonment. Others had to cope with similar problems and learned ways to defeat them with wild distractions and even stupid diversions.

Before retiring he would walk to shake off this sentimental yearning. He put on a jacket and went downstairs to the path between the trees standing sentinel as if they were friends he already knew.

6

Two days later John Nicholson walked through the entrance to the Shelbourne Hotel in Stephen's Green. It was twelve-thirty and he was in time for lunch with the Isselhergs. They greeted him in the lobby.

'Shall we go straight into the dining room?' Gustav gestured to John who nodded. Rachel and Karita led the way to their table.

'Thanks for accepting the invitation Dear John,' Rachel said as she gently touched his hand. When all were seated there was an awkward silence.

Karita was the first to speak.

'John I passed my final examination in May and will be conferred next week.'

Rachel scolded her.

'Now Karita, John has other things on his mind.'

John smiled and turned to Karita.

'Not at all. Life must go on. Congratulations on a wonderful achievement. I know it was well deserved as you've a gift with words.'

'Thanks John. You remembered. I got a first in English and specialised in Celtic mythology. The thesis dealt with the procrustean era in Europe. I found it so interesting ever since you told us those wonderful stories about your country when you were in Sweden. I was spellbound.'

He nodded, encouraging her to continue.

'While we're here dad promised to take us to Tara, Knowth, Monasterboice and other places I cannot pronounce.'

Her laughter was infectious.

'Yes John,' Gustav interrupted, 'maybe you'd advise. We've a car and maps.'

'Tell me your plans first and then we'll see.'

Gustav outlined the sites in a sixty- mile radius of Dublin. John made some suggestions.

'We will try to fit them in,' Gustav said, 'although time is limited.'

'These are the tip of the iceberg,' John said, 'the great sites are scattered widely on the west coast including some islands in the Atlantic.'

'What a pity dad,' Karita said looking disappointed.

'It'd take ages to explore them,' John said, 'they are vast.'

'Well maybe a kind person will take me to see them someday-- the really outstanding ones if I undertake a doctoral thesis.'

'Would you go that far Karita?'

'I would. I love the ancient history of this country, something similar to ours. I must explore it in depth.'

Her parents agreed. The meal was relaxed and the conversation was taken up with reminiscences of John's years working in the Helmuth Institute. After coffee Karita asked him for a walk in Stephen's Green across the road.

A warm wind was running as they entered the park. At times it grew excited and caused trees to shiver as if a flame brushed by them. Clouds causing light and shadow on lawns and flowerbeds tore the sky apart. There was a feeling of agitation in the air. Karita was aware of his anxiety, even though he walked with determination. His mind was elsewhere.

'Nice of you to show me around this beautiful park John.' She tried to sound appreciative. 'You probably have better things to do than walking with me.'

'Nonsense Karita. It's a pleasure to see you again.'

'Do you mean that?'

'Of course. You're such good company.'

'Remember the times we had riding in the countryside, doing all those exciting things together and … '

'Please.' He spoke with difficulty. 'Probably not the best time to talk about those things.'

'John don't you realise it is good to talk especially now.'

She linked his arm as she used to, almost pulling him along.

'I can't help it. I'm numb and forlorn.'

'Of course you cannot help it. I understand.' She was getting into her stride reminding him of the long discussions they had in the library of Kungsangen House. 'You are bound to feel that way and I do understand. At least I am trying to.'

'Thanks Karita. But I have to go through it.'

'Through what?'

'The grieving process.'

She stopped and faced him.

'Let's sit down John. We can discuss this better.'

They chose a seat facing the lake where ducks were quarrelling.

'You know, John, grief is part of life and living, suffering and bereavement come to us all. They are the root and flame of our existence. My father did not mention it to you but he is not well and may not have much time left. I must face that. When I say I understand your pain I am preparing myself.'

'Sorry about your father. I'm fond of him. He's more a friend.'

'He's also fond of you. He'd great admiration for your work. You know that. And there is no harm in repeating it.'

She pulled his arm closer. He made no resistance. Numbness was all pervading.

'Other things I might say,' she continued. 'You know me well enough not to take offence.'

'No Karita. I will not.'

'We live most intensely in contact with other humans. Not in isolation.'

He remained silent. He was preparing for more of Karita's fine words. She'd an endearing way with them.

'And that's what some of us run away from,' she said, 'we are too timid, too afraid to open up, to give our souls to others.'

'Not you Karita.' It was difficult for him to say much more. 'Unfortunately a lot of people do precisely that.'

She hesitated struggling with indecision.

'The next people you give your soul to, they must not be silly fools who'll abuse it with selfish ends. Be careful. Be brave and strong and time will come to your rescue and make you stronger than ever.'

'Just like your young princess in your epic poem.'

She blushed and looked away.

They walked the rest of the way in silence. He felt grateful for her kind words. Before saying goodbye she asked him to come to her room. He reluctantly agreed.

The lift took them to the third floor and straight to her room.

'Come in John. I won't keep you long.'

She opened her suitcase, produced a parcel and proudly held it out to him.

He was perplexed.

'What is this?'

'Open it and see.'

He removed the padded wrapping and found the large ancient hourglass that measured time with golden sand.

'Oh Karita. This is too much. I cannot accept this after all you told me about it. You really treasure it.'

'I do treasure it. But I want you to have it. When you invert it you can see how it measures time beautifully. Then it stops. Time stands still. But you can start it flowing again. You have a sense of control. A sense of being in control.'

'You haven't lost your lovely way with words. You express things so well.'

'Thanks John. That makes me happy.' She turned to look out the window and over the park. 'I don't know if it is the right time to tell you, but why not?'

'What is it?'

'It is my ambition to write a novel, a saga really or a heroic story. I could borrow from your wonderful Celtic mythology. I will have time now to devote to writing and my head is bursting with ideas.'

'That sounds wonderful. I wish you well with your efforts.'

'As I gain experience I realise human contacts may not be enough to fulfil our needs. That is why I want to become a novelist, to get immersed in fiction because in that way everything about us can be explored and explained. We can make things happen when we want them to and everything can work out for the best--if that is our wish. It's like magic!'

Her expression became serious as she continued.

'One wish would be for you to help me. You seem to know so much mythology.'

'You know that may not be possible. My work schedule is demanding. There's little time for anything else.'

'If I send you one or two drafts of the manuscript, perhaps you could look at it quickly.'

John touched her on the cheek and forced a smile.

'My poor Karita. You are so innocent and you've a lot to learn. What you ask is similar to a situation in medicine. I shudder when a colleague in hospital asks me to have a "quick look" at one of his difficult patients when he cannot figure out what is wrong. It is unfair to everyone. Most especially the patient. Quick looks are a menace and can lead to disasters.'

She sat down dejected not knowing what to say. Not for long.

'I understand what you say but this is different from medicine. If you were to say yes you'd feel committed to spending time on the project. Well I won't say anything further but don't reject it out of hand. There may be a way. Who knows? We can't see into the future.'

'That's true. It's a difficult time at present. Anyway I feel honoured you should think of me. The idea sounds terrific.'

'You started it all back in Sweden. Remember that wonderful night at dinner in our house with all the guests and you telling those wonderful stories. Everyone was enthralled. And I have never forgotten it.'

'You're very kind.'

'One last thing John.' She stood up and approached with hands out. 'I haven't yet been able to finish my epic poem about the Celtic princess imprisoned in the dark castle. Maybe, just maybe, you will help me finish it. There must be a simple ending and, hopefully, a happy one.'

She touched his hand.'I want you to have this hourglass. It's been in our family for a long time. Now it will have a new home. And when you use it, perhaps, you'll think of me and our happy times together.'

Impossible for him to say anything more. Instead he gently kissed her, held her hand for a long lingering moment and mumbled goodbye.

He had to leave as soon as possible.

7

John woke next day with mixed feelings. He'd read more of Linda's diary; it moved him greatly and yet Karita's words burned into his consciousness determined to stay there.

Another day ahead. He was resigned and stoical. Patients had to be seen and cared for. Some results were due back today, especially those in ward 3 A. Case management would take place at a clinico-pathological conference. These discussions could be helpful. Three children Carol Smith, Suzanne Murphy and Annette Nolan, presented major problems.

He went straight to sister's office and opened the path reports. His suspicions were confirmed; each had leukaemia and the most advanced was Annette Nolan--the lovely quiet girl he'd spoken to recently. Ward rounds with Sister Agnes, the house physician and junior nurse were next. Details were discussed in front of patients using polite and reassuring language.

Notes for the conference were prepared and ready for twelve

o'clock. The group consisted of consultants, registrars, junior doctors, nursing sisters and students. It was a democratic way of agreeing on each patient's treatment regimen.

Professor Walter Wainwright's expression was solemn as he tapped the table to convene the conference. Conversation ceased as he began to speak.

'Ladies and gentlemen welcome to our meeting. Before we start I'm afraid there's one matter I should report to you in confidence.'

This was unusual. People looked at each other.

'An anonymous letter addressed to the head of the pathology division was received yesterday. Its contents I found disturbing. I don't intend reading it out word for word because some of the language used is coarse. The drift of the letter states a member of the public accidentally gained entrance to our pathology museum, which as you know is housed in temporary quarters. It appears this person became agitated at the display of pathology specimens we use for teaching purposes. The person concerned did not report the incident to the authorities.'

'Instead, on returning home she told her husband. This letter was then written by him with threats, warnings and goodness knows what else. There appears to be no clear purpose of intent except to express anger.'

'However, I've a feeling this is not the last we'll hear about it. I don't feel we should discuss the matter in open forum at present. We can only wait developments--if any. I will, of course, report to the Chairman of the Board.'

He turned the letter upside down and looked around the room.

'Now down to business. Dr. Kennedy would you like to begin?'

Wainwright seemed to find solutions to any problems. John Nicholson was last.

'I've three patients with leukaemia in Ward 3 A. Two seem to be straightforward and I think will respond to treatment. The third, a twelve-year old girl, worries me especially because of this morning's report. This is the third report in as many weeks and each shows a rapid elevation in cells indicating an active marrow. She's been started on cytotoxics but they're not producing much of a response. We've a problem here that's not going to be easy to solve.'

Wainwright responded. 'What do the radiotherapists think? Dr. Conway.'

'Radiotherapy could be combined with other therapy. We would consider marrow ablation and donor replacement.'

'Yes indeed. Let's hope it doesn't come to that. It is difficult to find the perfect donor and there are ethical, legal, even religious obstacles to overcome.'

Wainwright turned to John and smiled for the first time.

'I'd be cautious with the patient. Don't rush into anything drastic. No unnecessary risks or heroics.'

'Enough said professor. Thank you.' John was not at all happy.

8

Tom Nolan sat in the garden of the house beside the little harbour. Dark hair was brushed back and smouldering eyes watched Ruth's every movement. A nervous tic flickered in his left temple--the only sign that all was not well. Something had to give; it was a question of who'd the shortest fuse.

'Why now? While Annette's in hospital.' Ruth suddenly exploded. 'Couldn't you have waited for heaven's sake?'

'It doesn't matter.'

'It does,' she shouted. 'If the authorities find out we're responsible what'll become of her? She's sick enough as it is without your crass interference.'

'You started it.'

'I was frightened out of my wits and had to tell someone. But I didn't mean to make a written complaint. If they find out we could be in deep trouble.'

'Don't you believe it,' he said. 'They could be in deeper trouble if the press finds out about them. It's worse than Frankenstein.'

'Shut up! For God's sake,' she pleaded, 'just leave it alone. I shouldn't have said anything. Just suffered in silence. I might have known what a fool you can be sometimes. What a mess we're in. Thanks to you.'

This stung him. In spite of the rebuke, right was on his side. He was sure of himself. She was impetuous, reacting on a whim and hysterical. He'd seen it before and this was no exception. She didn't understand him, his work, the ideals, the grand design, the permanent basis for what they stood for and she shouldn't question his judgement.

However, he'd have to be cautious and delay action because of Annette's illness, an unexpected interference in plans. But no way was it going to stop him. It was a matter of waiting. A matter of time. Then things would really happen. A smile of triumph flashed across his face.

9

Next day the Nolans had an appointment with a consultant. Ruth was the only one who turned up. She sat in the queue waiting her turn; her daughter was ill, her husband irrational and set to cause more trouble. He was impossible. Time dragged by. The magazines on the table were hideous; the television silly and mischievous children intolerable. Nobody seemed to care.

'Mrs. Nolan.' A voice came from behind. 'The doctor will see you now.'

A nurse approached with a smile and indicated a door to her left.

Ruth knocked gently.

'Come in.'

A striking man greeted her with an outstretched hand. No white coat.

'I'm Dr. Nicholson and work with Professor Wainwright. Please be seated.'

'Thank you.'

She sat and looked around the room. Just the doctor and herself then.

'I thought it best if we'd a word together before speaking to Annette. Incidentally was Mr. Nolan not able to make it today? I hoped he would be present.'

'Oh sorry doctor. He sends apologies. He couldn't make it today. Don't worry I'll tell him everything when I get home.'

'Very well then.' John appeared a little sceptical. 'As you know Mrs. Nolan,Annette's been feeling unwell and had several blood tests.'

He lifted reports from the table.

'These tests are incomplete. More will be required together with marrow biopsy. And perhaps some scans.'

'Yes doctor. I know they can be complicated. We're most grateful for your kindness to Annette. We're confident you'll do the best for her. She's such a good and loving child.'

He lowered his head before continuing.

'Nice of you to say that Mrs. Nolan. Sometimes it's hard to tell the facts as they are. The burden of truth can be a heavy one. Oh dear!' He smiled. 'That sounds a bit pompous. Wasn't meant to be I assure you.' He was holding back.

'Not at all. I understand. I want to know everything.'

'Very good.' He gave a little cough. 'Unfortunately your daughter is developing a fairly severe form of leukaemia. Each of the three blood tests has shown a rise in the white cell count.'

'What does that mean doctor?'

'It indicates an active bone marrow where abnormal cells are produced. Other children can have a slower form and sometimes may even go into remission. Sadly Annette's condition appears to be taking a relentless coarse.'

'Doctor this is awful.' She looked pitiful. 'I didn't expect things were so bad.'

He nodded and spoke gently.

'Once her tests are completed she'll have the finest treatment. We'll do our best to keep you and your husband informed.'

'Her progress or otherwise. I've no illusions doctor,' she said simply.

'I admire your courage Mrs. Nolan. We all have worries and have to do our utmost to cope with them.'

Recklessness overcame her as she said.

'Even you doctor must have had personal tragedies.'

A transient smile appeared; the eyes remained anxious and sad.

'Now it's time to go to the most important person in the whole affair--that's the patient. Will we go up together and have a chat?'

'Yes please. I'd love that.'

'One thing Mrs. Nolan.' She listened carefully. 'Please let me do the talking. It's good to make a child feel important. Then I'll leave the two of you together.'

He collected his papers stood up and held out a hand.

'Best if I lead the way. We wouldn't want you to get lost. Would we?'

Her heart missed a beat. She followed reluctantly. The bitterness was back again.

1 0

Professor Walter Wainwright normally had little time to spare. Today he'd take a chance. Why not? He deserved it. Recently things were getting get too much although he wouldn't admit it. The mid-sixties were approaching and each day accelerated the process; some strange effect made clocks and watches run faster than ever. It was maddening. No time for anything! He dearly wanted to ask others had they noticed this fact but held back.

Today he'd idle away a little time by strolling through the grounds of in Trinity, which he loved; they reminded him of Cambridge. He bought The Times and settled down to peruse it. Usually there was too much information for a busy full-time professor. He'd to be selective. Medical and medico-legal matters were his main interest. A battle was going on in the UK between parents and hospitals over the retention without permission of body parts of children who died while undergoing treatment. Parents were demanding huge compensation and hospitals said the procedure was necessary for teaching purposes.

Wainwright mumbled the main agitators were probably the legal profession. Greed is a terrible thing, he thought. For centuries universities and hospitals equipped pathology museums with specimens of major diseases. And they were splendid ways of instructing students to further knowledge and research.

Even the renaissance artists and physicians were the first great minds to inquire into these problems. Then the Royal Colleges were active in adding to their collections. The aim was altruistic. Now someone thought there could be money in it primarily for them and, maybe, for aggrieved parents and relatives. Once the press got the smell of scandal they went for it like a pack of hounds.

He put the paper down in disgust. What was the world coming to? He continued his stroll around the cricket pitch. Exercise stimulated the imagination. The days in Cambridge were good ones, happy ones especially with Gillian--until she died. It was a pity one couldn't save up the overflow of happiness and withdraw some when needed, such as in the past few weeks. Memories were not the same; good and bad ones got mixed up. With happiness, on the other hand, it's all wonderful and marvellous.

He looked at his watch. He'd better make his way back to St. Mary's.

A request from Nicholson for an appointment waited in his office. He lifted the telephone.

'I can spare a few minutes. Could you come now?'

'I'll be straight up.'

Two minutes later John knocked and entered.

'Please take a seat John. What's all this about?'

'I mentioned Annette Nolan at the conference. That's not the complete story.'

'Then what's the problem?'

'It's more to do with medical politics, research procedures and the like. I know the father and he's active in the ALF. As such I'd find it difficult to deal with him as a parent. I've nothing against the daughter Annette. She's a lovely, but tragic, little girl. Completely the innocent party. Her mother is a pleasant soul who's going through a rough patch. She's not getting much support and she's torn in two.'

Wainwright made a few notes. 'What you're saying is the girl's treatment could be complicated by more than medical matters. We may have unwelcome interference.'

'That's precisely why I wanted to talk to you.'

'What do you propose? The girl needs radical treatment and fast.'

'I have started it already. But I'm the one that should not continue to give it. Somebody else should be put in charge because no matter what I do, or not do, I'm going to get the blame.'

Wainwright thought for a moment. Nicholson was the finest oncologist on his team and Annette needed the best. It was true what was just said; there was potential trouble on the domestic and perhaps on the wider legal front if they were not careful. Also Nicholson had his personal problems.

'All right John. There's good reason to drop out of the case for the present. I'll relieve you of your duties there and I'll ask Dr. Kennedy to step in and take over Annette Nolan's treatment.'

John groaned inwardly as Wainwright continued.

'He's a good chap although a bit impetuous and over confident. Different from you. With his personality he should be able to handle any difficulties with the Nolans.'

'Let's hope so and he won't put his foot in it.'

Wainwright shrugged his shoulders and looked out the window. The interview was now at an end. Walter Wainwright felt the weight of years. The potential trouble outlined by Nicholson added to his sense of disquiet. He wasn't in the business of premonitions. If he were he could feel one coming on.

There was trouble ahead.

Dr. James Kennedy was recently appointed consultant to St. Mary's under Professor Wainwright. Although less than forty-years his hair was almost white and he'd a tragic look about him sometimes associated with actors. Only to look at him you'd realise how vulnerable he was.

Few knew anything of his past and he'd an ingenious way of avoiding questions. Although he might hint that he'd been injured and suffered some injustice; a glimmer of sympathy could arise from others in spite of his sulking self-indulgence. Female staff attempted to welcome him, went out of their way to sympathize with him at times, but were politely and firmly put down. Somehow things didn't ring true; his attitude made it difficult to gain trust.

A need for advancement appeared and a reverence for those in authority manifested itself. Targets were power barons in the health service who were expanding their grip on the healthcare system. Here was the future as far as he was concerned.

John Nicholson was alarmed about the Nolan case but there was no option. Wainwright reassured him he'd keep an eye on things. John wasn't to worry. He'd be released to do more research into genetics and computer medicine.

He still wasn't satisfied and watched Kennedy from a distance; he was indeed an actor of sorts. Apparently Kennedy wished to be seen as a fascinating character, but defects and deficiencies in knowledge became obvious. Also he wanted to give the impression he was warm and friendly. He wasn't. He only seemed so. He'd a cunning way, searching out means to increase his influence within the hospital hierarchy. Pledges of loyalty to "the team," to everyone were made. Ultimately there was loyalty only to one person.

Dr. James Kennedy marched into ward 3 A followed by Sister Agnes, two junior nurses and six medical students. He liked an audience--it appealed to an inner need. At the first bed he listened attentively to reports being read out, rather than do it himself. He believed in delegation. It was good for the other person as long as it was kept in check and not let get too far. A fine balance was needed. After all he was in charge.

'Very good.' He looked approvingly at Sister Agnes. 'Please continue on the present regimen. No need to change. No need at all. Understood?'

'Yes doctor. We'll do as you say.' No further comment.

The same posturing occurred at the next few beds. Students were not to ask questions. Only Dr. Kennedy was allowed that privilege. Students could be embarrassing in front of patients and that was not tolerated. The patient's comfort and welfare were always at the top of his priorities, he said, and everyone had to appreciate that. He should lead by example. Always the best practice.

The entourage made its way to Annette Nolan's bed. She was frightened and pale not knowing what to expect. Her pupils were dilated; her hands trembled as she gripped the bedclothes with white knuckles. Dr. Kennedy noticed her anxiety and smiled broadly.

'You are Annette Nolan. Is that correct?'

'Yes.'

'Very good. I'm Dr. Kennedy and I've been asked by Professor Wainwright to look after you from now on. So you need not worry about anything.'

'What about Dr. Nicholson?' She sank lower in the bed. 'He's my doctor.'

'Not any more my dear.' No explanation was offered as he turned to sister.

'Please could we have the latest reports on this patient?'

'Do we have to do so here?' Sister dared. This was getting uncomfortable.

'We do indeed sister.' He was ruffled. This wouldn't do. 'I'll remind you each patient will have the same care and attention. No exceptions at all. Understood?'

'Understood Dr. Kennedy.' She handed the blood report to him so he could read it. The students glanced knowingly at each other. He looked straight through sister then at the report and back at her. He hesitated and quickly took it from her. He read it briefly and remained silent.

Annette's anxiety increased. Ignoring the insubordination he faced the patient.

'Now my dear can you tell us all how you feel?'

Annette remained silent. Words failed her.

'Come, come my dear. No need to be shy. We are all here to help you. You must understand that. Isn't that right sister?'

'Yes. Doctor.'

'Very good. Now that is understood. Annette my dear, please can you tell us how you feel and what it was that brought you into hospital?'

She still could not speak.

'Young lady. This is not good enough.' Time to exert some authority and let it be seen. 'If we're going to help you we must have a little cooperation.'

Pitiful she looked. She found courage to speak, more by way of protest.

'Dr. Kennedy. I've already told Dr. Nicholson everything. He spent an hour with me and wrote it all down. Have I to repeat it again especially in front of all these people?'

The comments hurt. A flash of anger appeared and was gone. He gave an evasive laugh. It was time to defuse the situation.

'No. Of course not. We understand perfectly,' he said with vitriolic politeness. That smile appeared again and remained switched on. He turned to sister and ignored the little urchin. 'I'll speak to sister privately at the end of my ward rounds. Come gentlemen, we have others to see and cannot afford to waste time on idle chatter.'

Later that morning Dr. Kennedy finished making notes in folders. Before leaving he turned to Sister Agnes.

'By the way,' he handed her Annette's folder with an off hand gesture. 'You'll notice I've changed the medication for the Nolan patient. She doesn't seem to be making any progress. In fact she's doing poorly on her current regimen. Do I make myself clear?'

'Dr. Nicholson left instructions it must be continued for at least three weeks.'

'I don't wish to argue. Suffice it to say Dr. Nicholson is known to be somewhat unconventional. What I've prescribed is generally accepted good practice.'

'Naturally. I don't question your judgement Dr. Kennedy. Your instructions will be carried out immediately.'

'That's better Sister Agnes.' He affected indifference. 'We now appear to understand each other. Good-day to you.'

1 2

That evening Ruth Nolan returned to St. Mary's. Again she was alone. Visiting time was already started and most parents had arrived. A gentle chatter greeted her.

She walked towards Annette's bed at the window. It was empty. She waited,thinking her daughter had slipped out for a walk in the corridor. Five minutes passed. Nothing. Ten minutes. Still no sign of Annette. She became anxious. Where was Annette? She went to sister's office. No one knew where the patient was--she had been in bed at six o'clock and taken her tea.

Sister went back into the ward. 'Let me try the toilets. She may've paid a visit before you came, Mrs. Nolan.'

'Maybe. But she's been a long time.'

Sister searched the toilets and found Annette. She'd been violently sick in one of the cubicles, collapsed and was unable to get up. Sister called for help and the patient was helped back to bed. The house physician was called and carried out an examination.

She was physically unharmed but in shock. Ruth was assured everything was all right. Back to normal. Nothing to worry about. Just a tummy upset.

When they were alone Ruth asked her what on earth happened? What was the matter with her? It all spilled out. The episode in the ward that morning, the new doctor taking over from Dr. Nicholson was a cruel and nasty person. He was rude to everyone. She didn't want to stay in this hospital any minute longer. She demanded to go home.

'What's the new doctor's name, Annette?'

'I think it's Dr. Kennedy. He bullies everyone, frightens everyone and he was nasty to me when I mentioned Dr. Nicholson.'

'Poor Annette. I'll get to the bottom of this. I won't let anyone hurt you. You'll see everything will work out fine.'

'Thanks mum. I knew you'd understand. I've never been so upset. I want to go home as soon as possible or even have that nice Dr. Nicholson again.'

'Rest assured my darling. Everything is going to be all right.'

1 3

Tom Nolan gathered his coat around him as he strolled with Patsie on the cobblestone beach. It was a cold night and he had the sound of surf for company. It was calming and he needed it. Nature was a good healer. Always had been. The mountains to his left stood fold on fold preparing for night, blue snow changing to pink before disappearing. It was hard to breath in the still air. But no, it wasn't the fault of the air. After all he was an artist--a painter--with some success although inspiration had deserted him recently. Too much domestic upset.

Confusion filled his mind. Thick brows made the eyes almost impossible to be seen though he could well see. Ruth accused him of not caring about Annette. This hurt deeply. For once he didn't react immediately. He'd his reasons, his strategies to think about which were important. Yet he couldn't discuss them. It wouldn't be right. He couldn't trust his wife to keep things secret and it would be unfair to ask her.

He wasn't a conventional person. He'd his own way of doing things and was an independent operator. A conservative anarchist he was, which was somewhat contradictory. Perhaps cautious was a better word but it didn't have the same high aspiration. There was so much wrong today. Sometimes his thoughts scared him and there was no one to confide in.

One by one the arc lamps on the harbour gave a shudder and sprang to life. Overhead the sky darkened and was almost impenetrable although some early stars were brave enough to pierce the inky blanket.

He was tired and looked forward to settling for the evening with Patsie before the fire. Ruth would be home soon. The sound of the van on gravel outside told Patsie to welcome the mistress home. She stepped into the hall and Tom went out to greet her. She was still his lovely blonde soul mate, dressed in a blue skirt that almost touched the ground. She removed her coat. Her beauty was unapproachable, the strong blue eyes, the straight nose and the clear sallow complexion.

Even before she spoke there was obvious agitation.

'Come and sit down Ruth. I'll make you a cup of tea.'

'No tea Tom. Thank you.'

She went straight to her chair beside the fire. Her cheeks were flushed and she looked as if she'd been crying.

He was alarmed. 'What is it Ruth?   Is everything all right?'

'No Tom. Everything is not all right.'

She hesitated. His smile was reassuring. But for how long? His eyes could change in a flash. She could see his anger rising as the full story came out.

'How could they be so cruel to Annette? She must be frightened out of her wits.'

Shock hit him hard. He had to stand and backed against the curtains.

Unspeakable depravities on the hospital authorities flashed across his mind. It was bad enough to learn that Dr. Nicholson was in charge for a while. Now apparently a totally obnoxious bully had taken over leaving Annette terrified. She wanted to come home.

'This is dreadful. And must not continue. I'll go to the hospital tomorrow and demand an explanation. Wait and see Ruth. No one's going to abuse Annette and get away with it. This Kennedy imbecile is beneath contempt. He needs to be taught a lesson in manners and behaviour especially when dealing with sick children.'

'Don't do anything drastic Tom. Remember Annette is ill and needs treatment. We want her better.'

'I'll be careful Ruth.' Again there was silence. Then he banged his fist on the table and said in a loud voice. 'You've gone through enough. Leave it to me to settle once and for all.'

A sense of relief came over her. Her husband was strong and determined. If something had to be done she knew he'd do it. She fell into bed exhausted and happy things could and perhaps would start moving in the right direction.

Later that evening Tom Nolan slowly climbed the stairs to the bedroom. He felt awful. The burden of responsibility was now on him. Entirely. His thoughts raced ahead as soon as he closed his eyes. Bursts of words such as overbearing bastards, cruel monsters and selfish egotists came to him. Ruth must be protected, left out of the developing scene. She'd done more than her fair share. It was up to him now to stop any abuse and take it to the highest authority. Cruel people, no matter who they were, must be given a lesson and to hell with the consequences.

A wave of sickness erupted inside him. It seemed to run through the whole earth. That night there was little sleep only moments in a kind of twilight zone where large accusing eyes stared at him. He dared not make a move; if he did they would threaten dire consequences. Malicious forces were attempting to destroy him and blow his fragile ship off course.

Next morning he looked around at a normal world. It was amazing how daylight could dispel evils monsters.

It was clear what had to be done.

John Nicholson couldn't see the passing scenery from the car when darkness fell. Anyway he wasn't interested. An urgent call from a local doctor said Professor Wainwright was ill and had asked Dr. Nicholson to come as soon as possible.

John rushed out to Rathgar. Driving was difficult in the snow, which thawed, refroze and crackled under the wheels. He was uncertain of the house, although he'd been there before with Linda. Twenty-six was probably the correct number and he rang the bell. A shuffling sound occurred, the door opened slightly and an elderly lady peered out.

She'd a frightened expression.

'Yes. What is it?'

'I'm Dr. Nicholson. I believe I'm expected.'

'Yes of course doctor,' she said at last, 'thanks be to God you've arrived. We're delighted you came. The poor dear. He's not well and it was so sudden.'

The door opened widely and he entered. She took his coat and bag.

'I'm Mrs. Lewis the housekeeper. Grace, the nurse, is with him at present.'

He reassured her. 'You did the right thing in sending for me.'

'No. It was the doctor who asked. Unfortunately he had to go. He told us the patient had a bad stroke complicated by pneumonia and probably won't last the night. The doctor knows you're coming and is anxious the patient is transferred to hospital. But the professor absolutely refused. He's very stubborn you know.'

'Don't I know?'

'The doctor has done all he can and left this note for you. He's very upset. But the professor has always been strong-minded and will listen to nobody. Perhaps you can change his mind?' She looked at him pleadingly. 'He will listen to you Dr. Nicholson. Please make him see sense. It'll give him a better chance.'

They stood in the kitchen, which was heated by one bar of an electric fire. He read the letter. Everything possible had been done under the circumstances.

'Would you like a cup of tea Dr. Nicholson? You must be tired.' She went over to the sink to fill the kettle. 'It was an awful journey out here. I'll bring you tea and sandwiches if you'd like to go up straightaway.'

'That'd be very kind of you.'

He went upstairs and Grace met him in the landing. She was exhausted and glad someone had come to share the responsibility.

'Poor old soul. He's very bad.'

'You need a rest now. Go down to Mrs. Lewis and she'll look after you. Then you should go home. I'll take charge from now on.'

She nodded.

'Thanks very much doctor. I appreciate it.'

He hesitated outside the bedroom not knowing what to expect. Slowly he entered and was shocked at the appearance of his old friend; the face was shrunken and pale, the cheeks hollow and one side immobile with the head retracted.

'Hello professor.' He tried to sound cheerful as he approached the bed. 'It's me, John Nicholson.' The patient tried to open an eye. It was an effort. He tried to speak. The words were difficult.

'Can I get you anything?'

There was a confused gesture. John couldn't understand what was required. He asked how he felt and the question was left to echo around the room.

Mrs. Lewis arrived with a loaded tray. She glanced at John and then the patient, wishing to ask questions yet knowing it was wiser to remain silent. Before leaving she whispered. 'I'll be available if you need me.' She touched her eyes with a handkerchief. 'I've worked for the gentleman for twelve-years now and a nicer person never existed. Never raised his voice. I can't believe it.'

'You retire now Mrs. Lewis,' he said simply, 'I'll stay through the night. I can manage.'

She nodded, touched him on the arm and then as if remembering something she approached the bed, kissed the tips of her fingers and, for a moment, placed them on Wainwright's forehead. She turned and quickly left the room.

He moved towards the bed informing the patient he was merely carrying out a routine examination to confirm the diagnosis. When finished he said.

'Yes. It looks like a left sided stroke and pneumonia as a complication.'

The response was barely audible. 'I know John.'

He pleaded. 'You should be in hospital. Please let me arrange it. I can do so immediately. An ambulance will be here in minutes.'

The other raised his right hand slightly.

'No. No. No. Please do not.' The words were an effort. 'Let me go in peace.'

'I'll stay with you tonight and we'll see what can be done in the morning.'

'Thanks John,' he said deliberately, 'you are a true friend.'

The room was cold so John brought the electric fire up from the kitchen, replaced his overcoat and sat beside Mrs. Lewis's tray. He didn't realise how hungry he was. Perhaps he should call an ambulance and get Wainwright to hospital even against his wishes.

He moved to the window. It was snowing outside and nothing stirred under the white shroud. He went back to the patient and pleaded with him again. Wainwright was finding it difficult to speak, but his voice was completely negative. The hand was clenched on the bedclothes indicating he was implacable.

Typical Wainwright, thought John. Stubborn to the last. It was obvious he wanted to pass away naturally without technology and science that could only prolong his suffering for a while. Why bother? He was tired and weary. He wanted to go. Wanted to die. John wondered would he not wish the same. To pass away quietly in bed at night. He continued to talk, now about times past. He knew Wainwright could hear him; the hand was relaxed and face less wrinkled.

Even though John was aware of Wainwright's views on religion, he thought he should ask this once if a clergyman would be of any help to make his peace with God.

'Thanks for the kind thought John. Someone said a man's reach should exceed his grasp. Or what's heaven for? I was too busy trying to put this world right to bother with the next.'

'Yes. I know all too well. Anyway you did it brilliantly.'

'And besides John,' Wainwright tried to sit up a little but failed, 'and besides John I never knew that we had even quarrelled and that's unlike me. So if he's there at all I don't want to apologise. The right people don't need apologies and the others just take a mean advantage of you if you do.'

John went on talking, telling of his life with Linda, the strange and exciting times with the Isselhergs in Sweden and even going back to his childhood. The breathing became irregular and mixed with a rumbling cough. He recognised the signs. It wouldn't be long. Before it was too late he wanted to say 'thank you.' What he'd achieved was due to Wainwright. Thanks was such a weak word. He wanted to say more but fine words were never his strong point.

He went over to the window again. It was getting bright. Seventhirty was the time. Once more he returned to the bed and whispered. 'Can you hear me?'

The patient was completely still, the forehead cold. He felt for the carotid pulse. Nothing. His friend had slipped away almost unnoticed. He closed the mouth and pulled the sheet up. Emotionless he sat in the empty room--the episode hardly affected him. It was inevitable. There was no stopping it and, really, it looked so easy. Yes Wainwright had been right; he always was. He knew exactly what to do. There could be no other way.

John wondered at the numbness inside. Why was there so little effect? Others would probably be hysterical and irrational. Not him. He must be made of stone with no feeling. His reserves had been used up, drained away. Even in overdraft.

Kneeling beside the bed he tried to say a short prayer. Words refused to come, only an incoherent babble. Suddenly he felt exhausted and finished. There was nothing more he could do but wait. Others would be arriving soon and know what to do.

1 5

Tom Nolan telephoned St. Mary's to speak to Dr. Kennedy or his
deputy--at least. He took a deep breath. He must exercise restraint.
Must remain calm even polite.

'Hello. Is that St. Mary's?'

'Yes.'

'My name is Thomas Nolan,' he said slowly, 'I wonder could I
speak to Dr. Kennedy or his deputy please?'

'I'm afraid that's not possible Mr. Nolan,' was the curt reply.

'Eh. I don't understand.'

'I can put you through to his secretary. Will that be all right?'

'Yes. Of course.'

Tom took another deep breath and waited.

'Hello. Dr. Kennedy's secretary here. Can I help you?'

'Yes. My name is Thomas Nolan. I'd like to talk to Dr. Kennedy
about my daughter. You see she's a patient of his in St. Mary's.'

'Just a minute please Mr. Nolan.'

A mumble of voices could be heard. He tapped the table.

'I'm afraid Dr. Kennedy is not here at present. Perhaps I could take a message.'

'A message?'

'Yes. That's right Mr. Nolan. Perhaps you would like to leave a message.'

'Yes. A message. Let me see.' Again he tried his best to be polite. The strain was becoming intolerable. 'I'd like to discuss my daughter's treatment with him.'

'Yes. Of course you would,' she sounded damned condescending, 'but Dr. Kennedy doesn't discuss cases with people over the telephone. Only colleagues. Perhaps you'd like to write with your queries.'

'A letter you mean?' He couldn't believe this!

'Yes. Dr. Kennedy gets lots of letters. He'd prefer it that way and he'll respond in whatever way he thinks fit.'

Tom was ready to burst. This could not be true. This woman seemed to think she could boss everyone and get away with it. Well just a minute. There comes a time. But hold on. Remember restraint!

'I'm afraid that would be very time consuming. Time consuming for Dr. Kennedy I mean. He must be a busy man.'

'He's very busy Mr. Nolan.' Irritation could be detected. 'If a letter is not acceptable, perhaps you could speak to sister on the ward when you visit your daughter.'

'Speak to sister you say?'

'Yes. That is precisely what I said.'

'But will she ...'

'Mr. Nolan I'm afraid I cannot help you any further. Good-day to you.'

The phone went dead. He looked askance and slammed it back in place. Anger gripped him like two hands. He went to lie down and wait for the storm to pass.

The journey to St. Mary's was hazardous that evening. Traffic was heavy and everyone seemed to be going to a funeral. It was better Ruth didn't go with him. Yes, he'd give Annette a hug and kiss from her mother. And she'd be pleased to see her dad for a change. Besides he'd some business to attend to.

It was raining heavily when he arrived and parking was difficult. Damn the rain! It was always raining when he'd business in town. Rushing up the steps to the entrance he lowered the umbrella and inquired the way to ward 3 A. There was a hell of a lot of building material lying around making a terrible mess. No wonder Ruth got lost.

He was breathless at the top of three flights of stairs. And ringing wet. In spite of the inner turmoil he must exercise restraint. Entering the ward he looked around. He hated hospitals, the sickness, and smell of chemicals and accoutrements that went with the business of medicine. Ruth said Annette was in the end bed near the window. No sign of her. He approached and noticed a small face with eyes closed and sheets pulled up.

She was hardly recognisable, so thin and pale and asleep. He sat quietly in a chair beside the bed though there was noise all around.

'Annette,' he said gently. 'It's me. Your dad.'

No response. It was unlike his Annette--always full of life. He touched her cheek. After a long moment she opened her eyes.

'Annette. It's me. I've come to see you.'

The girl stared at the stranger in front of her.

'Annette. Are you all right?'

Slowly a smile dawned and she tried to raise herself.

'Dad.' She held out her arms. 'You've come at last. I thought I wouldn't see you.'

'Of course I've come. Why wouldn't I?' As they hugged she trembled and didn't want to let go. 'Mum sends her love but thought it best I visit you tonight. Hope that's all right?'

'It's great to see you dad. I miss you and Patsie so much.'

'Yes. We mustn't forget Patsie.'

They laughed together but it didn't last. Cautiously Annette looked left and right.

'Dad. Please take me home. The new doctor is awful to everyone and he seems to especially pick on me. He's so rude. Even the nurses don't like him.'

'Dr. Kennedy you mean?'

Putting her finger to her lips she nodded.

'I see.' His voice had a dogged determination. 'I've heard from your mother and rest assured I'm going to do something about it.'

'What can you do dad? He won't listen to anyone. He just shouts at people and the students are terrified of him.'

'Well. I'm not afraid of him and it's my intention to talk to him.'

'May not be possible. He's always in a hurry. And people are always looking for him.'

'I'll find him and find him soon.'

'If you do, dad, please ask if I could be transferred to Dr. Nicholson who used to look after me. He was so kind and spent hours talking to me.'

Tom was suddenly serious; he also remembered Nicholson.

'Talking about what Annette?'

'Why do you ask?'

'I've had some dealings with him in the past.'

'Oh good. That's great. Isn't he so nice and gentle and caring? I really like him.'

Tom was silent. Couldn't reveal past secrets. He merely replied.

'Yes. Dr. Nicholson's nice and he tries very hard.'

'Everyone loves him. He's disappeared over the last week. Nobody knows why.'

'That's another thing I'll try and find out. Enough of that for the moment.'

'I feel tired since Dr. Kennedy changed my medication. I've lost my appetite.'

Tom was surprised. 'Did you say Dr. Kennedy changed your medication?'

'Yes. Dr. Nicholson started my treatment, but when Dr. Kennedy appeared on the scene he was very cross with sister and insisted on changing it. Since then I've felt awful. I find it hard to walk around the ward. My legs are so weak. Even sister is worried but she hasn't said anything though she keeps checking my temperature and pulse. I think it's to keep me awake.'

An ice-cold anger gripped him; he had to change the subject. Small talk about school and walks along the beach occupied the rest of the visit. The great things they were going to do and places to see when she came home. They hugged and cried a little when time came to say goodbye. Even holding hands lasted longer. With head lowered he left the ward and a final look back showed a white hand raised appealingly. The impact was almost too much. He stopped in the corridor to regain his composure and looked out the window. It was dark outside and raining heavily. Her misery made him reluctant to go straight home.

As he turned from the window he pulled the wet coat around him and an imposing nurse in navy uniform approached. This could be sister-in-charge. He'd take a chance.

'Excuse me sister,' he said politely and tried to smile.

She stopped and gave him a cursory look.

'Yes. What can I do for you?'

'I'm Annette Nolan's father and I've just seen her. I'm worried about her. She seems to have deteriorated since she was admitted. She's tired and sleepy and says she's lost her appetite. I'm most concerned about her welfare.' His distress levels were rising. 'Quite honestly it was maddening when I telephoned this morning to talk to Dr. Kennedy or, at least, his deputy. I was put through to an obnoxious secretary who told me Dr. Kennedy was not available and did not speak to patients or relatives on the telephone. She suggested writing a letter. That was ridiculous and I said so. She then suggested I might like to talk to sister-in-charge on my next visit. Maybe I'm lucky in meeting you tonight.'

Sister looked around. Perhaps he was a person she could talk to. There was much unhappiness in her staff since Dr. Kennedy appeared on the scene. He'd caused a lot of friction. A word with Mr. Nolan probably would do no harm. And maybe some good.

She drew closer and said in a subdued voice.

'Mr. Nolan could you spare a moment in my office. It's too public here.'

She led the way to her room.

'A good idea. I'd welcome it. That woman on the phone was infuriating. Kennedy only wants letters sent to him. Sister, I couldn't believe my ears. All I wanted to ask was about Annette's progress. He wanted a letter to ask the same question. All my life I've believed in a one-to-one contact with anyone--anyone no matter whom--to look them in the eye and ask a direct question. If the answer is straight and true I feel I can trust the guy. This business of hiding behind God almighty secretaries and excuses about being too busy. That's just unacceptable and quite honestly I don't believe it. I think the man has something to hide and won't come out and face simple questions.'

Sister Agnes closed the door and listened carefully nodding her head. Here was a forceful man who demanded answers. He was coming up against a wall of obstruction, obfuscation and deliberate none cooperation. This aloof consultant had chosen to throw his weight around, to antagonise and turn people against him. Of course, he was merely exerting his authority and everyone should do exactly as he said with no question. That was the efficient way forward.

She put a straightforward suggestion to him.

'Mr. Nolan you feel strongly about what's going on and you are a determined man. Why don't you see Dr. Kennedy at his outpatient clinic on Thursday morning? The clinic runs from 9 a.m. to 12.30 p.m. Surely he could find a minute to speak to you and you can put your concerns straight to him.'

Tom picked up the cue swiftly.

'I'll do it. Seems much better than writing letters. I must thank you.'

1 6

As John Nicholson walked in the Phoenix Park the light faded off the hills to the south, the world grew darker and a breeze blew in from the west. A moon crescent challenged the failing light. Shadows grew longer and more menacing. Even the birds were muted lamenting the loss of another day. It was the evening before Wainwright's funeral and John's fatigue intensified. He wished to be alone. There was a peace about this place. It was close to the city and St. Mary's. For two hours he walked with a lot on his mind, then at the Furry Glen he gazed over the water reflecting on years of rapport and turmoil.

This place was remote. Another world. Some mystical element could speak through the silence. Wainwright was gone--gone suddenly--and was irreplaceable. It was like being kicked when one was down. Linda's death was hard to cope with. Now this. Fate certainly knew how to lay it on thick and fast. The double grief was like a physical pain--only worse. Treatments were available for most pains. This was different. Attacks came in waves and sapped his energy. Few people or places were open to go to and pour one's heart out. Maybe that was his fault. It was too late to change. Words flashed past him; frustration, anger, rejection and uncertainty. Yet loneliness was low on the list as there were two escapes; the memory of years with the warm hearted Wainwright and Linda's diaries.

After the air had cleared his brain he drove home, a little older and wiser. Karita said grief was the fire of life. Perhaps she had a point.

A notice was placed in the papers saying the funeral was private and flowers should be donated to charity. It was Wainwright's wish to be cremated and his remains returned to the family plot in Cambridge.

A group of close friends were invited to the crematorium and the rector of St. Anne's officiated. About twenty people attended a reception in the house in Rathgar; among them was the general manager of St. Mary's, senior administrative staff, John Nicholson and James Kennedy. One surviving brother travelled from London.

There was muted conversation in the house; most found it embarrassing to talk to others but felt obliged to do so. Not so James Kennedy who went to the general manager and Chairman of the Board of Governors. Observing from a distance John was undecided to join them. One look from Kennedy showed he wasn't welcome.

A booming voice came from behind and a large hand placed on his shoulder.

'John my dear friend. How are you?'

Gustav Isselherg apologised for being late. He only heard the news and got on the first plane to say goodbye to one of his dearest friends.

'I was shocked to hear the news about poor Walter.'

'It was a great loss to all of us.' John projected his voice in the direction of the Kennedy group. There was a ripple of recognition. 'A wonderful man and probably impossible to replace.'

'I knew him a long time. Ever since we were students in Cambridge,' Isselherg said. 'No one could touch him in experimental pathology. He's done so much. Look at his publications. Truly extraordinary.'

The many facets of Wainwright's career were discussed. John informed Isselherg about the problems facing the department from now on.

'It'll probably drift for a while. That's obvious,' Isselherg said in a loud voice, 'but I hope it won't be let drift too long. It could go down hill rapidly if there's no strong leadership at the top.'

He placed his hand on John's shoulder again and looked around the room.

Every morning Dr. Kennedy rushed through the ward stopping at each bed, hardly listening to results he'd requested. He'd interrupt sister or the house physician in mid-sentence.

'I know the rest of that report. It's the same as yesterday.'

'There's more to come, doctor.' Sister reminded him sternly.

'It's essentially the same. Carry on the treatment. Next case.'

So it went on, getting more hurried and flustered. He always left Annette Nolan to the last minute, his mind on other things. Lots of other things.

'Dr. Kennedy,' Sister Agnes said, 'you should know this patient has deteriorated recently. She sleeps all day, can't walk around the ward and her appetite is poor.'

Dr. Kennedy gave a sigh.

'I remember the girl. She refuses to answer my questions and is totally uncooperative. We should arrange a psychiatric assessment.' He turned to the house physician. 'Doctor please arrange an appointment with Dr. Levine to see if he can throw any light on her behaviour. It's most odd and I cannot think why.'

'Perhaps her new medication is not agreeing with her, Dr. Kennedy,' Sister Agnes volunteered.

He stared at her in disbelief and gave full reign to his fury.

'Sister Agnes how could you! Of course it's agreeing with her. Only it will take time. You above all people should know that. These are not overnight miracles we perform. It's a matter of time. It's a matter of time for all of us.' His voice was rising. 'You'll have to be patient. That's all. It's simple and you should know that.'

He looked at his watch, which he did frequently.

'I must be off. No time to waste in useless argument. There are more important things to do. Understood? Goodbye.'

She looked at him sailing out of the ward oblivious to the frightened eyes that followed him. She had to find a way around this. Experience of adversity had stood to her in the past, yet this was one of the worst cases she could remember. A lot of planning was needed.

And Annette Nolan continued to deteriorate.

1 8

Dr. Kennedy had several meetings scheduled with Colin Smith, the general manager. There was a strategy ahead and nothing was going to get in the way. He made straight for Smith's office after ward rounds and demanded to be seen. It was urgent and could not wait. The message was passed on and he was invited in.

'Mr. Smith you're probably aware,' he sat down, 'that there's an obvious vacuum in the department after Wainwright's death. Even today I could see untidiness and indiscipline at all levels of staff. It's my duty to point these things out. I've a greater opportunity to observe the activities of the clinical staff and the way they go about their duties. You have more important things to do in your office, and let me add you and your large team are doing a splendid job in monitoring the hospital.'

'Thank you so much Dr. Kennedy.' Smith sat back and smiled benevolently. 'Your comments are most welcome. It's difficult to establish a management team to monitor work. Information gathering using performance indicators on the professional staff is horrendous. It's a thankless job so I appreciate your kind words. I sometimes feel sorry for my staff. Their efforts are not always appreciated. The sooner we get funds for surveillance equipment the better.'

'That's wonderful Mr. Smith. Something to look forward to.' Kennedy half shuddered as he said the words. 'It'll make your work easier to account for every item.'

'That's right Dr. Kennedy.' Smith agreed with a triumphant smile. 'More importantly, however, monitoring will enable us to objectively measure how long each doctor spends with patients and if time is wasted we can take corrective action and potentially save a lot of money. Efficiency is our guideword. That's what we're paid to do. To save money. Efficiency is the name of the game. Efficiency at all costs. Yes that's our motto. We've estimated there's so much time wasted by clinical staff that it could be reduced by at least half. Then think of the savings that could be spent on other things. Doctors talk too much to patients. We could double the number of patients seen in outpatients, for example, and thus greatly increase productivity. It's obvious doctors are wasting time and we could show them the way. But it will cost a lot more money--although well spent. Don't you agree Dr. Kennedy?'

'Yes. I do. It sounds logical I wonder why someone didn't think of it before.'

'We weren't here before.' Smith said simply. 'Well don't worry. Better late than never. I must say it's nice to get agreement from one of the senior consultants. It makes a welcome change. I think we can work together, Dr. Kennedy.'

'Yes, indeed. Why not?

1 9

Tom and Ruth Nolan sat in front of the log fire occupied with their thoughts. She'd made sure the room was neat and tidy; the fire built up, flowers on display beside the violin stand in the corner--straight in front of Tom was Patsie spread out wallowing in the heat.

Three days to the outpatient clinic--too long for Tom. If tomorrow he could get the confrontation over. Restraint was proving difficult though he must learn. It was a time of preparation, planning a strategy and not putting a foot wrong. Also time to compose a letter, a polite one, which seemed mandatory and he was determined to deliver it personally. No obstructive secretary would stand in his way.

Ruth also felt the strain. She was aware of Annette's deterioration but the authorities were doing their best and accepted it without question. And she still trusted her husband. It seemed the whole family were on trial playing a waiting game. It was not time that set the pace of activities it was her anxieties, a distress she suffered in silence.

On Wednesday evening both parents visited Annette. The ward was bright and warm when they arrived and conversation mixed with laughter was a good sign. They approached Annette. Her face was turned away and eyes closed. She was asleep--again. A pale arm rested listlessly on the white sheets. Ruth called her name. Slowly she turned to face them. The eyes were sunken dark and dilated. Emaciation was beginning to show. This is not progress, it's progressive, Tom said to himself. Something must be done. It was torture.

Annette had a sense of hopelessness; her childish joys were growing dim. She tried to smile but felt she was looking at someone a long way off. Attempts at conversation were made. Soon the parents realised the efforts were too much. Tom looked at his watch and signalled it was time to go.

2 0

Tom Nolan was determined to be in plenty of time for the clinic on Thursday morning. At eight-thirty he was the first at reception. Nurses and clerks began arriving about ten minutes to nine. Immediately he approached the girl in charge when the blinds were raised at the desk.

'Is Dr. Kennedy's clinic this morning?' He asked amiably.

'Yes. Have you an appointment?' Was the sharp reply.

'Well. No. I wondered if he could spare a minute to talk about my daughter Annette Nolan in ward 3 A. She's not well and we're really worried.'

'That may not be possible Mr. Nolan. Dr. Kennedy's busy and has a full list.'

'It'd only take a minute. That's all.'

'Well. I don't know.'

'Please.'

'Why don't you talk to sister-in-charge in ward 3 A?'

'I already have and she suggested I come to his clinic today.'

'Well. I don't know,' she repeated in an off hand manner.

'It was not possible to talk to him on the phone. He was too busy. I spoke to his secretary. She suggested I write him a letter.'

'Well?'

'I have the letter and brought it with me. I'd like to deliver it personally.'

'Well. I don't know. It'd be better if I give it to him. Perhaps you'd like to wait in the queue. He may see you after he reads the letter.'

'Are you sure?'

'I am sure. I'll give it to him and tell him you are waiting.'

'That sounds a good compromise. Here's the letter. I'll wait over there and hope it won't be too long. It's very important I see him you know.'

'I'll pass the message on Mr. Nolan. Please take a seat.'

At nine o'clock patients arrived and filled up most seats. No sign of Kennedy. Nine-thirty came and went. Still no sign. Then a flurry came from the entrance and Kennedy rushed in with two briefcases and a pile of hospital folders, said nothing and disappeared into his room. A nurse appeared and read out a patient's name. The person called disappeared into the room and rapidly reappeared. A regular feature. No call for Tom Nolan.

Eleven o'clock came and went and yet no call for Tom Nolan. Half an hour later he went to reception to ask the girl if the letter had been delivered. To his surprise the previous girl had disappeared. She was on her midmorning break.

'How long will that be?' He asked.

'Oh about forty-five minutes approximately. If you'd like to try again.'

"Suppose I've no choice.'

He returned to his seat and waited half an hour. Restraint was wearing thin. Twelve-fifteen arrived, as did the first girl who was on her break. He returned to the desk and asked if she'd delivered the letter.

'Of course.' The reply was abrupt. 'I left it on his desk at nine o'clock. He's bound to have received it.'

'But he only came in at nine-fifty. He may have ignored it. Please could you find out if he's received it? Please.'

' 'Fraid not sir. I'm on my lunch break. You'd better ask one of the other girls, or better still, why not ask his nurse next time she comes out?'

'All right then. Probably my last hope.'

Another half-hour passed and a glamorous nurse emerged from the consulting room intent on ignoring everyone as she hurried passed the benches. Tom stepped into her path. She had to stop.

'Excuse me nurse. My name is Tom Nolan. I've been here since eight-thirty and I asked that a letter be delivered directly to Dr. Kennedy by hand. I was promised it would be. Please could you check?'

'Dr. Kennedy gets lots of letters Mr. Nolan. He's a very busy man.'

'I know he's busy.' He stood towering over her. 'Everybody keeps telling me he's busy. It seems he's no time to talk to the parents of one of his very ill patients. Now would you please return to that consulting room and find out if he has received my letter delivered by hand four hours ago and if in his busy schedule could he even spare a minute to talk to a concerned parent. It's a sad thing we've no communication from him about her progress.'

'Mr. Nolan I should remind you that Dr. Kennedy is most concerned. The referring doctor, a Dr. Sutton, is informed of all the clinical details and really you should go and see him for a progress report.'

'I'm sorry nurse. I've waited four days to come to Dr. Kennedy's clinic and now waited nearly five hours this morning only to be told he cannot spare a minute to talk to me. He's too busy and I should return to my GP. That's all the bad news I need. Each day I see deterioration. Her GP doesn't. We do. He can only go on an occasional letter he might get from the consultant.'

He guessed she knew more but wasn't going to give an inch.

'I'm sorry Mr. Nolan. Dr. Kennedy cannot spare the time. He wishes to say your daughter is making good and satisfactory progress.'

The fuse in the time bomb ticking inside was lit. Defiantly he stood up, pushed the nurse aside and burst into the consulting room to confront Kennedy. Total surprise appeared on each other's faces. Kennedy, holding a golf club in his hands, was gently practising his swing across the carpet.

'Dr. Kennedy,' Tom exploded, 'I only wanted to get some words of reassurance about our daughter Annette. She's getting sicker by the day and even the nursing staff are fearful about her. What can you tell us about the future?'

Kennedy put the club down looking uncomfortable and foolish.

'She's a difficult child Mr. Nolan. Difficult in many ways. Now that I've seen you I'll see if there's anything further can be done. For the moment you must excuse me. I've got an important meeting at two o'clock which I cannot miss.'

Looking at his watch and mumbling to himself Kennedy hurried to the car-park. Before getting into the car he checked the clubs were complete and in order in the booth. The match was due to tee off at two o'clock and he'd only thirty minutes to get there. The intrusion in the hospital caused him to miss lunch. Hopefully Smith would understand how hard it was to keep to strict schedules--not to blame him, as he was a victim of circumstances. He deserved a few hours of golf, though he really didn't like the game that much. It was a way of meeting people that counted. Many senior executives in administration played an incredible amount of golf and were always looking for suitable partners.

That evening Kennedy wanted to go home for a well-earned rest. Another busy day tomorrow. When was it otherwise? Yet something wouldn't leave him alone. The pleading, even the restrained arrogance of Tom Nolan had a lasting effect. Was there an option? He was in charge and had several warnings the child was not responding. They were only fussing. Conventional treatment took weeks to have an effect, although he hadn't checked recent blood results. That was a mistake. He turned left off the main road and headed for St. Mary's.

In spite of his tiredness he made for ward 3 A. Lights were dimmed to allow children to sleep. He crept up to the girl's bed. The light was a little stronger here. She could be awake even though the eyes were closed. A pink eiderdown covered the bed, probably her own, and one hand held a well-worn teddy up to the pathetic face.

'Annette. This is Dr. Kennedy,' he whispered, 'Are you awake?'

No reply. The eyes remained closed. He repeated the words a little louder. Still no reply. For a fleeting moment he met her eyes, dark and hostile, sunk deep and red rimmed. She did look very ill and the sight shocked him. Fine lines of the immature bone structure, black lustreless hair and hollow cheeks were clearly defined.

She lay motionless in the half-light like an old master painting; the almost angelic countenance had the potential for profound beauty. That is if she was to survive the illness and given the chance to pull through. He remained a further minute then shuffled out of the ward, his movements followed by the dark, sunken eyes.

What did Dr. Kennedy want at this time with no nurse or sister? She'd little energy left to be frightened; any feeling she had was almost one of hate although she barely knew its meaning. What she found difficult to understand in Dr. Kennedy was his aloofness; he was either loud and obnoxious or quiet and sarcastic with no compassion. What made him so? She could think of nicer people. Her dad for example. So much fun and excitement about everything and her mum who cared for her beyond all doubt and her greatest pall, Patsie. She was stuck in this hostile atmosphere where people were horrible and seemed to fight all the time. She longed for home.

Kennedy went into the ward office where patients' folders were filed. Annette Nolan's was easy to find; he sat down and studied recent reports. There certainly was a significant increase in white cells. It was a progressive acute leukaemia--out of control. Current treatment seemed ineffective. Something more radical, even courageous, was needed if the illness was to be halted and stabilised. Radiotherapy or even marrow ablation and donor replacement. That would be a last resort and not always possible. He flicked through previous pages and found Nicholson's detailed entries to start her treatment, which was to last three weeks at least. Nicholson had a flare for the most advanced chemotherapy and was prepared to take risks and even added unconventional items. He studied these and came to a decision. This girl would probably die if left on the present regimen. If Nicholson's treatment was tried she could also die or possibly respond.

Who was to know?

2 2

Sister Agnes set out on her two-mile walk from Liffey Mansions to St. Mary's early next morning. The showery weather she was well used to and yet the blustering attempts of fate to find her off guard, to contend with adversity such as a handicapped son, an unfortunate mother in a special home and a husband who disappeared off the face of the earth were a constant worry. Dr. Kennedy's behaviour only added to her problems. His ward rounds she dreaded; his occasional smile at staff--rarely at patients--as if he used his exalted position to dispense happiness through gestures. He was a contradiction. It was unpleasant for everyone except Dr. Kennedy, as he appeared to enjoy others' misery.

It stopped raining when she reached St. Mary's. Typical. You travel drenched and it stops when you arrive. Another day ahead. Did Annette have a restful night? Strange how she thought of the little patient slowly disappearing before her very eyes.

Her wet clothes were changed and she tidied for the wards.

There was a compulsion to go to ward 3 A first expecting the worst.

'How are you today Annette?' She asked kindly.

'Not much change sister.' Annette was not at all happy. 'I couldn't eat breakfast and had a terrible nightmare last night.'

'Oh dear.' She sat on the bed. 'That's awful. Care to tell me?'

'Of course.' Annette tried to sit up. Sister helped her.

'Tell me what happened.' Sympathy was in her voice.

Annette began with a shudder. 'It was late, the ward was quiet and the lights were out. I was asleep when I heard Dr. Kennedy's voice beside me. It was unmistakable and he was whispering something. I was so frightened I kept my eyes closed. He insisted on calling my name. He stayed a few minutes but I remained as still as possible. He turned away slowly, quiet as a mouse. I peeped and saw he was dressed in curious sports clothes I think but I could be mistaken. It was all so strange and there wasn't a soul around. It was like an apparition or a ghost. I couldn't get it out of my mind all night.'

'You poor child, Annette.' She touched her on the cheek. 'As if you hadn't enough problems. Now this. It's intolerable.'

Annette started to cry, gently at first, but then she gave in. The other children watched and some cried in sympathy.

Under normal circumstances sister would come down on them like a ton of bricks. Not today. Stalemate was in the air. Something must be done for this girl and her parents who'd already tried to redress an abusive situation. Even though she was a decisive person there were times she wanted to runaway from stress. Why did one person have to be so superior that no one else mattered? No one else had a say in the care of the most vulnerable in society. Annette was not going to be given that chance--if Kennedy had his way.

His treatment was only effective in mild cases. He hadn't the courage of Dr. Nicholson to take a major risk to attack a major illness with the most powerful therapeutic agents available. There were risks but surely a fatal outcome was the greatest risk of all. It was maddening.

Sister Agnes held Annette's hand and then placed it under the bedclothes.

'Annette I must leave you now. I've lots of work to do. But I'll be back soon when I've read night-sister's report. Just rest now.'

A cup of tea and biscuits were waiting in the ward office. Annette Nolan's folder was on top of the others. A message, written in red ink and dated nine-thirty the previous evening, was addressed 'for the attention of Sister Agnes Lynch. Please see inside for instructions.'She turned to the last page. Her eyes widened as she read: 'all present medication to cease forthwith. Please start the Nicholson regimen, see page 38, for full instructions. This is a more radical form of treatment, but it is now my judgement that it is called for and urgently. Please implement immediately. (Signed) James Kennedy.

Interviews for Professor Wainwright's replacement were set for March. This would give the successful candidate time to work through notice and start at the beginning of the academic year in September. Advertisements were placed in Ireland, the UK and in selected US journals, which were circulated in most continental countries.

One of the first applications was from Dr. James Kennedy. It was an impressive document listing things Colin Smith never realised he'd achieved. Compared to his previous application there was a marked difference. A PR firm probably had a hand in it. Two applications came from the UK, one from Germany and the USA--a total of five. A comfortable number, but why no word from Dr. Nicholson? It was well known he was Professor Wainwright's favourite colleague and even friend. Years ago Wainwright appointed him as Lecturer in Pathology and supported the appointment out of his reserve fund. Rumours and speculation were rife. Would he go forward? If not would his present position in the hospital be worth keeping?

John Nicholson had his reasons. It was uncertain the new appointment would continue to fund his specialised genetic work. Many professed they couldn't understand it. He'd contacts abroad that were more in line with his ways, including Germany, Sweden and especially Cambridge. He'd published extensively in journals that only accepted highly technical science. One of his outspoken critics was Dr. Kennedy who questioned the value of the computer analyses and risk factors, the detailed mathematical calculations-- more like pure science than commonsense medicine that would be useful for sick patients in hospital.

Yet John Nicholson knew what he was doing. If James Kennedy was deliberately blind to the ultimate benefit of population screening John would leave him to continue to impress students and staff with static and unimaginative medical practice that was above all, safe for him but maybe not for patients. Kennedy hated taking risks and wished to be known as dependable and not putting a foot wrong. And administration always admired that kind of behaviour.

John had prepared a curriculum vitae, which was initially too long, a whole twenty-two pages, containing the esoteric papers in lesser known journals, details of his current research and work for the future. He deleted a lot of it so that the final submission was seven pages long. He placed it inside Linda's diary and retired to bed.

It was difficult to sleep. A wind reaching storm force and heavy rain were forecast and Nature kept her promise. Even though all windows were sealed she insinuated herself; the scream overhead, sound of trees and debris flying about, sheet rain clawing at everything and eerily moving curtains made it an uncomfortable night.

Tomorrow he'd booked a day off work and it was the last date for submission of applications. He longed for peace and quiet to weight up his decision but tonight's bedlam was not helping to induce a state of calm; it was more like a multiple replay of Mussorgsky's Night On A Bare Mountain.

Next morning he woke early. Still chaotic outside. Slowly he walked downstairs. Linda's diary was on the floor near the front door. His job application lay beside it. How strange! More strange the page that was open was the last entry made when they took the trip to the "valley of the two lakes", which reminded her of Dalarna and Mount Velkon in Sweden. Glendalough was her nirvana or Shangri-La. The scene came flooding back; walk by the lake, tall trees, cliffs, silent water leading over to St. Kevin's Bed and then arriving at the waterfall at the end of the lake. The sound of the moving water was magical as she prepared a picnic.

She patted the rug beside her and said.

'Come John, let us make our own memories.' The rest of the afternoon was indelibly printed in his memory.

He picked up the application and looked out the window. The rain had stopped and the sun shone brightly. Nature was calling him back to the valley of the two lakes and this time he'd take Linda's diary. As he drove through Enniskerry the sky was still unsettled. The back road past the Sugarloaf Mountain had little traffic. On through Roundwood, Annamoe and into Laragh across the bridge over the Glenmacnass River before joining the Avonmore River. All in flood after last night's rain.

Laragh is a village that boasts a few shops, a petrol pump and a pub, which provides a decent lunch. As it was still raining he decided to try the speciality of the day. The forecasters promised it would clear later.

The pub was deserted so there was a good choice of seating. His order given, he chose a seat at the window with a view of the crossroads. A turf fire smouldered in the grate, wooden benches rested along the walls with pine tables. An old man with a velvet voice spoke to his dog as they sat at the fire, encouraging more life into the flames.

All was quiet and peaceful. Suddenly a Range Rover pulled up outside the window and a girl jumped out. She was in a hurry. John had a good view. And what a girl! A goddess in skin-tight breeches and leather boots. An open neck white blouse, which barely covered all the essentials and thick blonde hair blown hither and thither. Above average height she'd a figure that would play havoc with the pulse of any decent man. As she strode into the pub the shiny boots enhanced the beauty of long legs. She placed a rucksack on a high stool at the counter, sat on another and ran her hand through the hair to get it in shape. Vigour and wellbeing shone from her like a light; her voice was cultured, her face classical. Although he was reluctant to know about her he was enchanted. When finished her snack she threw the rucksack on her back and moved towards the door. Before leaving she looked directly at him. His heart missed a beat. Where had he seen those piercing chinablue eyes before, the straight blonde hair flowing back in waves over the ears and half way down the neck, and the exquisite gold earrings, which dangled provocatively from a small chain?

She hesitated as if deciding whether to ask a question--thought better and left. Shock from this intrusion went through him, that was in no way unpleasant and a sense of unreality came over him. Even though he did not recognise her, one instinctively knew when one had met an angel like Linda in the hills; it had real impact.

The man with the velvet voice noticed the encounter yet contin-

ued talking to his dog. John struggled through his lunch. Some
friendly overtures were made to him and the man got talking about
events that occurred in the area. Even though they were years ago
his tone made the stories seem as if they'd just happened. The sight
of his collie, hanging on to every word, eyes fixed on his master was
one of the most radiant pictures of intelligence John had ever seen.
After lunch John set off determinately to cover the walk as far as the
old tin mines. The weather was unsettled but he'd come prepared.
Threats hung in the wind, and the mist. In empty places there's always a temptation to look around and skywards with an ill-defined
anxiety. It's almost as if something is following and might show
itself at any time

He longed for company on this trek. Instead there was the sound
of distant thunder. Like some wild beast that had been rudely
awakened it rolled over the hills and now set to searching desolate
places. A sudden zigzag flashed like gunfire followed by a distant
roar in the hills.

He took shelter in the boathouse opposite St. Kevin's Bed and
waited for the worst to blow over. Across the lake flashes of light-
ning occurred as the storm leapt down from Lugduff, Camaderry
and Brocknagh Mountains and as far as Table Mountain. It leapt
through the air with the force of artillery and roared with ear-deaf-
ening sound and ripped through adjacent glens exploding in de-
creasing magnitude.

Then silence. Cascades appeared across the road rushing over
stones and heather. A mixture of fear and exhilaration filled him;
it was almost like being possessed by an elemental fury. The glens
caught the thunder and flung it to each other as in a game.

An hour later all was calm. He continued walking and found
the exact place of their last picnic. Beside the tumbling stream was

chosen for the spot to relax. He fell asleep for about half an hour. The sound of the water woke him and as he stretched his hand he touched the diary. He read about that magical day.

… In front in the bright sunshine is one of the world's glories. The hills fade into a blue haze and the quiet stream is nature's harmonious sound. Everything is complete …

… People can differ a lot in their experience of Nature. Dickens said that Glencoe in Scotland was <u>terrible</u>. When passing through the glen he found the massive rocks, sprinkled on the ground God knows when, like a burial ground for a race of giants. And a dwelling there was so bleak and mighty in its loneliness. An awful place. It is shut in on both sides by enormous cliffs from which great torrents rush down in all directions. Here one might find oneself wandering in the very height and madness of a fever …

… It's June today. What a difference to Dickens' nightmare. It's like my town land in Dalarna and the day is perfect. Alas for poor Dickens the sun was not shining. The valley is not awesome;it is not frightful, although it is like the wild mountains anywhere and gives one a lesson in humility. We have never existed for it and it is oblivious to us. Here is scenery without mercy. The walk is half in sun and half in shadow. In the upper heights are gullies broadening into streams as water descends into the valley. In some gashes trees hide from the wind as we would when sheltering from the elements. The sun goes in--for a while. The glow dies in the valley as if a light has been switched off. Everything is grey and hopeless. I imagine strange and dark creatures harbouring in some of the gullies. This soon passes. Sun appears again and the pleasure of the two of us together enjoying a simple picnic is unforgettable. The imagination can run riot. Whatever way one's fancy takes it. If you chose to be sad, you will be sad. If you chose to be happy, then you <u>will</u> be happy. And that's always the best choice …

John closed the diary and gazed at the changing merciless landscape.

His decision was made.

2 4

The appointments' committee was selected. In addition to Colin Smith, General Manager of St. Mary's, there was a senior professor and Fellow of Trinity College, a Fellow of the Royal College of Surgeons, the incumbent professor of pathology in University College Dublin and a representative from the Department of Health. An external assessor was required and Sir Kenneth Richardson from Addenbrooke's Hospital in Cambridge agreed to join the committee.

The Board Room of the College of Surgeons was chosen and the great windows showed a fine spring morning in Stephen's Green. The enormous table rested in the middle of the elegant room where distinguished world leaders had received Honorary Fellowships of the College.

Today the atmosphere was less glamorous as the committee assembled at ten o'clock. Six applications were short listed to three; Dr. Gerhardt Stein from Frankfurt, Dr. James Kennedy a graduate from University College Dublin and Dr. John Nicholson from Trinity College Dublin. They were asked to wait in the adjacent Banqueting Hall.

Colin Smith, as chairman, smiled at committee members and outlined the strategy for the proceedings.

'I think we should begin. May I suggest we interview Dr. Stein from Frankfurt first? Perhaps we can establish some baselines for other candidates and who knows learn something about pathology in Germany.'

He asked the supervisor to invite Dr. Stein to join the committee. The interview went smoothly. After Colin Smith introduced members to the candidate he asked was there anything else he'd like to add to the application. Nothing further.

'Very good,Dr. Stein. Can you tell us something about yourself and then I'll hand you over to my colleagues for some specific questions.'

Dr. Stein's English was almost perfect as he explained his background and his academic qualifications. Members quizzed him on aspects of his research. It transpired he used many animal models to test the complexity of chemotherapeutic agents. Germany had many world famous companies and work was expanding. The professor of pathology then asked.

'Dr. Stein if things are well organised in Germany and you have streamlined your research programmes so well, why do you think you could do better in Ireland?'

'That question is an important one. You see professor our work is progressing rapidly, with exciting results and these are reflected in our publications but there is one drawback for me--a personal one-- the profession is overcrowded in Germany and I can see little room for advancement if I stay. The competition is just too intense.'

'And you think you might have more freedom and less competition in Ireland?'

'That's precisely my reading of the situation. There could be greater scope for individual development and I understand you have some fine research work already in progress. I knew Professor Wainwright and was a great admirer of his work and teaching. I would hope to continue his ways and methods.'

The chairman smiled at him and looked around the table.

'Any further questions gentlemen?'

None was forthcoming so he nodded to Dr. Stein, thanked him for coming and suggested he return to the Banqueting Hall. Dr. Stein stood up, bowed slightly and left the room.

'Gentlemen,' Colin Smith spoke softly, 'I suggest we keep our discussion to the end of the proceedings when we've had the opportunity to interview all the candidates.'

Dr. James Kennedy was invited to join them. He was immaculately dressed and wore his confidence like a suit of armour. He knew exactly where to sit and took his place without being invited to do so. He wished members a good--morning and gave a special welcome to the professor of pathology from UCD, his old teacher. The most obsequious greeting was reserved for Sir Kenneth Richardson.

Some were uncomfortable at the way the proceedings were going and looked at Colin Smith.

'Now gentlemen we must get down to business. For a moment I was a little uncertain who was interviewing whom. Well Dr. Kennedy we have your CV and it looks impressive.'

'Thank you Mr. Chairman.' Kennedy grinned at him across the table.

'Is there anything you'd like to add to it?'

'There probably is chairman,' he said with a shrug, 'but we can cover the additional items during the interview.' He glanced at the UCD professor.

'All right then who'd like to start?'

The TCD representative raised a hand.

'Dr. Kennedy, do you approve of using animals in medical research?'

'Of course I do. They are useful in many ways and will probably be increasingly important as time goes by.'

'Thank you. No more questions Mr. Chairman.'

The UCD professor smiled.

'I believe you run a very busy hospital practice mainly in St. Mary's and I've heard reports of your brilliant regimens in treating leukaemia. Can you expand on some of your more innovative results you've achieved?'

'Yes. This has been exciting work. As you're aware St. Mary's children's unit is the most specialised in the country and treats the more serious forms of childhood leukaemia. We've been pursuing a policy of individually tailoring regimens of chemotherapy for each patient using intensive computer analyses to help titration, doses and times of administration. We have to feel our way carefully. The intention is to try and postpone or avoid total marrow transplantation if we possibly can. Although I realise there are times when it has to be done.'

The professor smiled and said in a loud voice.

'I must say your work is highly commendable, almost in a sense pioneering. There must be risks'

Kennedy leaned back. 'Indeed there are risks but I'm willing to take them.'

Sir Kenneth Richardson was invited to speak. He hesitated,

looking down at his papers and then turned to Colin Smith.

'Yes Mr. Chairman. I would like to add a few short points to help things along. They're not really intended as questions although, at any time, I'd be more than glad to hear Dr. Kennedy's observations.' He gave a gentle cough more to emphasise his remarks. 'For many years colleagues in Cambridge have worked with that excellent centre in Sweden called the Helmuth Institute. The Director is Gustav Isselherg and for years a stream of excellent papers has come out of that Institute. Most have been world leaders in the treatment of leukaemia in children and originate from their superb laboratories using a great range of animal models. The principles for many successful regimens have come from this source and I just wonder if Dr. Kennedy is using these same recommendations already known in the international literature or has he come up with even newer and perhaps superior forms of treatment. If so does he propose to publish them in the near future? Or better still perhaps he might like to outline them to this committee this morning.'

There was an embarrassing silence from Dr. Kennedy. He was desperately gathering his thoughts on how to gloss over the searching comments.

'Thank you Sir Kenneth on your kind comments on our apparent excellent results. Of course we do read the international literature. You should also realise we have our own excellent team working in St. Mary's and Trinity College, all under Professor Wainwright. And these teams are still working here.'

'Of course. But how long can you depend on these teams, as you call them?'

'I cannot answer that question. Obviously there are many unanswered questions flying around since the tragic death of Professor Wainwright.'

'And we've already had some unanswered questions this morning Dr. Kennedy,' Sir Kenneth turned to Colin Smith and said. 'No more comments chairman.'

2 5

$\mathbf{D}$r. Nicholson was the last candidate. A feeling of <u>déjà vu</u> came as he walked across the sumptuous Donegal carpet. He thought he detected a faint smell of sulphur; and was at a disadvantage in waiting the longest.

Wearing his professional smile Colin Smith extended a hand for him to be seated.

'Welcome, Dr. Nicholson.'

Formalities were gone through, introductions, glances at CVs and bland questions. The professor of pathology indicated he'd like to start proceedings.

'Dr. Nicholson you've been active in animal research in the past. Some time ago this activity seemed to occupy you to a great extent but little appears on your current curriculum vitae.'

'A lot of my research was carried out in Sweden and major obstacles were overcome, laying the foundations for modern chemotherapy.'

'That's right Dr. Nicholson,' interjected Sir Kenneth, 'this committee has acknowledged your valuable work when we interviewed the last candidate.'

'So you realise what is in Dublin is mainly based on Swedish work.'

There was a mixed response except from Sir Kenneth.

'Yes. Indeed we did recognise this work. Then you returned to Dublin alongside Professor Wainwright. For some reason your work went in a different direction. What a pity you didn't continue. You were diverted into the field of genetics and computer analyses.'

'There were some circumstances in Dublin that militated against medical research as it's routinely carried out elsewhere. These made it difficult to continue.'

'A simple fire can make cowards of us all.' A low voice came from the left of the chairman. Not everyone heard it, or didn't want to hear it.

John certainly heard it and knew exactly where it came from. He glared at the source and his expression said more than words could do.

Colin Smith realised the committee should be wound up as quickly as possible. Another gentle cough and shuffling of papers indicated the proceedings were over.

John Nicholson withdrew almost unnoticed from the Board Room. Candidates were asked to remain in the Banqueting Hall.

Colin Smith asked for tea and coffee to be sent up to the Board Room. He had a feeling things hadn't gone smoothly.

He drew a breath and asked for silence.

'Gentlemen the task ahead is not easy. Professor Wainwright was a wonderful research worker; a superb teacher and clinician almost in equal measure although I've heard his skills in administration were not always up to the standards we expect today. However we're not all perfect.' He gave a gentle laugh. 'The question we must ask now is which of our three candidates can match his qualities? I hope you'll agree these are the important requirements to allow us to come to our decision. Agree?'

Silence reigned. 'Very well then. Any views on Dr. Stern?'

Sir Kenneth spoke first.

'Good candidate who would do excellent work and also perform well. You'd probably get good research out of him but I'd have some doubt about his teaching ability. Would students take to him?

I think not but I may be wrong. As for his clinical skill I've a feeling this is probably his weakest point. There's little reference to his duties and even the referees tended to shy away from this aspect.'

'Thanks Sir Kenneth. In summary you'd feel we'd have a good medical scientist producing lots of papers with little else. Almost a full time laboratory worker.'

'Yes although perhaps a little strong, it does sum up my feelings.'

Nodding of heads occurred. The chairman invited further comment. None came.

'Can we pass on to the next candidate, Dr. Kennedy, who holds a consultant appointment in St. Mary's and has expressed a keen interest in laboratory research. Who would like to start?'

The pathology professor raised a hand.

'I've known Dr. Kennedy a long time. Always a true gentleman.'

'Of course professor,' Colin Smith interrupted, 'but I must remind you of our criteria. Research teaching and clinical medicine.'

'Indeed chairman. I was coming to them. His research is somewhat lacking with few published papers although he said he'd be willing to undertake research especially in animals. And he's a splendid teacher. All the reports coming to me show his students respect him and he exerts great discipline. Lastly his ability as a clinician seems to be very good. He's made remarkable breakthroughs in advanced leukaemia. His success rates are truly remarkable.'

Sir Kenneth leaned forward in his chair.

'Professor does he intend publishing the results of his breakthroughs? Suggestions made to me indicate his regimens have been tried out elsewhere and there's nothing new in what he's doing. Could be a reason why he's reluctant to go into print.'

A silence followed. There was no answer from the pathology professor.

'Now let's move on to the last candidate, Dr. Nicholson,' Smith said. 'He worked closely with Professor Wainwright for some years and also in Sweden where many research papers were produced. His work appears to be remarkable but for some reason stopped when he returned to Dublin. This would worry me. Any comments?'

The Trinity professor spoke first.

'I found his CV fascinating and it was by far the best. His interview didn't go well and he seemed uncomfortable with the process. Maybe he's reserved or has personal problems. And I cannot speak for his medical skills.'

The pathology professor was next.

'His CV was commendable. Why wouldn't it be with Isselherg's name on most of the publications? Where's the real credit? Also it's baffling he stopped his animal research on returning to Dublin and this while working with Wainwright. Indeed there were many rows over the issue. Wainwright urged him to continue the Swedish work in Dublin but he was reluctant. Instead he went off into genetics and computer analyses and new fangled technology that nobody else understood. As for the final criterion--his medical competence--he has a good reputation and appears popular with patients but seems to find it difficult to teach students. They almost seem to get in his way.'

Colin Smith looked at his watch.

'I think we've had enough time to assess each candidate. You've read the CVs, had the opportunity to speak to each one and we've had our discussion. It's decision time. Perhaps a vote would be the fairest. Could I have your votes as a figure out of ten?'

The votes were collected and he read them out carefully.

'Your votes go as follows Dr. Stern six out of ten, Dr. Kennedy eight out of ten and Dr. Nicholson gets seven out of ten.'

He wrote the results down carefully on official papers and passed them around for members to sign.

'So gentlemen the winner of the chair in experimental pathology in TCD along with the Head of Oncology in St. Mary's hospital is Dr. James Kennedy.'

2 7

The appointment went to the person who'd made it to the top by various means. Some felt he deserved it; others said there were other reasons. Professor Kennedy ignored the rumours. It was a city of begrudgers and unfortunately such scum existed. They should be treated with contempt. Out to make trouble and best avoided. Kennedy gathered around him the favoured ones. Those who did not support him, or were indifferent, were shunned. No two ways about it--for or against. His empire was going to be built this way and would influence research especially in cancer. It would be the main factor in educating students in St. Mary's and satellite hospitals under the control of TCD. Because he was well in with the UCD authorities arrangements could be made if they were willing to play ball. As for patients, there was always the staff such as consultants, registrars and house physicians who'd carry on treating ungrateful patients. Nicholson and colleagues could adequately undertake this.

*

The whiff of sulphur that John Nicholson picked up in the Board Room proved right. Conspiracy was in the air. The questions, or most of them, were not really questions. They were rhetorical to entrap him leaving no means of escape. And the comment that a fire in a research hut could make cowards of us all. The chairman should have insisted the source be identified and action taken.

The following days were grey although adversity was beginning to have less effect. He'd the security of a consultant post although one aspect of his work caused concern--the future of research. A programme of genetic profiling groups to assess risk was being developed and a basis for screening certain populations. He saw beyond the present. Yet people said he was wasting time and should be treating established disease, which was already a problem in cancer clinics. The message of prevention was hard to get across and the sooner widespread studies were carried out the better the health of the nation would be. Some said he was a man before his time. Others like Colin Smith and the new professor of oncology were not impressed. Their concern was to cope with present disease and let the future take care of itself. And all these fancy screening programmes would be expensive to run and drain precious resources. Under the new regime the more John tried to promote his plans the more resistance he encountered. Don't rock the boat Dr. Nicholson. We've enough problems as it is without examining apparently healthy populations and looking for trouble. What's the point in that?

Yet John knew it was where the future lay. He could prove it and many papers were appearing in the literature, pilot studies that showed significant drops in death rates because of early detection. The harder he tried the deafer the authorities became. Gradually things started to go wrong. He needed items of equipment to maintain the running of projects but for some reason funding was refused on the grounds the budget was overspent. Next month, perhaps, he might like to make a further submission. Next month the same answer came.

Frustration he could cope with and was good at getting around it. Then he found evidence of deliberate blocking procedures in place to prevent the flow of funds. He became worried. This wouldn't happen in Professor Wainwright's day. The matter would be settled immediately.

Now it was different. It was difficult to get an appointment with Professor Kennedy. He seemed to be always at a meeting, or conference or away and could his secretary take a message and the professor would ring back. He rarely did. Things went from bad to worse.

The research was being run down by means outside John's control. It was not a happy situation and he saw little way out of it. A concerted effort was being made to make him feel uncomfortable, nothing direct, nothing open, but a creeping paralysis of all his brightest ideas and hopes for the future.

Frustration turned to anger.

2 8

Annette Nolan was allowed home after a three-month intensive course of treatment in St. Mary's. She was in remission thanks to new treatment discovered by Professor Kennedy she was told. And to think for the first two weeks she was so poorly.

She'd put on some weight and could walk along the shore with her mother and Patsie up to the school gates. What a welcome especially when it was discovered it was her thirteenth birthday. Regular blood checks were still required but she didn't mind.

'If that's all I have to do to stay well along with the iron tablets Professor Kennedy wants me to take I'll be the happiest girl in the world,' she told her mother.

Even Tom Nolan was a changed man. Since Annette's illness a further dimension came into their relationship.

They had been a happy family, struggling but complete in many ways with no major worries. Life was simple and fulfilling. They didn't ask for much yet were interdependent. Then came Annette's illness. What were they to do?

A new doctor had set up practice in nearby Greystones--a Dr. Peter Sutton. Previously he'd been in Westport but a domestic problem caused him to travel east and look for a suitable area to set up practice. He chose their little town, although not as nice as Westport there were many similarities. He was well regarded by everyone and couldn't do enough for his patients. The word got out; however, that one should avoid his wife who thought she was in charge of everything. She was totally obnoxious. Some outspoken patients advised the doctor he should get rid of her as she was a liability and could ruin the practice.

For the present the Nolans were settling down to a domestic routine complete in every way with a good doctor looking after them. Tom felt adversity could work wonders sometimes. Annette's return brought about a flowering of a kind of love new to him. It was deep and demanding. Ruth was reaching beyond anything before to hold his heart and affection. There was a new attitude to existence and it began to appear in his work. A hope and confidence in times to come.

Times were different for John Nicholson. Clinical work was satisfying but research was not progressing, as it should. It dawned on him the reasons put forward for lack of funding were only a cover-up for something more fundamental, more sinister in the academic environment. Apparently elements in the new regime did not want him to succeed. The same old story he'd gone through before repeating itself, success was frowned on and not easily forgiven.

Life became dull and unreal, a struggle as never before. Why even bother? What's the point? Numbness came back and clouded everything--everything was becoming a useless effort.

It was time to take stock. He could opt for another way out and ignore obstructions and jealousies. Opt for the easy life. Do some clinical work only, then golf and a social round. Lots of others were doing it, getting well paid and playing hard at life. No,this was not him. He was a loner and still ambitious--maybe his curse. There must be another way. Other distractions like art, poetry, music and even writing.

Karita flashed through his mind. She'd such wonderful plans and was most anxious for help. Sometime but not yet. It was too soon. Forming a new relationship with someone could have its merits. It required a lot of energy and <u>joie de vivre</u>,which was in short supply at present. It was again too soon. Only nine months. Caught in a dilemma. There was no easy answer.

The present situation was becoming intolerable made deliberately so. A crisis was looming in his career. A crossroads was some way off. Slowly and inevitably he was approaching it.

He had to change.

A message was waiting for John on the answer machine. Unusual. Few people knew his home number, as it was ex-directory. Pressing the response key he heard the distinct voice of Sir Kenneth Richardson.

'Hello Dr. Nicholson. Richardson here. This call may come as a surprise. Well let it be. I'm in Dublin for a conference and it is four o'clock on Tuesday. I'd like to see you for a chat when it would be mutually convenient. I'm staying at Jury's Hotel in Landsdowne Road. If this message gets through in time say before seven o'clock, and you are free, could I invite you to dinner at the hotel? It is important we talk directly. I hate letters and even phone calls. Would this be possible? If so please phone me in room 2007 and take a chance. I wish to talk about something important. Say yes if you can possibly make it. I await your call. Thank you and hope you're keeping well.'

John was flabbergasted. What on earth was all this about? There was no indication why Sir Kenneth wanted to see him.

He looked at his watch. It was six o'clock. Plenty of time to make it. Sir Kenneth was the only one in the interview that gave him a fair hearing and seemed a pleasant person. He'd nothing to lose. He phoned the hotel and asked for room 2007. It was answered immediately.

'Richardson speaking. How can I help?'

'Sir Kenneth. Nice to get your message. This is John Nicholson returning your call. Hope you're enjoying the conference. There are so many going on here it's hard to keep up with them.'

'Indeed Dr. Nicholson. The conference is informative and well organised. In a way I was hoping I might have met you at it. Certainly Professor Kennedy was there and I'd to hear about the studies he's doing and the changes that are necessary since Wainwright left us.'

John cringed at the thought.

'However don't worry John. May I call you John?'

'Yes. I'd be delighted.'

'It's hard to talk on the phone. I do hope you are free for an hour or two this evening. I'd welcome an opportunity to discuss some important matters in private. And what better place than this lovely hotel? How about it?'

'Yes. That would be wonderful. What time would suit?'

'Could you make it between seven and seven-thirty? I'll order dinner in my room.'

'I'll look forward to it. See you later then.'

He replaced the receiver and checked the time. It was six-fifteen. Just enough time to prepare. He arrived in good time and was shown up to Sir Kenneth's room, a sumptuous suite on the first floor.

A perfect county gentleman, white hair and plenty of it, ruddy complexion, and an obvious taste for tweeds, an agreeable wit and eloquent tongue and probably a roving eye for women, welcomed him. The manners were the height of perfection, his welcome generous and warm.

'Dr. Nicholson--sorry John. It's so good of you to come. I much appreciate it.'

'Not at all. I was free.' John dropped his voice to a murmur. 'I received your call on my return from a long walk in the country. It's a good way to get rid of worries.'

'You're bothered with worries then?'

'I have my share like all of us.'

'Some have more than others.'

'Maybe. But we do our best to cope.'

'I suspect you were troubled about the recent interviews.'

'To be honest I was devastated.' John was subdued.

'I'm not surprised. There was bias operating against you. It was obvious to me.'

'Could you not have voiced your opinion?'

'I did very strongly. The chairman put the decision to a vote. Of course I voted for you.'

'Thanks Sir Kenneth. That means a lot.'

The more he saw of Sir Kenneth the more he liked him. He was polite true and honest, a cynic with malice, a dreamer and a hard nosed pragmatist.

'There's something I have to ask you John. Are you happy now that there's a new regime in place?'

He probably knew the answer but was obliged to ask it.

'Happiness is too strong a word Sir Kenneth, especially over the past few months. They've been turbulent. I prefer contentment and even that's incomplete. There are things that irritate and seem to be getting worse since Wainwright died.'

'Yes. He must have had a stabilising effect on you. I know he has given you wonderful support over the years. It was a great loss. Well John we can't live in the past.   We must be concerned with the present and ask if we want that present to continue into the future.'

'Lots have no option. They have to accept their present life will continue until they retire. They've no choice.'

Sir Richard stood towering over him.

'That's the point of our meeting tonight John.'

John hesitated. 'I don't understand.'

'Well then I won't beat about the bush. I was impressed with your CV. It was the best by far. Your publications are extensive and have made a great contribution to medical science. Now from what I hear--not just from you--there's a systematic dismantling of your research programme in college, perhaps by subtle means and maybe not so subtle. I can see trouble if you stay here in an environment of obstruction and to use a good Irish expression begrudge appears to be alive and well.'

John looked at him wondering what was coming next.

'You're probably aware of the Newton Foundation in Cambridge. It's associated with Addenbrooke's Hospital. It's making advances in genetics and probably is one of the world leaders in computer medicine, which seems to be the big thing of the future. I know these are your special interests and we're trying to recruit the best brains around. I'm only one of the senior professors on the staff but I think I have some influence with my colleagues.'

John was beginning to enjoy himself.

'You're asking me to join your team and … '

'The answer is a guarded yes. I personally would like you to join us. I know more about you than you might think and I like what I see. We could work together. There are some pleasant colleagues already in post in college. One or two may have Nobel Prize potential.'

'What you say is intriguing. But it would be a complete change in my ways. I found it difficult to settle down in Sweden under Isselherg.'

'My dear John. Cambridge is completely different to Stockholm. We speak the same language and it's not a million miles from your hometown. If you agree I'll do my best to smooth the way. There will be an open competition and interview process. However I'm chairman of the selection committee and that should make a difference. Now what do you think?'

A smile dawned on John's face.

'My reaction is one of delight and excitement. The offer to work in the Alma Mater of my friend Walter Wainwright seems ironic--as if the wheel has turned full circle.'

'Then your feelings are positive but not fully decided on. I can understand that. With your agreement I'll arrange a list of terms of employment, salary, and other details to be forwarded as soon as possible and, of course, in complete confidence.'

'You've made me think Sir Kenneth.'

'Well now we should relax. It's time for a spot of dinner. Let me ring for room service.'

John went home after an excellent dinner--a little light headed. The conversation was polite yet entertaining. Sir Kenneth painted a tempting picture of the glories of Cambridge. He was hearing another point of view of a fabulous city. Walter Wainwright sung its praises and even Gustav Isselherg who spent some years doing a doctoral degree spoke in glowing terms.

John hadn't changed much over the years in spite of major tragedies. Success in life was his greatest aim; and he'd a ruthlessness to achieve it that almost frightened him. In the past he tried to explain it to others including poor Diane Sutton. His kind of success was individual to him. There was no yearning for recognition. He didn't believe success could be counted sweetest by those who never had it. That was just a sham. Some said for one to succeed others must fail--manifestations of mindless jealousies. One thing made him see red was when people said blithely that success was relative. What nonsense. Relative to what?

And the stupid idea that success could spoil people making them vain, egotistical and self-complacent. In truth, it should make them kind tolerant and even humble. In contrast, failure tended to make one arrogant, bitter, cruel and aloof. One of the toughest things was to keep on being successful. And the greatest insult was that it was a matter of luck. Ask any failure!

If Linda were here today she'd have scolded him for thinking like a true Dubliner. Maybe she'd be right. Now he had to make his decision.

PART TWO

1

Cambridge has changed little in hundreds of years. The location beside the Cam River is ideal; the streets and buildings are better than any film set and colleges with immaculate lawns and gardens go on forever. It takes time to explore. So what? No hurry. John Nicholson's no tourist. He'd arrived and was settling in. Sir Kenneth was right about formalities, which were gone through according to college regulations and it took a short time to be informed of his success. The interview was a pleasant experience and he was sorry it had to be concluded when Sir Kenneth asked.

'One last question, Dr. Nicholson. Do you have any qualms about coming to a frankly pagan country?'

'No qualms Sir Kenneth. A lot of religion in Ireland but little Christianity.'

Senior staff lodgings were arranged, well equipped and comfortable, an adequate bedroom with bathroom, large sitting room with a pleasantly stocked library and small kitchen. Porters helped in obtaining provisions and a major communal room was available for dinner. Sir Kenneth advised him to attend when he felt up to it--a convenient way of meeting people.

The first weeks were similar to Stockholm except he could understand everyone; politeness and good manners were almost a shock. He was entitled to college residence as long as he needed it. Other options were private lodgings or purchase of a property. He preferred to keep these open as he still had a house in Dublin. After all he was a bachelor now and only had to think of himself. Some items of furniture, a few cases of books, a music system and Karita's lovely hourglass were moved to Cambridge.

The laboratories were within walking distance, a blessing after commuting in Dublin. Cambridge was a large country town with beautiful parks and amenities, easy to get about especially on bicycle. Life around the river was its special attraction. Even with thousands of students there was a feeling of unity, and most people seemed to know each other.

Sir Kenneth introduced him to various staff and showed him the facilities in the Institute close to Addenbrooke's Hospital. The new offices in the science block were well equipped; he'd fought so hard to get a fraction of this equipment previously. And all he got were excuses.

Everyday was a gift of exploration, every project an adventure, every word spoken a fresh experience in human contact and learning. It was like school again, walking to that first flash of discovery, as if all spring blossoms had come out together. It was overwhelming. His exuberance to Sir Kenneth was expressed although his efforts seemed dull and ineffectual. The change of environment including the solitude, no friends from younger days, although an abundance of new ones, all affected him.

In residence sadness felt more acute. One feature was difficulty with sleep. He'd go to bed fatigued. Several hours later he could still be awake, he'd try to read some useless novel or magazine until sleep claimed him for a period. This was a roller coaster situation full of emotional explosions, which he must expect if he'd chosen such a radical change. He could still be in Dublin in the grip of bureaucracy that blocked most steps he made. Here it was the opposite. Everything he wanted or wished for was supplied as soon as possible.

And yet a gremlin whispered in his ear, something about desertion disloyalty and abandoning people who needed him. It was a matter of conscience. Even though the message was disturbing he felt he was forced to do the right thing, especially having read more of Linda's diary.

2

A small car pulled smartly onto the N 4 heading west in the spring morning. The search had begun for the old and ancient. At home Karita Isselherg read extensively about Celtic mythology, collected books and manuscripts, made copious notes and studied maps. Now the real quest had started in earnest--to see those fascinating places with mysterious beginnings. There was no substitute for experience. Embarked on the odyssey, the route was planned and she prayed the weather would hold.

Crisp sunlight flung shadows about her. Everything looked calm as she sailed along against light traffic, most coming into the city. The motorway went on through flat rolling country. That evening she reached Sligo whose roads, flinging themselves around the shoulders of hills, rising and falling ran on in bleak solitude. The tourist season had not yet begun.

The Ox Mountains with their great physical drama was her introduction to the place. The coastline was also one of the glories, superb white beaches at Enniscrone and Mullaghmore. Knocknarea rose mightily west of Sligo town on top of which sat an enormous cairn of stones--the burial place of Queen Maeve. Carrowmore Megalithic Cemetery, which is the largest Bronze Age chambered tomb system in Europe, apart from Carnac in Brittany was nearby. The tombs in the late afternoon were an awesome sight.

Clouds sailed in close contact with hillcrests, crows screeched in the upper air, battling against the wind and arguing. Bleak stone walls built about breast high to delineate a few acres of soggy grass amazed her, along with miserable looking sheep, perpetually optimistic, seeking out scant nourishment.

The sea glimmered in the distance with not a sign of humanity. She was alone and the place had a spirit of its own. Little pools of bog water filled in her footsteps and the smell of decay was everywhere. It was a foreign landscape of wind, heather terrain and dark hills. A dying drone of insects, solitude of sky and sea combined to distil an emotion that both calmed and excited her. This was what she'd come to experience for behind this world she felt an immortal presence. She'd not read mythology in vain; it was here and near the surface. The spell gripped her even more as Knocknarea silhouetted in the distance. Few other places existed where people had undertaken more daring deeds, where love and hatred were of arresting importance, almost as if their passion had seeped into the very rocks and grass.

Light gradually faded from the sky and mist thickened, allowing her imagination take over. The first star appeared and an uncanny watchfulness rose from the earth. Things seemed to listen and wait. A bent tree or an upright stone could move at any moment if watched long enough, or out of the dark forest Queen Maeve might ride out in all her glory and pageantry to go on another raid or conquest with the sound of swords clashing in combat and the mad gallop of horses adding to the clamour. All fantasy. Yes, she'd come to find fantasy for her work. It was here on the slopes of Knocknarea. The place was haunted and things slept with one eye open.

It was time to head back to the hotel where she hoped for a good night's rest.

She had booked into one of the finer hotels in the centre of Sligo. It was old and well appointed. She preferred places with time and character on their side, rather than brash plastic edifices mushrooming everywhere. She liked atmosphere. It helped her work. Time was the enemy of history, the more it progressed the more history regressed.

After a light supper she retired to her room, which was large prim and bare. A white iron bedstead clashed with oversized mahogany wardrobes capable of holding clothes for a family. A hard chair, dressing table and one ancient picture on blank walls greeted her.

She was always particular about bedrooms, being in her nature and upbringing. Couldn't help it. Things had to be right; if not, she was uncomfortable. Private places they were and yet they pretended not to be. What kind of head had rested on that pillow before and what strange thoughts, dreams or nightmares came to that imitation of death known as sleep? Some things she disapproved of; in a drawer a torn up bill for drinks served in the room and the wardrobes had the faint fragrance of another woman--always, to the lonely traveller, the most intriguing or vexing ghost in a strange room.

Only one thing to do--arrange things, as they should be. She draped all her belongings everywhere establishing a claim and most importantly spreading her books everywhere. There were plenty of books. She piled them on the table, the chair and the floor. Even the most hostile room could not resist being turned into a library.

She climbed into bed filled with that delicious drowsiness midway between dream and sleep. External noises including street conversation, car doors shutting and farewells faded into the night. Eventually the cumulative effects of the day's effort claimed her for restful oblivion.

The road west from Sligo leads to Ballycastle. Great sea cliffs stretch for miles out to Benwee Head with no evidence of habitation. The coastline is fearsome in its desolation though it was not always. A Stone Age community farmed here for thousands of years. They built dwellings, demarcated fields with stone walls and buried their dead in court tombs. Evidence was found over a seven-mile area and probably supported a community of ten-thousand people. Agriculture started in the area about 3,500 B.C. What became of the people or where they went is not known. The encroaching bog blanketed the region for 4,500 years--until now.

The site, known as the Ceide Fields, is located a few miles from Ballycastle and is recognised as the most extensive Stone Age settlement in the world. Nothing like it anywhere. What secrets are still buried there, yet to be revealed? The place was empty. For miles around there was nothing but space, the sky was north and empty, the sea was cold--and empty, the cliff face invisible--unless she stood on its edge and the light was fugitive. Where had everyone gone? Haunted Sligo had followed her here.

On to the Mullet Peninsula. Belmullet was one of the remotest villages. She stocked up on supplies and travelled south past Elly Bay. The western seaboard was visually more exciting where beaches rocks and small islands breasted the onslaught of the Atlantic. South of the Bay she turned right towards an elegant beach called Carricklahan and she instinctively knew she'd arrived somewhere special.

White foam moved around the feet of Iniskea Islands, further north was Inishglora and due south the striking cliffs of Achill. That morning was unforgettable. Here legends had merged with Christian remains and transition was long and difficult. Maybe the restless power of Nature had an effect on the people. Ancient customs were partly assimilated into Christianity. Through generations attitudes were passed down through generations as a collective memory giving insights into the world of Celtic mythology. She found scattered cairns, megalithic tombs, standing stones, cross slabs ancient graveyards and promontory forts with little or no history.

Except for the saga of the Children of Lir. Inishglora was the setting for the final stages of this beautiful story in Celtic mythology. Lir and his wife Eve of the fabled Tuatha de Danaan had four children called Fionnuala, Hugh and twins Conn and Fiachra. Eve died soon after the twins were born. Lir married her sister Aoife. The stepmother became jealous of the children and decided to have them killed. However courage failed her, so she cast a spell changing them into four swans that would have to spend 300 years on lake Derravarragh in the midlands, 300 on the sea of Moyle between Scotland and Ireland and 300 on Inishglora in the Atlantic.

One day they were awakened on Inishglora by a strange sound-
-a bell calling for prayer. They flew to the church and their long
exile finally came to an end. It was here that a monk--a follower
of Patrick--witnessed an astonishing sight. The swans were transformed back into human form--but they were old and feeble. Soon
after this they died and were laid to rest together in one grave. So
came to an end their wandering, searching and suffering. Now
whole again because they'd responded to the sound of the bell and
found peace.

Karita spent several days in the area especially around Fallmore
looking over Blacksod Bay towards Croaghan in Achill. She imagined she heard the bell that restored humanity to the Children of
Lir. Have we been deafened to the sound of beauty, not realising
'til it had faded away into time?

The road through the bog of Erris was astonishing bounded to
the east by The Nephin Beg Mountains running south to Corraun.
Only one road south from Bangor made this the largest roadless
area in Ireland. The Nephins were a shimmering green and gold
as the sun poured light on them like honey and later they took on a
mantle of blue and purple, which contrasted with the golden ochres
of cloud and bog. They stood sentinel over two hundred square
miles of emptiness that is both physical and mental.

It rained with grim determination further south; water falling in
sheets everywhere producing grey mists over mountain and sea.
Ballycroy was drenched in the downpour, houses huddled together
as water gushed in torrents from roofs, splashing into gutters, gur-
gling and rushing along the roadside. For ages the very rain seemed
to weep rather than fall over the land. And how it could rain!

Karita promised herself a visit to the Aran Islands to end the
journey. Why people ever settled there was a mystery. She was

determined to find answers. Was it a Shangri La or Tir na nOg for its primitive way of life among the beauty of the limestone plateaux falling away into the enormous vertical cliffs, ending in the white fury of the Atlantic's interminable sound? The monuments and tombs, especially the great Dun Aengus Fortress, which many regard as the most magnificent barbaric monument in Europe, were awesome. The mystery of the fortress was fascinating. How old was it? Who built it and why was it built here? No answers were available--only legends. She would try to supply answers, embellish legends, perhaps even invent.

These were enchanted islands, shadowy places surrounded by golden clouds hinting at eternal peace, a kind of paradise.

Before leaving Aran Karita felt a bewitching country had, for a time, drawn aside her veil and let her look into another world, making it come close to hand, to her hand in which was grasped an instrument for writing a cauldron of melting mythology.

4

John Nicholson grew in confidence and time was a friend. Karita's hourglass made him feel poetic.

Work absorbed him. When he was growing up, talk was conversation, in Cambridge it was communication benefit with others willing to teach him as well as listen. In this milieu everyone was keen to learn, pool resources and work as a team. Politeness and charm were prerequisites for advancement with many unwritten rules. So it seemed at first.

His position was senior lecturer and deputy head of the department of clinical pathology. The work ethic was different to previous experiences. There was freedom for innovation, with no one inquiring about a move for each new protocol or looking over his shoulder. Sir Kenneth arranged an honorary consultant appointment in Addenbrooke's Hospital so he'd access to patients. Several clinics a week were his responsibility in the oncology division. John asked that his speciality be narrowed to a study of blood dyscrasias. It'd fall in with his experience and further his research in chemotherapy.

'I like your approach John.' Sir Kenneth sat back in his chair. 'I'll introduce you to the people in haematology and you can explain your requirements.'

'They're quite simple. All I need is blood from leukaemic patients to explore their cellular biology. Simply the cellular universe'

'And what about animal models? If so you'll need a Home Office licence.'

'No need Sir Kenneth. I'll want to concentrate on the pathology of individual cells in culture and study behaviour under a range of different environments with the back up of computer technology. Digital design and analyses can be phenomenal.'

'All new thinking. We've the right people here to talk to.'

'I know. That's what makes me feel so privileged.'

'Nonsense John. You deserve it on your record. You were the right person I was looking for. A balance between a good clinician and a brilliant record in research. Just what we needed.'

He paused.

'Thanks. You're very kind.'

Sir Kenneth's eyes challenged him.

'That brings me to the next point.'

He rummaged through papers on his desk and produced several sheets. 'There's pressure on universities to take postgraduate students on Masters' or Doctoral courses. Our medical schools are full. The powers that be want us to increase our overseas candidates. I'd like you to start with three or four M. Sc. students and see how things work out. What do you feel about that?'

'It'd be wise to start with M. Sc. students and leave Ph.D.s to later.'

'Masters Degrees seem to be more attractive to the developing countries. There's also a financial consideration.'

'I understand that.'

'Well John. Could you take four students?' He persisted.

'I could try. There'll be plenty of work to do. As supervisor I'll need help from junior staff and technicians.'

'Jolly good idea.' He conceded. 'You can't be expected to look after them full-time. You'll have your own clinics and research besides teaching duties.'

'It'll be a pretty full schedule.'

5

Advertisements were placed in medical journals for degree courses in clinical pathology in Cambridge University. A large response resulted and ten applicants were considered. These were short listed to four--one male doctor from Saudi Arabia, one from Kuwait and two females, one from Jordan and another from Thailand.

September came and students arrived. John interviewed them separately. The first was Abu Khalil from Saudi Arabia, an imposing young doctor who'd qualified in Riyadh and done two years clinical work there. Now he wished to 'climb the academic ladder' in medicine. The Cambridge Master's would be an excellent starting point. He could see himself going on to Ph.D. and maybe a Fellowship of one of the Royal Colleges before returning home. Everything was so well organised there and he had lots of people to do things for him. That was the way he was brought up.

John was taken aback at this soliloquy. He didn't expect demands on his desk from a prospective who intimated others would do the student's work.

'Dr. Khalil things are different in this country. If you're expecting to get a higher degree from this university it is you who will
have to earn it. Nobody else. You must understand that.'

'Surely supervisors will be appointed for me--naturally. Won't
they?'

'Supervisors are only meant to supervise your work. They do
not do your work. Do I make myself clear?'

'You do not make yourself clear,Dr. Nicholson. I have come
here at great expense--although that's irrelevant--and I expect to be
taught by the best brains around to do research and at the end of
the teaching process a M.Sc. thesis will be produced.'

'Produced by whom Dr. Khalil?'

'By the authorities I assume.'

'That's where you're wrong.' John's anger was apparent. He
should slow down.

'If the university is going to grant a Master's Degree that degree
must reflect the work undertaken, carried out and finished by Dr.
Khalil. And nobody else.'

'But there must be guidance.'

'Guidance yes, like teaching you to drive a motorcar. In the end
you must prove you can drive that motorcar alone. Similarly in the
final examination you must prove you have done all the experiments, you understand them and be able to stand over the results.'

Dr. Khalil had a puzzled expression.

'I never expected this kind of insubordination. I may find it difficult to be present all the time. I have other places to visit and
commitments during my stay. You're going to make things difficult
for me.'

'Dr. Khalil I've explained everything to you. The choice is yours.'

The next candidate was Dr. Shaba from Kuwait--a much less assuming gentleman. He qualified in Kuwait and hoped to specialise in children's medicine. He had a choice of doing higher studies in Egypt, Jordan or the USA. The UK examination would be the only qualification his colleagues could not question and it would mean a great deal for his future career.

Dr. Shaba listened to John more than talked. No need for questions. Although he was reserved about his background there were leadership qualities there. He'd a good idea of his thesis title and knew his way around a literature search.

The third student was a graduate from Jordan University. A tall attractive good-looking woman who'd strong ideas on politics in her own country and a lot of others as well--or so she thought. She'd no hesitation in explaining her needs, ambitions and wished to work mainly on laboratory techniques collecting clinical material from patients with a limited group of diseases. Emphasis must be on the laboratory investigations and data analyses would be her prime concern. John was impressed at the maturity of her plans and the departmental biochemist could give useful advice.

The last candidate was a complete puzzle. She was a young doctor from Thailand who shuffled into John's office. No eye contact at all, to begin with anyway. She remained silent and only spoke in monosyllables when questioned. He looked through her CV and references--all glowing with praise from her Dean of Faculty and teachers at home. It was almost impossible to interview her on the first visit. She didn't know what field she was interested in and hoped someone would guide her. She emphasised most politely she didn't want to cause trouble. If she were given a task she'd do it to her utmost ability. She was so uncomfortable in John's presence he should leave any further questioning. He thanked her for coming and her good manners were almost an embarrassment to him. Even as she left the room she joined her hands and backed away slowly to the door.

John reported to Sir Kenneth.

'Enjoy yourself with the new recruits John? We'd over thirty applicants and narrowed them to four. Even there we don't have to take them all.'

'They're a mixed group. Different from our own students who are genned up on protocol and more interested in advancing in the hospital system to consultant.'

'That's the state of play on the internal scene. We've to give this a try. What did you think of the material?'

'The Saudi chap could be a handful. Expects everyone else to do his work. He'll soon learn. The Kuwaiti doctor--completely different--probably no trouble. The Jordanian lady--maybe a handful also--very liberated and knows where she's going in every sense. The last poor thing--the gentlest Thai lady--I just don't know. Her CV and references are brilliant. Maybe she'll turn out to be the surprise of the bunch.'

6

Weeks passed into months and students settled into work schedules. Dr. Khalil was a burden. It would be unfair to hand him over to other supervisors especially in the early stages. Battles were fought on who was going to do the literature search. Surely the librarians could do it; he was too busy with other things. He could be generous if they would only cooperate and see sense. Then there would be no trouble. John nearly exploded at the proposition. Khalil had no right to bribe others.

He sent for Khalil.

'Come in doctor. I was expecting you.'

'I understand you wish to discuss an important matter.'

'I do. Although it's not important to me.' He looked at Khalil, both standing, neither giving in. Khalil was first as he chose the chair nearest him.

'I don't understand Dr. Nicholson. If it's not important why do we have to discuss it at all? Perhaps it can wait.'

'Dr. Khalil it's not important to me. I've my work and career to keep me occupied and I'm doing precisely that. But now the government wants universities to cooperate with countries like yours to forge a flow of scientific information and technology. You are not doing the work expected of you and you've asked others to do it. This is not how this university works Dr. Khalil. You do all the work, ask for guidance and guidance will be given only but you do the work right to the end. Otherwise when the final examination comes I'll have to say some or most of the work in the thesis was not done by the candidate.'

'In our country there are ways of delegating work and it proves satisfactory.' Dr. Khalil said with an expression of complacency. 'We merely ask those whose jobs were given to them to do the work expected. The goods are produced.'

He stared at the smiling Khalil for a long moment. He hesitated, not knowing was he going to provoke a major diplomatic incident. He wouldn't pull any punches and came out with his opinion.

'Dr. Khalil if you wish to continue in the system you've outlined then I think the best thing would be to go back to your university and delegate others to do your research and you probably will receive your Master's Degree or something higher still.' He banged the table with anger flowing from every pore. 'This has never been the system here and never will. If Dr. Khalil is to get a degree from Cambridge he will have to earn it and only with guidance and help but nothing more. Understood?'

'Dr. Nicholson you make yourself abundantly clear.'

Dr. Shaba was no trouble and amenable to suggestions he was offered and always made a point of thanking people. John trusted him from the start. His interest was in assessing the impact of illness on physiological function by setting up parameters and, if possible, to carry out a double blind trial with an antidepressive drug and a placebo on postoperative patients who gave informed consent. Details were worked out and he contacted a drug company who'd supply the medication and placebo in sealed containers and the company was willing to finance the project. A psychiatrist should be brought in to supervise the project. Sir Kenneth suggested Dr. Cashman, the newly appointed psychiatrist. She was young hard working and seemed ambitious. John asked to see her.

Rachel Cashman floated into his room. Yes, she was ambitious; he could see that and wanted to go far, fast, hopefully not too fast. He explained the project and she grasped the requirements immediately.

'Don't worry Dr. Nicholson,' she said, 'I get the picture. I've been involved in these trials before. Some are difficult, and others are easy. It depends on how you handle it and how helpful the research student is.'

'Dr. Cashman,I've every confidence in Dr. Shaba. He has excellent references and he is amenable to any suggestion.'

'Amenable to any suggestion,' she repeated sounding intrigued. 'That should make a very interesting trait. I wonder how it could work out.'

He watched her quite puzzled. 'I'm grateful to you for agreeing to take over his supervision. If there are problems please let me know. I'd like a progress report.'

'Of course Dr. Nicholson. Leave it to me. I'll get the results we want.'

That was a strange comment but he let it pass.

'You'll get credit in the list of authors in the final publication.'

'I should hope so. After all the work involved. But again leave it to me.'

The extrovert lady doctor from Jordan was easier to organise. She knew precisely what direction her work should take. It would involve analysis of laboratory samples from cancer patients. This was John's special study and he'd supervise progress himself.

The student from Thailand was a puzzle. He interviewed her several times and only got indefinite answers. She wished the thesis title to be someone else's idea and whatever it was she'd humbly accept. John racked his brains thinking of something suitable. What work did she do at home? She wanted to help the poor in her country especially children. She loved and adored children and hated to see them sick. He suggested an investigation into the nutritional status of groups in geographical areas in Cambridge, which would take social class into consideration. She'd need the help of an epidemiologist and social worker and access to population distribution. Maybe the work would be too much for her.

Time would tell.

7

John Nicholson was struggling with a research problem when a knock came to his door.

'Come in.'

It was Emma, one of the nurses that helped Dr. Cashman and Dr. Shaba. She also assisted in his clinics and he was aware of her thoroughness. Today she was distressed.

'Dr. Nicholson. I don't know what to do.' She was almost crying. 'For weeks I've noticed Dr. Cashman adding five or ten patients with strange names to the end of her morning clinics. They're not our patients. They're not seen here and I don't know who they are. They may be fictitious names. I don't know what Dr. Shaba is doing. He keeps his own records and I've heard them arguing about the matter.'

Alarm bells rang. John smiled pleasantly at her and said he'd look into the matter.

'Thanks Dr. Nicholson. I was worried that something was wrong.'

Emma's visit upset him. Something improper may be going on. Dr. Shaba was sent for in the first instance.

'Good morning Dr. Shaba. Please be seated. Nice of you to come and see me so quickly. I merely wanted to check if everything is going as planned.'

Dr. Shaba was reserved but that was his manner anyway. Yet he was uncomfortable and reluctant to speak.

'I hope you're pleased with your progress,' John continued, 'and you've enough patients to gather data from.'

'I'm pleased with my progress and I've enough patients who are very cooperative. Everything is fine in my clinic and Emma is a wonderful help.'

'Good to hear it. Then everything's all right then?'

'Everything is all right with me. And I'm happy with my results so far.'

'Excellent. Then if there's nothing to worry about I won't keep you.'

He was slow to leave. Something bothered him yet his politeness was a barrier.

'Dr. Shaba is there anything else you'd like to tell me? Is there something I should know that you are embarrassed to tell me?'

'Dr. Nicholson. You have me in a difficult situation. I am in two minds, one to say nothing and hope the matter will go away.'

'And the other?'

'No one gossips about others lightly.'

'I suspect you've more to tell. There's something wrong and you want to tell me but are afraid to do so.'

'There is something.'

'Don't be afraid. I'm your supervisor and responsibility ultimately rests with me.'

'Thanks for saying that Dr. Nicholson. For several weeks Dr. Cashman has been adding fictitious patients to her clinics and filling out false results for medication. She's told me to do the same and I refused. I do not know what to do.'

'You have told me. Haven't you?'

'Yes. Now I could be thrown out of college to my greatest shame.'

'That will not happen. I'll see to it the practice is stopped immediately. The rest of the disciplinary procedure is up to me.'

'Thanks Dr. Nicholson. I thought I was in trouble and would be expelled.'

8

John Nicholson faced a dilemma. Perhaps one of the projects was proceeding dishonestly but there was no absolute proof. He'd have to talk to Dr. Cashman and let her defend herself. He wrote a polite memorandum inviting her for a discussion.

A knock came on his door.

'Come in.' She entered with a big smile.

'Dr. Cashman how nice to see you. Please take a seat. Would you like coffee?'

'That'd be lovely. White. No sugar.'

She looked around the room wondering what this was all about. Nicholson being polite wasn't natural. Didn't happen often.

He handed her the coffee and pulled a chair up beside her--no desk between them.

'Dr. Cashman. Incidentally may I call you Rachel?'

Her defences increased.

'Of course.'

'Rachel. You know I carry responsibility for research in this department.'

'I realise that. And we're asked to help out.'

He hesitated.

'It has come to my notice there may be some irregularities in the day-to-day working of your project with Dr. Shaba.'

'I don't understand. What irregularities?'

'Quite by accident I've discovered the actual numbers attending your clinics are consistently lower than the numbers that are reported back on the daily record sheets.'

'That can't be true.'

'I'm afraid it is. You see I like to check each person's working procedure and I've here the record sheets for daily attendances and the actual folders of patients seen each day. They don't tally.'

'There must be some mistake Dr. Nicholson. We try to keep accurate records of everything. It's important we get an ethical result to justify the grant from the company.'

'I couldn't agree more. Can you explain why there are apparently more patients seen regularly than actually attend the clinic?'

'I've no explanation.'

'Are you sure?'

'Yes. I'm sure. What do you take me for? Perhaps you should question Dr. Shaba. He may be increasing numbers so the overall results will be impressive. After all it's his project. He hopes to get a Master's Degree out of it and a good result would make that almost a certainty. He has all to gain.'

'And what would you stand to gain out of it Rachel?'

'Just a thank you and well done I suppose.'

'I think there's more to it than that. I understand it was you who made out the original grant application, which can be very complicated and involve intricate procedures and you were successful in getting the money. It just happened we'd an appropriate trial waiting to be done, and you were in the right place at the right time. It only needed me to approach you in all innocence and you eagerly took over.'

She looked at him with an increasing frown. The truth was becoming uncomfortable.

'With your training and expertise,' John continued, 'it was easy to set up the protocol sheets and all Dr. Shaba had to do was to fill them in as he was told to do. I don't believe he could have the intention or the opportunity to deceive the workings of the project in such a consistent way without you noticing.'

'I see.'

'So therefore I can only conclude it was you who set out to mislead as many people as possible, cover-up the daily working and in the final analysis produce a brilliant result for the company for which you would receive considerable credit. Am I right?'

She looked blankly at John saying nothing. The game was up. And she knew it. There was an awkward silence. She put her head down and appeared to be defeated. He'd arrived at the truth and things would have to be corrected. She said softly.

'What are you going to do?' She said softly. 'And what can I do?'

'Several options are open to me now. One would be to report you and the whole incident to the Dean and leave it up to the college authorities to take appropriate disciplinary proceedings against you.'

'That could be disastrous for me.'

'The second option would be to remove you from this particular project completely and ask you to go and find something different. That shouldn't be too difficult and I could get someone else to take over Dr. Shaba's supervision. There would be questions asked, which may be difficult to answer.'

'Is there any other option?' She pleaded knowing her career was on line.

'Perhaps there's one last option.' He took a deep breath and looked straight at her. 'If you promise faithfully to stick to the original protocol as planned--never deviate from it--and get Dr. Shaba to do the same it may not be too late to repair the damage done. Extra work will be needed to correct the phantom patients, but this will have to be done. Will you do it?'

'Yes. Dr. Nicholson. I will do it. I'll have to. I'm sorry for being so foolish. I realise it was terribly stupid.' She smiled with a hand extended.

9

Dr. Terese, the student from Thailand, worked on a comparative study of the nutritional status of groups around Cambridge and an epidemiologist was called in to help. John Nicholson arranged an interview to review progress. Deprivation and poverty were uncovered. She expected such cases at home but not in one of the most beautiful cities in Britain. It made her sad and she went on to give a mini-lecture on the poverty in her country. She asked what could be done by way of international cooperation.

John was amazed at her command of English. This was a sensitive human being--a rare type who cared less for themselves than others. Several times she asked was there anything she could do. The findings would be a revelation to local bureaucrats and John looked forward to disclosing the social secrets in their midst that only a foreign social scientist could uncover. They might even make headlines in the press.

Weeks went by.

One afternoon a message came through that one of his M.Sc. students was rushed to Addenbrooke's as an emergency. A friend in the students' residence found her unconscious and an overdose was suspected. Desperate attempts were made to save her life. She almost succeeded but excellent facilities at the hospital managed to bring her back from the edge.

She remained in hospital for observation and had psychotherapy. Some days later she requested an appointment with John. He'd already discussed the situation with staff members who advised that Dr. Terese should be dismissed from the university forthwith; this behaviour should not be tolerated. She must be thrown out. John was disgusted with this vindictiveness. He agreed to see her.

She entered the room slowly and humbly. There was no eye contact. Was she to be deported home in disgrace?

'Of course not. No question. Although perhaps you could explain why.'

'I have no hesitation in answering that Dr. Nicholson.' She responded quickly. 'My husband is a pilot with Thai Airlines and is having an affair with another woman. My disgrace is enormous. I had to protest in the strongest way possible. I did what I did. And I deserve to be punished.'

'Nonsense. You were grievously hurt. Other staff members have stronger views. But I have complete sympathy for you. You've done no wrong. All is forgiven.'

She fell on her knees and placed her hands on his feet. She bent down and each one she delicately kissed as a token of appreciation. She whispered she did not expect such a response from anyone. She was astonished and greatly relieved.

Graduation day came and went.

1 0

A letter arrived from Riyadh. It was from Dr. Khalil. It contained little information, merely inquiring if Dr. Nicholson would be prepared to see a patient in the Middle East for a consultation. Location was not specified. Someone would be in contact by phone and more details forthcoming. The affair sounded strange. Two weeks later a phone call came from London. A Mr. Omar wished to speak to him.

'Is that Dr. Nicholson?'

'Yes. I had a letter from Dr. Khalil telling me to expect a call.'

'That's right doctor. We'd like to make a proposal but it's difficult over the phone. If I travel to Cambridge could we meet somewhere at your convenience? I should add the proposal would be to your advantage.'

'Intriguing. If you come in the next two days we could meet in your hotel.'

'Splendid. I'll do that and make all the arrangements. Do not worry about a thing. I know my way around your country very well. I'll telephone as soon as I arrive.'

'That would be fine.'

Two days later Mr. Omar phoned about three o'clock in the afternoon from the Moat House Hotel. They would meet at seven.

What was all the privacy about? Was it necessary? John walked to the hotel within easy reach of his apartment. A tall gentleman dressed in Arab headgear and plain suit approached him in the lobby.

'Dr. Nicholson,I presume.' Mr. Omar extended a large hand.

'And you must be Mr. Omar.'

'Nice to meet you doctor. I appreciate you coming this evening.'

'No trouble.' The man had a cultured accent--probably an Oxbridge graduate.

'Shall we go up to the apartment? We'll have more privacy. It's crowded here.'

'Please lead the way.'

'It's on the top floor. The only available suite but views of the city are superb.'

'Sounds wonderful.'

They entered the lift. No words were exchanged until they were inside the penthouse.

'Now doctor. Please make yourself comfortable. Anywhere you choose.'

The choice was enormous; a huge sitting room with a long conference table, seven or eight easy chairs, soft lights and high windows that showed panoramic views of the city. He'd never seen Cambridge to such advantage.

'Dinner is arranged in about half an hour. There are some things

I'd like to mention before we become distracted with eating.'

They sat at the mahogany table. Mr. Omar produced papers from his briefcase.

'Doctor what I have to say I'd ask you to treat in confidence. Not a word to anyone including Sir Kenneth Richardson.'

Something odd about this request. John had always been open with Sir Kenneth. The other felt his alarm.

'Don't worry doctor. What I've to propose has no political overtones. They're purely medical and probably in your field.'

'Good. I don't wish to be involved in an international incident. I try my best to advance the science of treating serious diseases.'

'Our people know that only too well.'

'Incidentally, who are your people?'

'I am the travelling representative of the Sheik of one of the Gulf States. I'm told to do something and I try my best.'

John was uncomfortable, the conversation out of his depth.

'There's someone who needs the advice of a specialist. Our physicians are not confident in handling the case and would appreciate a second opinion.'

John was still puzzled.

'Why couldn't the patient come to London or Cambridge?'

'Be most logical. But it would be unsafe for him to leave the country.'

Mr. Omar was aware of John's concern. He added two other specialists, French and Swiss, had already agreed to travel to the Gulf.

'What about half-way?' John asked. 'We could meet in Geneva and the facilities there are first class. Geographically it's a good place for your team.'

'Geneva has already been considered. But there's a special plea on safety grounds and that means safety for everyone concerned. In our country we have total control of security, and I assure you if you agree you will be impressed. Here's the list of the other international experts who've agreed to come along.' He handed John a sheet and the names were recognised immediately. 'You may like to phone them to confirm the arrangements.'

Mr. Omar had done his homework.

'One last thing,' he continued. 'After you've consulted your colleagues that this is a genuine call for help you can be assured you will be rewarded handsomely. Please remember it must be kept a secret mission. I assume you can arrange a few days leave from your department--perhaps three or four at the most.'

'That'd be no problem.'

A Mercedes drew up outside John's apartment on Friday at two p.m. Cases were packed and the car sped south for Heathrow. The Gulf Air flight was scheduled to take off at six-thirty and he had plenty of time to check in. Every comfort was in the special waiting area. Time for boarding. He was escorted to the last aisle seat in the first class lounge. A stranger with an Arab appearance was seated at the window.

The flight to Paris was uneventful. Then the long haul southeast. John slept several hours helped by several cocktails supplied by the cabin crew. Touch down in Dubai was seven-thirty local time. Already the sun was blazing on the tarmac as he walked to the terminal where eight men in dark suites and sunglasses were waiting. No need to go through customs and his cases were loaded into the first of a fleet of twelve Mercedes outside the entrance. Mr. Omar asked John to get into the third car. He then got in and used his mobile to check whether the others were ready to move in convoy.

The all clear was given and he gave the signal to start.

He turned to John.

'Dr. Nicholson there's a long journey ahead and the scenery will not exactly match your beautiful countryside. However you may get a surprise.'

As conversation flagged John could see the shimmer of heat outside, the sand dunes were about 45 degrees centigrade and yet he was in a cool 22 degrees in the limousine. The scenery did not change for about 150 miles until they entered Abu Dhabi. Green lawns, bushes and trees along the road and in public parks suddenly appeared. It was like entering an enormous oasis.

The convoy arrived at the hotel and, after Mr. Omar arranged registration and other formalities, John was shown to his suite of rooms. Before leaving Mr. Omar told him he'd have a few hours to rest and, if he'd like a drive later this could be arranged.

'That would fine, but what about the patient? When … '

'Don't worry. Special arrangements are being made.'

'I don't understand.'

'You will. I assure you. For the present unwind a little and enjoy our hospitality. Please telephone reception if there's anything you require.'

He lay down for a siesta. Two hours later he woke refreshed and had a shower and shave. The telephone rang at six o'clock. It was Mr. Omar who suggested a drive to see the sights and perhaps a little entertainment.

'That's fine,' John said, 'but I'm still wondering about the patient.'

'Don't concern yourself doctor. Arrangements are still being made and you'll be informed when all the preparations are completed.'

'Well I'm in you hands. I'll have to wait.'

'Indeed. I'll introduce you to our guests from France and Switzerland.'

'Very good. I'll be down in five minutes.'

Introductions were made in the lobby and two cars were called to the entrance. Mr. Omar again took charge.

'Firstly gentlemen in the cool of the evening we'd like you to see our zoo, which is not too far from here. It contains rare specimens that are a delight to the eye.'

They only had time to see a small proportion of the stables for horses belonging to the mystery patient. Mr. Omar let it slip that his client only yesterday received delivery of 150 new thorough-breds to add to his collection. Regretfully there was no time to see them now.

It grew dark suddenly and they returned to the hotel. He was asked to be available at nine o'clock the following morning.

'Now we're making progress,' John smiled at Mr. Omar who cautioned him with a gesture.

John Nicholson waited in the lobby at nine o'clock next morning with the other guests. Two tall men in Arab regalia accompanied Mr. Omar into the lobby and shook hands with John and colleagues. Preparations were complete and the client was ready to receive them. Four cars took the party to a large palace with enormous security arrangements everywhere.

Cars stopped at the entrance. A white-gloved soldier in impeccable uniform opened the door and saluted. John got out followed by Mr. Omar. The party was escorted up the steps to the main entrance. A corridor led into an enormous assembly hall crowned with a glorious circular dome. Light trickled from alcoves along the walls giving an ethereal appearance. Biggest surprise was the gathering of fully robed local nobility.

Mr. Omar explained before they could be received it was necessary for them to be introduced to members of the ruling council, the local dignitaries and close relatives of the client. John glanced around the hall. No females insight. Mr. Omar went on to say this was the private section of the hospital for use by the royal family and the reason for the delay was that the entire hospital had to be evacuated before visitors could examine the client.

The situation dawned on John and others. They exchanged glances knowingly.

Mr. Omar gestured for people to step aside and he slowly lead the men to the top of the hall. There stood a young man of about thirty-three years dressed in the most immaculate white robes; about six foot four in height, with a short black beard and his brown eyes looked kindly at them. He extended a hand of welcome to each one but said nothing.

Several people acted as interpreters. It was decided the group should adjourn to the clinical suites. One of the local doctors had noticed a swelling on the cheek mucosa and throat of the client. John asked for the word <u>patient</u> to be used, very well then the patient. It did not respond to local measures and no diagnosis was made. The doctor had read some recent papers on oral and pharyngeal cancer that Dr. Nicholson was associated with.

Now the story was out. The local team were reluctant to commit themselves to a definitive diagnosis.

The best and safest way out of the dilemma was to call in international specialists. The development of a white lesion on the cheek mucosa and lining of the throat, which was getting worse over several months, was the relevant history. No apparent cause. It was a mystery. And a great worry.

That was all the information offered. It was not enough for John. With his two colleagues he asked the clinical area be cleared of the large crowd. All that should remain were the patient, three clinicians and Mr. Omar as interpreter.

'Your Highness let us begin the examination,' John said and the patient lay back obediently. Operating lights were switched on. John and colleagues using gloved hands carried out a full clinical examination and took notes. When finished the three discussed findings in a quiet corner of the room. John was first to speak.

'I think you and I have seen similar lesions many times in our own parts of the world. The diagnosis merely on clinical grounds is fairly extensive leukoplakia. There are different names for it, each with their own advocates. There may even be added candidal infection present and today we cannot get away from HIV playing a part.'

The others nodded and one suggested somebody should ask if the patient smoked tobacco and drank alcohol. The interpreter refused to put these questions forward so John approached the patient directly. The reply came back in perfect English that he did both these things. As to HIV infection he was doubtful--the opportunities were not readily available to him. The situation was becoming clearer now. The small group retired to a private room to make out a plan. Two biopsies would be carried out and John elected to do them. A full blood profile and specific scans would also be carried out. The findings would be reviewed in three to four weeks. The patient agreed. He was made aware of the causes of the problem and listened carefully. He was warned the condition was sometimes precancerous and the causative agents must be removed if at all possible. Samples were taken and placed in frozen containers for transit to Cambridge for independent analysis. The results would be sent back to the director of the hospital.

1 3

It was difficult for John to sleep that night. At seven-thirty a.m. he showered and shaved, packed his cases and went downstairs. All was quiet in the hall and dining room. The others were already waiting. No sign of Mr. Omar. Eight-thirty came and went. Nine o'clock came and still no Mr. Omar. Panic set in; they'd miss their flights to Paris and London. That was inevitable. What an end to their adventure to be left stranded like this. A complete anticlimax.

At nine-thirty Mr. Omar rushed into the lobby with a beaming smile.

'Gentlemen. I'm sorry to keep you waiting. Please don't worry. A few arrangements I had to make before coming to collect you and the delay was unavoidable.'

'The flight has been delayed then?' John asked anxiously.

'There's no delay on the scheduled flight. That's due to take off shortly.'

'Without us obviously!' Said one of the others.

'Yes.' Mr. Omar was still beaming. How could he be so complacent?

'To put your minds at ease our client, as a gesture of good-will, has put his personal Boeing 737 at your disposal. His father would have preferred you to have the 747 but unfortunately it's in Switzerland. The 737 is being prepared and a crew have been instructed to be ready in one hour. We'll go to the airport shortly and the flight will take you to Geneva. From there I'm afraid you will have to complete your journeys by scheduled flights, which have already been booked and Dr. Nicholson your flight to London is on Swissair. Unfortunately we could not get clearance to land our 737 at Heathrow so we have to do it this way.'

To enter the aircraft was an experience. Towards the front was a large seating area with exquisite décor and separate office space for working in private. Two or three bedrooms, a large kitchen, bathroom and a small comfortable cinema were further back.

As the plane took off John and others sat together putting final touches to their report, exchanging telephone numbers and addresses. Then they settled in a comfortable corner, each quiet with their own thoughts.

A ravishing stewardess informed John that lunch would be served shortly.

'Is there a menu?' He asked.

'Sorry sir. We don't carry a menu. The flight is well stocked you may have anything you wish and we can supply it. You name it, we have it.'

'Now that makes life difficult.'

'It really shouldn't sir. I could suggest a few things.'

'Please do.'

'You might like to start with special Russian caviar with a little vodka to taste.'

'And then?'

'Perhaps the finest venison with a classic Claret especially good at this time.'

'And I'm sure you've lots of supreme exotics to follow.'

'Of course sir. You've only to ask for anything, anything at all and it will be supplied graciously. These are our strict instructions.'

He looked at her for a long moment, thinking of things not necessarily connected with food. Finally he turned away and said simply.

'After all I've been through in the last three days I think I'll be happy with a Spanish omelette. Is that possible?'

Her smile melted his heart as she replied.

'Of course it would. You know you can ask for anything you want and it will be granted. We are only here to serve you.'

'Thanks again. I'll look forward to the omelette.'

A gentle flourish of her handkerchief left the faintest fragrance in the air.

1 4

As the Swissair flight touched down at Heathrow that Monday morning in late autumn Karita Isselherg walked into the library of Kungsangen House in Stockholm. Laden with books, notebooks, maps, photographs and a collection of writing accoutrements she sat at the French windows overlooking the garden. Outside a dusting of snow covered most things giving a glowing sameness to objects and foretelling ominous times.

Not really concerned with weather was she although the brightness added excitement to her work. The family were relieved at her safe return. Details of the journey were explained; places, climate, times and people she met were described. These were precious to her and would be used for different purposes. It was a fact-finding odyssey gathering material for a work on mythology like never before. Prior to the tour she'd read books, which were esoteric, scientific, erudite and mostly boring, some ridiculously way out she couldn't finish them. Fortunately none came near to what she had in mind. Her parents said they understood, but did they really?

Autumn was a good season to start; darker evenings meant fewer distractions and winter months allowed the imagination greater scope. Preparation could be daunting and blank pages she found terrifying. First thoughts were best and once started she was obliged to move forward; not to stall to cross out or correct spelling and grammar, not to think much or use logic but to give into the urge to almost lose control. She placed energy where it was unobstructed by an internal censor, to express her thoughts with no cover-ups or polite excuses, to explore emotion right to the edge. First thoughts could have great energy and uncensored by decorum or whatever would grandma think? She was going to be a great character along with her warriors. It is what is--writing down the bones. To hell with propriety.

Her aim was to convey truth and not tell the truth. It wasn't necessary to write what really happened; she'd write word images creating rhythms and structure and a riveting plot as the story unfolded. Great writing was meant to crush us, entertain us, move us to tears and lead to a greater understanding of ourselves and our place in the world. The global plan was to imagine Aranmore as the magical island, describe its fascinations, enlarge these to include the whole country with strong characters acting out dramas, first in the west, then the south and finally in the east around Newgrange in Meath. All taking place well before Egypt ever crowned a Pharaoh. This was a minor country with a major history; a lot of it hidden and still speculative.

She opened a notebook where she'd written an initial impression of Aran:

… As the sun goes down a strange stillness falls on Aran. Unusual for here. Streams and pools scattered in the small fields turn yellow and then the colour of blood before eventually giving way to silver. No trees to give shade or shelter, only walls. But what walls! They were built before the start of time and stand today in defiance especially round the great fortress of Dun Aengus …

… The magic of Aran burns into memory. When day is done and night, full of secrets, waits before unfolding her wings. One can sometimes hear her whispering high in the wind. As day's fierceness dies all things lose their shadows and without shadow lose substance. An all-pervading darkness creeps over the earth …

…Night-lights shimmer but are few and far between--between the monuments and standing stones, which take on a life of their own. One is compelled to seek out a lighted dwelling as a ship searches for a beam of light to indicate that all is not lost….

… The events that follow convey the truth about this extraordinary place; a place where anything is possible if one possesses an imagination that can cope with happenings that took place in a time before the glories of Egypt, when people lived their lives in an unrecognisable way to a visitor from this end of the spectrum …

Enough for today! It is a scattered start but enough is enough. Tomorrow will be the real test when she'll scribble flow charts, write an introduction explaining the purpose of the epic, when and where the action takes place and explain the consequences of such a great history on people, their land today and international consequences.

Over the next months pages grow into hundreds and words into thousands. In the beginning the islanders struggle with the ocean

about them. Then the island is conquered by a proud and courageous people who build a great fortress that is the wonder of all.
From here they sail to the greater island, the mainland, and discover a land of beauty beyond measure. In Part One many conflicts
are faced, including clashes with local chieftains and kings. They
experience hardships, loneliness, tender love, worshipping, starva-
tion and abandonment in despair. In the end villains are destroyed
and through amazing acts of valour the heroes overcome crises to
achieve a state of contentment and peace.

She is exhausted yet fulfilled. The manuscript is sent to
London.

1 5

Following John Nicholson's visit to the Middle East his research work was productive with some lucky breaks. It's strange how a distraction can give renewed energy or make one see a problem in a different light. For months there was a major problem facing him about DNA analysis in certain diseases. He'd tried different cell cultures, always with the aid of his own formulae in the computer and persistently he came up against a brick wall. At times he was tempted to consider the use of animal models as others were doing. The greater the frustration the more the temptation. Easy to set up an experiment and an answer would be more straightforward.

But no. The struggle with his conscience in Dublin together with his writings in Cornwall came back and his pledge to avoid animal work. It had cost him dearly with Professor Wainwright. Being a matter of conscience he could not go back. His work had to be focused where there was no cruelty and yet results could be achieved. Already strides had been made; he must not deviate. His work was appreciated by some who regarded him as a man before his time. Not by all. Others scorned him hinting at a lack of courage. Wasting time by 'going the long way round.'

Frustrations seemed to resolve. Answers stared him in the face. Why hadn't he thought of another procedure? It would complete the blocked linkages in his equations and enable another safe combination therapy for cancer. The discovery was so great he'd to share it. Straight away he reported to Sir Kenneth.

'John. Please come in and sit down.'

He entered with a pile of papers and placed them on the conference table. Sir Kenneth looked wearily at them; he knew what was coming.

'What a tale to tell your grandchildren. Amazing how a story improves in the retelling.'

'Maybe so.' John smiled. 'But remember I've no children let alone grandchildren. What you suggest would be a little difficult.'

'Of course. You need a wife first.'

'I already had a wife Sir Kenneth.'

'I do recall and lost her tragically.'

'They say it's a matter of time to recover. I'm still waiting.'

Feeling uncomfortable Sir Kenneth asked. 'Your work?'

'It's really exciting. Since I came home everything seems to have fallen into place. One procedure staring me in the face and I couldn't see it. Now it's clear and I think it will work.'

He drew several diagrams on a sheet of paper and explained each one carefully. Sir Kenneth was delighted.

'My word, John, you have an original mind. I admire your approach. Please go ahead and finalise the work and do all the fine-tuning necessary. Then let me have a copy of the definitive paper before submitting it for publication.'

'I'll see to it straightaway. Is there anything else we should discuss?'

Sir Kenneth hesitated a moment, then went to his desk and found a letter that had arrived a few days ago. He frowned when he reread it and mumbled something about trouble again and why didn't they leave it alone?

John was puzzled. 'What's the problem Sir Kenneth? Can I be of any help?'

'Well,no harm in telling you. This letter is from the secretary of the Oxford Union. They like to debate contentious issues and there's usually a lot of public interest. For some mischievous reason they want to invite two speakers from Cambridge to face two Oxford speakers on a motion--let me see the exact wording, "This house agrees that the benefit of animal research outweighs the harm." '

John's face dropped; it was obvious he disapproved of the statement.

'The wording is biased from the outset and makes it sound simple.'

'I know what you're saying. It's in the usual short snappy sentence they use for other debates. Anyway they've asked for two speakers from each university and suggested two from here would be divided, that is one for the motion and one against with the same combination on the Oxford team.'

'That could be a lively debate. I'd like to go along and listen.'

'I agree. The sparks will fly I'm sure. Who can we pick that will do us justice?'

'Dr. Juniper would speak in favour of the motion. He's strong views on animal models and will not be deviated. I know because I've had several battles with him.'

'And what about you John?'

'How do you mean?'

'I know you are against the use of animals and do your work in a different way. I think you'll be ideal in disagreeing with this motion.'

'I would disagree. I'm not a great orator and haven't an easy facility with words.'

'Perhaps not. And yet this could be a chance to prove yourself right if you feel strongly enough about your work. You'll probably find those fine words you wish you had. It could be a golden opportunity to have your views made known to a wider audience. I believe the BBC will be there.'

'That's a frightening prospect in itself.'

'Seriously you should consider speaking. I'll endorse it if you wish. At least it should be great fun. I believe the audience can be lively at times.'

'I'll think about it. Thanks for letting me know.'

'Not at all. They've given us four months to prepare, which is a comfortable time to get one's thoughts together.'

'Four months,' repeated John thoughtfully.

'And John. If you decide to accept please discuss anything you wish with me, anything at all, awkward details, difficult problems. I'd be delighted to help.'

'I'd welcome that. It will be a challenge. Although maybe I don't realise what I'm letting myself in for.'

He left Sir Kenneth's room felling he'd been handed a poisoned chalice.

1 6

Two concerns remained with John Nicholson. His <u>in vitro</u> research had taken on a new meaning. He'd learnt the technique in Sweden from Professor Isselherg on relatively undeveloped equipment. Advances in information technology made the work more feasible enabling significant breakthroughs. Yet he was reluctant to reveal the findings.

The invitation to speak at the Oxford Union was also a worry especially the wording of the motion. Certain opinions were gathering strength on either side of the argument. A lot of publicity and even violence by animal rights people had occurred. The police were concerned at the escalation in attacks on vulnerable establishments. To crown it all Cambridge University was chosen for a huge expansion in its research laboratories devoted to animal research. It had obtained some government funding but most was due to come from private sources that expected huge returns on investments.

It was wise to keep his results quiet. Let things be. If they were released too soon anything could happen, blocking tactics, withdrawal of support or worse. The only person he trusted was Sir Kenneth and even he voiced concerns at their weekly meeting.

'I appreciate you want to lie low for the time being John. There are some unpleasant things happening and the university does not want unsavoury publicity during our negotiations with big business. The expansion will cost millions and worth a great deal to the university.'

'I'll quietly continue with my work. It's turning out better than I ever dreamed of. No one else is bothered with it. There's a certain glamour in using animals as clearing houses before humans can be tested.'

'I do hope your work continues. Another thing, and perhaps not unrelated, I get the feeling the Union debate is not as simple as it seems. There's a possibility, or more a probability, big business will do anything to get the motion passed. I'm sure they'll get top speakers, perhaps coached by a QC, to put the best case forward. It's a high profile public forum with lots of media coverage.'

'I'm having doubts about speaking against the motion,' he said. 'Emotion will only carry the argument so far and I'm reluctant to mention the in vitro findings in a public forum before publication. Do you see my dilemma Sir Kenneth?'

'I do. You have my sympathy. It's a tightrope not too much emotion or sentiment. They won't buy that. And how much science can you reveal to a mixed audience? It's developing into a can of worms.'

'I would've loved to discuss it with Walter Wainwright. He was solid as a rock and knew exactly how to get out of a tight corner.'

'Is there anyone else you can talk to? Perhaps outside this country.'

John thought for a moment.

'There's the Helmuth Institute in Stockholm where I started <u>in vitro</u> work with Professor Isselherg. He was enthusiastic but handed over most of the initial development to me. It was slow and painful. Now it's making progress.'

'Why not take a trip to Isselherg and discuss the problem. Maybe he could throw more light on it. Dr. Juniper will have no difficulty in persuading people of the benefits. Everyone wants to hear good news. He'll spell them out thick and fast and get a lot of sympathy. Your difficulty is to prove the harm is greater than the benefits. There's bound to be a preconceived prejudice in many.'

'When you put it like that I almost want to forget about the whole thing.'

'Please don't John. I've faith in your abilities. I think you could come up with some real surprises. This is what we need in this country, active intelligent debate on important issues if we're to go forward and hopefully lead the world in cancer research. With a little help from the appropriate source, John, you are the best man, the only man for the job. And you'll do it.

'Really?'

'Telephone Gustav Isselherg and have a talk with him'

John telephoned the Helmuth Institute and asked for Professor Isselherg. An excited voice answered.

'John Nicholson. This is a pleasant surprise. How are you?'

'I'm fine and working hard in Cambridge.'

'I heard you'd left Dublin. Perhaps the prospects were not good?'

'How right you are. Everything is here and I've made good progress with the in vitro testing you introduced me to in Stockholm.'

'I remember. We'd little success and it was very slow.'

'Well Gustav. Good news. The process has been speeded up with modern technology. I find it incredible.'

'Sounds fascinating. But why are you telling me? Why not go ahead and publish as soon as you can.'

'There's a potential problem, more a dilemma, looming here over the next few months. It's not easy to discuss it over the phone, but I've been invited to speak at the Oxford Union.'

'The Oxford Union. My God. Congratulations John that's a huge compliment.'

'Thanks Gustav. The motion is clearly worded in favour of the status quo. It reads as follows. "This house agrees that the benefit of animal research outweighs the harm." '

'What a simple, yet complex, statement! And you're against it. It needs lots of thought and preparation.'

'I realise that only too clearly and am getting cold feet.'

'Nonsense John. That's not like you. Nothing was too difficult. We were sorry to lose you when you went to Dublin.'

'That didn't last and it's when I lost poor Linda.'

'How can I forget? A terrible tragedy. It's not time that will heal the loss. There has to be something else.'

'I don't understand Gustav.'

'I've said this before more than once; there's always an open door with us in Stockholm. You might benefit from a week or two, or even more, we'd be delighted to have you with us. You could call it a holiday, or a working holiday. Perhaps put together the bones of your address. Our combined word power may have some impact on prejudiced blockheads whose only function is to support the easiest way out and to hell with morals.'

'You haven't changed Gustav. You've still got fire in your belly.'

'Then John put your foot down. You're a free man now, unfortunately, but you're free. Take a holiday with us either in the city or in our country house. Springtime there can be glorious and incidentally for some time Karita has locked herself away from the family. She's just completed an enormous volume on Celtic mythology called "Truth behind the legend." She'd be thrilled if you were our guest for a few weeks--or whatever. As you know I'm semi-retired and more or less my own boss. Please say yes.'

John replied impulsively.

'Gustav I'll come. Your invitation is so persuasive I'd find it almost impossible to refuse. Although it was not the reason for my phone call.'

'Of course not. I know that. It was I who invited you. Remember? Nothing to do with you.'

Three weeks holiday was arranged with no difficulty. Sir Kenneth was pleased he was going to stay with the Isselhergs.

'I used to know Gustav in Cambridge, along with Walter Wainwright when we were students. Walter and Gustav were close friends and I was in the background. I'm delighted you're going back. They seem to approach things differently over there and you could learn something useful for the Oxford Union.'

Another reason for John's visit was his wish to discuss <u>in vitro</u> techniques with Dr. Knutson, the brilliant biochemist who had recently joined Isselherg's department.

Isselherg's private car waited as the plane touched down at Arlanda. John was glad of his topcoat, as there was a difference in temperature compared to London. Eriksson welcomed him politely and they drove to Kungsangen House. The same elderly gentleman dressed in black greeted him with genuine pleasure. Inside the real welcome waited. It was evening about an hour before dinner. What better timing? Rachel embraced him as did the daughters and Gustav gave him a bear hug. He was then shown to his room.

'You might like to freshen up first sir,' said the man in black, 'dinner will be served at seven o'clock. Just the immediate family this time.' There was a twinkle in his eye as he recalled John's first visit.

'That's nice.' John answered frankly. 'A comfortable number.'

He unpacked, had a short nap and it was time to smarten up. At seven o'clock he arrived downstairs. Conversation was polite although subdued when the family were seated. Several years had passed since he was a guest here. Lots had happened since, tragic things that were difficult to talk about; the girls were quiet as the parents inquired about events after John and Linda left Sweden for Dublin. The hesitancy, the unintentional silences at times were awkward--a lot of words with little communication, thought Karita.

Gustav decided to liven things up.

'John who asked you to speak at the Oxford Union?'

'Sir Kenneth Richardson. He knows my views on research methods. He's also asked me to play down the in vitro results for the present for several reasons including patenting and legal considerations.'

'Understandable. You can't be too careful. This is a cutthroat business--sorry for the pun but you know what I mean. If I can help please let me know although I've slowed down considerably. Dr. Knutson's the one to discuss pure science with. He confuses me at times.'

'I'll remember that.' John smiled uneasily. 'I must speak to him.'

Karita was listening carefully biding her time.

John continued.

'I hope to write the outline here away from the distractions of Cambridge.'

A good time for Rachel to interrupt.

'As you know John you've the run of the house--as before. If you want to work in your bedroom that's fine. Or you might like the library. It's beautiful in there at the moment with views over the lawns and flower gardens.'

'Sounds great.'

She continued with more enthusiasm.

'Karita used it writing her novel. She found it inspiring.'

'I don't want to disturb her work.' John said cautiously. 'I'll leave her alone.'

Karita realised her opportunity.

'Please do use the library John. I've finished the first novel and it has been sent to London. So I'm waiting and at a loose end.' She glanced at her parents. 'I don't want you to take this the wrong way John ... '

'Of course not.'

'Even little me might be able to help.' She admitted quietly. 'Not in a scientific way. More in a presentation PR approach and placing your priorities in the right sequence. That's where my journalistic experience may come in handy.'

'You're absolutely right Karita. You have a lovely way with words and a concise mind. You know lot of dos and don'ts about literature.'

'You're very kind. So there you are. You've my father to oversee the presentation, you've Dr. Knutson to guide on the fine-tuning and you'll have me, hopefully, to give impact to the emotional and moral arguments that may sway the hearts and not the heads of the audience.'

John sat back with a sigh.

'What a stroke of luck I've returned to the Isselhergs in my hour of need. It's wonderful all this help is available. '

Karita raised a hand.

'May I make a suggestion? We give John a couple of days to collect his thoughts, make notes and telephone Dr. Knutson. On the third day I could discuss ideas on presentation based on rough ideas. This would be the best time because everything is fluid and flexible. If my contribution were left to the end it would be more difficult to change things. He'd be too set in his ways.'

She turned to John with a pleading look.

'Please agree to this. I'd love to see the initial plans. They are easier to move around. Look on me as one of your eventual audience; one of those you'll have to convince that you're right. Firstly you will have to convince me that you are right!'

He smiled and nodded.

'It's a deal Karita.'

John wrote pages of notes and discussed them with Dr. Knutson over the next couple of days. He met Karita in the library on the third day.

'Please sit down John beside the French windows. That's where I did my work. It brings back happy memories.'

'Lovely view of the garden. Must be inspiring.'

'It's lovely. Now John you may think I sound like a schoolteacher with what I'm going to say. Even a little surprised. Take it all as well meant. I like meeting people and learning things I don't know. Conversation should be communication. We have people talking a lot and saying nothing. The first thing to get clear is whom are we communicating with? And this applies to you John.'

'Mainly university students from all faculties, special guests and a fair smattering of the media and press. I don't communicate well.'

She smiled gently.

'In the old days people were ashamed to talk. They failed to reveal what sort of people they were.'

'Me all over. I'm too hesitant.'

'People are interested in people.' She said quietly. 'Yet a lot of us wear masks, which do not allow us to tell the truth.'

'Again that's me. Afraid of hurting people.'

'You mustn't,' she said, 'what we need is transparency and honesty. Especially honesty.'

As she leaned towards him a fragrance arose.

'A few questions you could ask yourself. You needn't tell me the answers though I'd like to know.'

He looked straight at her. 'Such as?'

'What have been your priorities in life and have they changed?'

'Karita that's so complex. Long ago I was blind with ambition and never considered cruelty a problem. It took second place to compassion. After three years working here I changed drastically and discovered compassion was more important.'

'What's your greatest fear?'

'Simple. Fear of failure though it's not easy to admit, except to you Karita.'

She mumbled to herself. 'Wonder why?' And then. 'Have your fears changed?'

'The older I get the greater the fear of failure.'

'I see. That's why this Oxford Union thing is so important. It's not just like a simple experiment going wrong.'

'Got it in one. It's of paramount importance.'

'What about friendship and love and family.'

'Karita you know I've been through that. The fallout is still with me.'

'Are you going to let that continue?'

'I don't understand. What do you mean?'

'I think you do but you don't want to admit it. I digress. I apologise.'

'Don't apologise,' he said, 'I think I had it coming. Remember you spoke about the need for honesty and people wearing masks? These are qualities I find it hard to live up to.'

She appeared more relaxed. 'I said it was good for people to talk, one-to-one.'

He looked at her quizzically. 'I could ask isn't life difficult?'

'What would you say John?'

'Again you're so straightforward. I haven't been thinking of you, your needs, and priorities even your curiosities. What your prospects are. I apologise. Still I don't see where all this is getting us. Is it relevant?'

'I don't know yet. I cannot say anything about the benefits or the harm of science but I am trying to get to know you better, your true inner feelings. Perhaps things you don't realise yourself. When I've read your draft I can put the two aspects together. Leave it to me for the present. Just let it simmer, think over the whole issue and the cream will come to the top.'

'You make me feel guilty especially after you asked my help with your manuscript.'

'Oh that!' She dismissed it with a gesture. 'That's finished and gone. So there's nothing more to it.'

'We'll be patient. Lots of luck with it anyway.'

'Thanks. It was lovely talking John. Don't worry. My needs are less important in the short term. You've got an important problem to solve and we've to try and solve it.'

'You're so understanding. And I'm a selfish bore.'

'Nonsense. You're far from it. Sometime before you leave maybe you will listen to me and my worries.'

'I promise Karita. You'd make a great schoolteacher.'

She would read the draft in a quiet corner. She needed to be alone.

He pushed the chair back and walked over to the French windows. For the first time that afternoon a smile brightened her lips and eyes. It was eerie how memories came back and his body came alive like a flower in rain. Even in her voice there was a kind of splendour.

2 0

Karita returned to her room with the draft and placed it on the bed. She went to the window. It had stopped raining. Far away the sky opened and large clouds hung over the hills glowing with amber light. On impulse she decided to walk through the garden as far as the stream. She wrapped up in a woollen shawl--a present from her Irish trip. Days were getting longer and the countryside was drenched with an expectancy of spring. She watched the stream slipping over grey stones and away through a tunnel. John's interview occupied her.

The last flush of sunlight faded as she returned to the house and the lights were on. She'd have liked to stay in the garden longer but the wind whistled like clashing swords. The blazing log fires never looked better; they'd their own seductive quality that was hard to resist.

That evening dinner was quiet and subdued. She excused herself early. The reason--a headache--but there was more to it. She went to her room taking several books from the library. The curtains were closed and the reading lamps switched on. She slid between clean sheets with the script and notebook in hand.

It took about half an hour to read. She stared at the ceiling with excitement and disappointment; excited by the force of argument about harm--and harm to everyone--and, yet, she couldn't understand what benefit could be obtained by other means. It sounded wonderful. It also sounded confused disjointed and not plausible. Disappointment set in. Where was the passion? Oh yes it was mentioned but only in passing. Serious editing was needed. For now she was tired and exhausted. The script was placed under her pillow and the light turned out. She was going to sleep on it.

The sun was a surprise next morning when she drew the curtains. This day would be different. She'd make it so with a major task in hand. John needed help although he hadn't asked. His helpless way brought out an instinct in her to point him in the right direction, to organise him whether he liked it or not. She was determined. The feeling reminded her of passages in her manuscript when, in olden times, women loved to set their men folk difficult tasks or send them on hazardous journeys. It was a peculiar trait in women. Some would even take pleasure in sending a reckless youth on an impossible task to face appalling dangers. It was a way of weeding out suitors. However she hadn't this problem.

She sat at the desk beside the French windows where the light was good. Notebooks, references, dictionaries to the right and John's manuscript to the left and in the middle a pile of blank writing paper staring straight back at her--defiantly.

The writing started. This time it was not about dark islands in Atlantic mythology and magic. She wrote about tears in women and children and men who were neglected all over the world by uncaring cruelty. If only one could hear the lament as a living sorrow, and imagine it preserved in some indestructible urn. She wrote about compassion with more intensity than anything she'd ever written before, page after page.

Several hours later she was forced to return to her bedroom with headache and exhaustion. For a while she slept and was partially wakened by a voice downstairs calling her name. As there was no answer it was assumed she'd driven into town for shopping and would be back later. She dosed off again. Not for long because a knock came to the door.

That was the way it happened in her semiconsciousness; not just a simple knock on the door. This knock took its time to arrive and in a dramatic fashion. She suspected its imminent arrival by gentle steps down the corridor--far off, a manifestation that was not yet a knock but as steps grew louder an expectation of an approaching knock was almost inevitable. It stopped outside in a frightening pause before surrendering itself to the door.

'Who's there?' She cried a little desperate.

'Don't worry Karita. It's only John.'

'Oh, that's all right. I was only resting.'

She got up quickly, put on a silk dressing gown and tidied her hair.

'Please come in.'

He hesitated a moment and then accepted the invitation.

'Let's sit at the window and look over the lawn. There's a lot of green about.'

She was fully awake and refreshed.

The writing papers were on her desk. Looking through them she explained the sequence of events in the script. Good scientifically but lacking in emotional appeal. She'd tried her best to rewrite parts starting at ten that morning and only finishing at four o'clock.

'That's too much Karita. I never expected all that work. Just a few suggestions.'

She handed him both versions.

'First read yours and read my adaptation. Then put yourself in the audience and see which you'd prefer. Go ahead John. I'll leave you for half an hour. I'll go and have tea and biscuits and come back later.'

'Fine. I'll do just that. See you.'

She disappeared downstairs. He put his feet up and read his original and then her draft. He was astonished, appalled and amazed at the different approach. Her interpretation was naked passion, empathy overflowing with startling examples of cruelty and the consequences for animal life. At the end there was the most masterly dissertation on compassion he'd ever read.

John's draft lacked conviction. At one stage in the past Wainwright gave him a lecture on pity; it had an effect but didn't last. He had tried to include kindness mercy and sympathy yet a subtle weaving and powerful appeal to the goodness in everyone came through brilliantly in Karita's writing. Even though he was ten-years older she revealed a maturity in life and the living of it. And the university course in humanities must have given her a special perspective.

His background was different. Life had been tough. Massive blows of fate had blunted his sensibility and this episode was a revelation. Natural upset changed to gratitude, gratitude that he'd met this family, Gustav and Rachel, the sisters especially Karita. There was also a dilemma. She appeared to be attracted to him; not in words but in how she did things, and the way she'd poured her heart and soul into improving his presentation. He would be eter-nally grateful. Was that enough? That night he slept badly.

Sun streamed into the bedroom next morning--a change from the last few days. He shaved showered and went down for an early breakfast. Outside the dining room the garden was preparing for a joyous day and scents drifted though the open window. The peace quiet and tranquillity were just what he needed. A few days remained and he was determined to make the most of them.

All of a sudden there was a commotion in the hall. Karita's voice preceded her as she rushed into the room. Her excitement was boundless and she had to share it with someone. Who better than John?

'What is all the fuss about Karita?' He asked. 'Has something happened?'

She flung her arms around him.

'Guess what John?' She showed him a letter. 'This arrived in the morning post. It's from London and the publisher is thrilled with the manuscript. There are two more planned so they've offered a wonderful contract to accept this one provided I promise to let them have the other two in a reasonable time. What do you think?'

'Fantastic news.' He stared at her open mouthed. 'Congratulations Karita. It's what you deserve. You've worked hard. You'll be able to complete the trilogy.'

'I'd love to do it.' She admitted. 'And you were the one who started it all. Your story telling was enthralling.'

He paused trying to find words.

'Can I make a suggestion? Let's go for a long walk. It would be a pity to waste such a beautiful morning perhaps we can talk about future plans.'

'Future plans?' Her eyes brightened.

'You have a bright and important future and must be given every opportunity to fulfil it now that the chance is there. As for me there's a crisis looming. In my bones I feel it and I've to plan for every contingency. Let's plan and enjoy the few days together in this lovely place.'

They wrapped up well and walked through the garden past the stream and out into the great woodlands beyond, through copses, clearings and dark passages where trees closed ranks over them. It was good to forget recent events. She loved spring best of all; it filled her imagination with new ideas.

They talked endlessly as he explained the new developments in his alternative research, which could be a thing of the future. These few days allowed an intimacy develop that was hard to define, but it was there. Both felt it as she talked about poetry. They lunched at a local inn and walked further through the woods.

The air was warm and bright but not for long. A mist slowly covered the face of afternoon. In the west the sun melted into a golden glow, changed to red, darkened and disappeared behind cloud. They pulled their coats tightly around and made for home. Passing the water pool at the end of the garden great black shadows swept above their heads; the swishing noise was deafening. Karita was terrified and clung to John. A family of swans was searching for shelter like all creatures looking for places to rest when dark- ness falls. The reflection of a half-risen moon was shattered into flecks and splashed across deep shadows. The air echoed with the sound of wings and more reflections were rumbled, scattered and dispersed. A haunting spectre they were as they drifted into obscu- rity. A spasm went through Karita as the Island of Inishglora came back to her.

They waited until the noise abated and mist wreathed the area like ghosts meeting and greeting.

Before they arrived home the sky cleared to the east over the woodland and the moon appeared again. They watched the unfolding spectacle.

She turned to him, her wide eyes challenging him.

'When my time comes for help John will you be there for me?'

'I'll be there if I possibly can.'

'Thanks. But you are so serious tonight. What is it?'

'I don't know. Maybe I have little talent for contemplation.'

'It must be the moon,' she said, 'I feel happy and glad and have lots of lovely ideas. I like things to sparkle and laugh and look wild. I'm still so excited! The night shouldn't end.'

2 2

Sadness filled the air around the dining table. Rachel smiled weakly as she touched John's hand.

'Thanks for visiting us again Dear John. We thought you wouldn't make it.'

'I'm glad I came. There's such a welcome here it's almost like coming home.'

Gustav opened his hands. 'Always remember this is your second home. We are now a complete family around the table. And tomorrow … '

The others lowered their heads as Rachel came to the rescue.

'You'll have lots of work when you return to Cambridge. And the Oxford Union debate. Are you worried or is that a silly question?'

'I am worried about it. Gustav's been a great help on the scientific content.'

'I've tried to get John to be more forceful and positive.' Gustav said. 'I can visualise the bullying from the opposition. It's tough and cruel and once the crowd goes against the speaker it's like feeding Christians to the lions. The verbal slaughter can be ferocious. I've been to a few debates and witnessed the carnage first hand.'

Rachel glared at him. 'How could you say such things? You'll terrify poor John.'

'I won't.' Gustav smiled back at her. 'I know John far better than any of you ladies, I think.' He hesitated as he looked around the table. Nobody challenged him. 'John must face reality and be prepared for a rough ride. I also know he's capable of giving back as good as he gets. I've seen it in my department. It's a rare spectacle but it can and does happen.'

John gave a laugh. 'I don't know how to take that--a compliment or fault. I prefer to think the former.'

'That's the way it's intended.' Gustav took a sip of wine and lifted his glass. 'Here's to your continued progress in your new work and outstanding success at the debate. I'd love to be there but probably won't be able to make it.'

'I understand. I'll let you know how it goes anyway.'

'Thanks John,' Rachel said, 'that would be good of you. We always have your welfare at heart.'

A feeling of compliment overload came back though it didn't affect him as much as it used to.

'Rachel is right,' Gustav said. 'I won't be going to the Institute. A day off. Eriksson will drive you to town. I believe you've another meeting with Dr. Knutson.'

'That's in the afternoon. I'll stay in the city overnight and fly out next morning.'

'Sensible. No point in rushing things.'

John noticed how quiet the others were.

'Karita has been a wonderful help with the speech.' He added over coffee. 'I gave her a draft copy, which modestly I thought was quite good. She kept it for a night and a further day and rewrote-- not the content--but the whole flavour, the appeal, the empathy and compassion.'

He turned to Rachel and Gustav. 'You've a remarkable daughter in Karita. She has a fascinating way with words and certainly knows how to use them. She's going to go far. And she's a treasure.'

An awkward silence. There was no answer to his remark.

'I suppose we'll read about the results.' Gustav changed tack. 'We'll look out for the English papers.'

'Enough said about work and serious things,' Rachel smiled. 'Anyone wants to play games or listen to music or just do what they like.'

Silence. John was the first to respond.

'I'll retire early if I may be excused. I've paper work to prepare for Dr. Knutson.'

'Of course Dear John.' Rachel held her cheek out for a goodnight kiss. He obliged, stood up and bowed slightly to everyone and left the room.

Arriving at his bedroom he found an envelope under the door. He opened it. Inside was a message from Karita reminding him of his promise. He did remember--a promise was a promise.

Also enclosed was an exquisite photograph.

No writing,no message anywhere.

Just the image.

Next morning a fog collected outside making the garden and trees a mere outline. Hopefully it would lift. Eriksson helped him with his bags. The family remained out of sight as he was driven away from the House towards Stockholm. John had his own thoughts for company.

He booked a comfortable hotel for the night near the airport bus terminus and walked around familiar places, ending up in the restaurant in Gamla Stan where he met Linda Lindstrom. Memories and more memories. The meeting with Dr. Knutson was purely business and there was an extensive agenda to get through.

The last evening in Stockholm was going to be entirely his own. He'd lived here for three years and knew places he wanted to see again. There was the small bar beside the florist shop that he'd visited, not too often--only when necessary. His favourite seat was still there in the corner where he could get a good view of the action as it trickled in. The same barman had some difficulty in getting reciprocal recognition.

His feelings were mixed as he visited old haunts. As he sat alone in the corner--one usually sits alone in Swedish bars--a kind of sickness of an exile crept over him. As he'd wandered the streets soaking in the spirit of the past it felt that present times were haunted. Later as he strolled through the quiet streets, which were again threatened with the same morning mist, the white neon lamps stood alone amongst the trees as if they were dark pencil sketches by a crazy artist in a hurry. The penetrating darkness was acute as a voice within calling for security, to end this purposeless memory lane. It served no useful function; its main purpose was to upset and yet he wouldn't listen.

He arrived back at the hotel in confusion and went straight to his room. He'd tried the nightclub he enjoyed in his bachelor days. Things then were full of excitement and discovery and impudent hopes. The expectation of things to come;immediate things too, now all that was gone and couldn't be rekindled, even though he half expected it might be. Nothing left for him here. Just feelings of why bother? He was tired and the flight was early next morning. He asked for a wake-up call at 7 a.m. He noticed Linda's diary floodlit by the bedside light. He opened a page at random.

… My dear askling John. It is a strange feeling that if you're reading this I will probably be already gone from your life. I have no idea how long after I've gone that you may find this special letter to you, but when you do I long to know that you will have started on your way to recovery. I would feel dreadful for a long time and probably never recover. You are different; you were always emotionally stronger than me. When I was ill I had a strange feeling I wasn't really going to make it in spite of your courageous efforts. I didn't want to think about it too much even though you had no family to fall back on for support. It was a great distress to think that you would be alone and abandoned. Since I became sick I've worried so much about you. Remember askling I always love you no matter where I might be. My heart would be broken if I knew you would never be happy again. So please go out and find happiness again, find that special kind of person who will make you happy again. Perhaps it's not possible but please try. The world you live in would be more wonderful for it.

… I'll watch over you. I love you into eternity. Linda

23

Great excitement was present in the cottage by the harbour. Tom Nolan's exhibition was scheduled to open in the Osborne Gallery in Dublin in six weeks and last minute preparations were hectic.

Even Annette felt the pressure as she woke to sunlight dancing around her bedroom. And no school today. It was Saturday. No hurry to get up. She thrilled at the colour of the sky framed by the window; it could almost be a painting itself although occasional objects intruded on its stillness. Birds in the garden below added to the elation as they called to each other. She was happy with her life and family.

Ruth was also heavily involved. In addition to running a busy household she also had to keep a lid on Tom's enthusiasm. It could easily overflow and get into trouble with those damned last minute things.

'Never mind them,' she reassured him. 'All the paintings are finished and with the gallery. They're being framed and taken care of.'

'The owner of the gallery wants me to write a booklet to accompany the show. He thinks there could be a great story in the journey from Malin to Mizen. He may be right.'

'You could easily produce some impressive tales and describe the process of painting like the lovely talks you gave me after each trip.'

'You're very kind. Although spoken words are easier than writing them.'

'How do you know? Just try it.'

'I'll have to now.'

'Right then. I'll make it as easy as possible. You can have the sitting room all day. A fire will be lit and no one will disturb you unless you call for something. Annette and I'll be quiet as a mouse and so will Patsie. So you've no excuse.'

'Sounds great. I'll remember what I discussed with Mark O'Neill last year.'

She looked crossly at him.

'On second thoughts I might give it a miss. A good underlying theme could be <u>Faithful To More Than Reality.</u>'

She smiled.

'Brilliant Tom, now in you go and settle down to work. There's plenty of paper and pencils on the table. I've got everything you need. So off you go!'

He entered the room with the glowing fire, the flowers beside the violin case and the large table pulled over to the window for light. There was no excuse. He made himself comfortable.

And he started to write.

Painting the Irish Landscape -- *A Journey from Malin to Mizen*

Introduction

... Ireland stands alone on the fringe of Europe and, until a few hundred years ago, its Atlantic coast was the western extremity of the known world. The ever-changing weather that comes rolling in from the ocean produces light and shade effects that are both ravishing and unforgettable. Like the weather the western seaboard is infinitely changeable and can scale heights of geological drama. This landscape is probably our greatest national asset and yet is under attack more than ever before ...

... To capture the landscape on canvas a journey was undertaken commencing at Malin and ending at Mizen. Malin Head, being the northern--most tip of Ireland, seemed an obvious starting point. The road led through the wilderness of Donegal with its roaming deer, wonderful beaches that go on forever and from where, on a fine day, you can see Scotland. Then through Dunfanaghy, Horn Head, Falcarragh, Bloody Foreland, Dungloe, Rossbeg and Glencolumbkille. On to Sligo and Leitrim's legendary countryside with its strange mountains and haunted valleys such as Glencar, Eagle's Rock and Glenade. Sombre Ben Bulben and Knocknarea framed the serene beauty of Drumcliff, Raghly and Lissadel. Mayo, with its vast mountains, hungry hills and glorious bogs, was next. The road was a long one through the extraordinary Ceide Fields, remote Belmullet, Corraun and, of course, the island of Achill with Europe's highest sea--cliffs rising 2000 feet from a silent sea. On to the utter sadness of Killadoon, Doo Lough and Delphi. South was Galway and Connemara where hundreds of lakes overflowed with light, the occasional tree grew horizontally and tiny fields were veined with stone walls. The road continued southwest passing the rocks and turloughs of Clare, the mountain gaps of Kerry, the lonely roads and beaches of west Cork to end at Barley Cove nestling at the foot of the glorious cliffs of Mizen …

… This was not a single mighty journey but an amalgam of many over several seasons; spring and early summer in the north--west, summer in the mid--west, autumn and winter in the south-west to give a more complete picture on a sequential basis.

The Journey, Landscape and Art

… We can travel far and wide searching for something and then come home to find it. This was my feeling that bright morning on Malin Head when spring was clothing a naked world in preparation for better things. The smell of flowers that came out to greet me, the sight of crocuses and daisies--white as angels--and the silence of rising sap gave a wonderful expectancy to everything, everywhere. And the sound of great waves breaking on rocks below was like a living pulse. On any journey we travel back in time and forward in space. On Malin, the sense of place was deeply moving; I was aware of the myriad journeys of others here, including St. Columbkille's life--long exile, the tragic Flight of the Earls, the Spanish Armada and the naval convoys in the Great Wars. But it was not so much the time measured on calendars; it was more the character of seasons I really wished to record …

… The atmosphere at Marble Strand was extraordinary. The rock face of the hill was so dark under a shrouded sky; the sombre clouds were almost too oppressive for this world. The trembling light on the brow of the hill redeemed the scene. Other Donegal memories include the great scroll of evening sky rolled back above Muckish and the Derryveagh Range showing a blood--dusky presence spreading down to Errigal and beyond. Later the first stars burnt as a majestic prelude to the unveiling of the Milky Way. The road through Bloody Foreland allowed panoramic views along the coastline. Then there was the time spent on Cruit Island watching the waves staggering in from a green sea, falling with a thud followed by the hiss of withdrawal. The view from Kincasslagh towards Aran Island was sublime with blue shining from 'the floor of heaven' making an unforgettable experience. The desolation around Errigal had a profound effect as I visualised the crippling rents and evictions that continued the work of the Famine. The beautiful, but cruel mountains were never meant to sustain man or beast--yet thousands were thrown out into the cold, their miserable homes burnt to the ground. The fate of some was to roam the pages of the past, of others--probably the majority--was to fall into the anonymous dust of time ...

... Then there was the walk on Rossbeg Strand that was one long lingering with moving reflections for company. On to Glencolumbkille where the sea was blazing white behind Glen Head. Here the mists of history can blow aside, if you let them, to show a time when the twin torches of faith and learning were being extinguished all over Europe and the vandal hordes were massing like vultures over the corpse of Rome, when the Island of Ireland experienced its golden age. Columbkille, perhaps more than anyone, kept it alive by establishing monasteries including that at Kells where the famous book was written ...

... Leaving the desolation of Donegal the journey led to Sligo and Leitrim, a land of enchantment, legend and antiquity. Awesome Ben Bulben was seen from selected points, usually with water. Streams cascading over its cliffs could be startling when strong winds caused the water to flow upwards. Drumcliff River, beside one of Columbkille's monasteries, was liquid gold in the evening light. Along its edges the trees, lonely in their crowds, had red rents between their foliage like a sprinkling of sacrificial blood. An evening spent on Sligo's mountains was an eerie experience, including the slow heartbeat around Eagle's Rock and the sad pagan silence of the stones in Carrowmore Megalithic Cemetry. In the ghostly half--light they were like giant sleeping beings and, with a little imagination, they could actually move. There was something unearthly about these places, something that went back beyond ancient times, something elusive and eternal …

… A treasured memory of Mayo was the falling waves on Portacarn Beach, in remote Belmullet. Recurring in a fragile rhythm they made the silence so eloquent; it was here that the Children of Lir heard the bell that would restore humanity to them. How intertwined landscape, literature and legend can be. Another was the thrill of waiting for dawn over Croagh Patrick when the black mountain had its edge slowly eaten away by a wonder light--increasing and powerful--until the sun lifted itself, naked and molten, spilling over the glassy waters of Clew Bay. And then there was light--everywhere….

… Mweelrea was another mountain that profoundly impressed especially the view from Leenane. The capriciousness of chance showed the profile of this beautiful mountain with the touch of God on its brow …

… The Burren in Clare was unique--a bizarre, yet lovely, world where colour had a language all of its own. Colour was everywhere--surely a way to express joy especially the colour of wild flowers, which express it supremely …

… Kerry was such a contrast. The landscape was lush, majestic and accessible. Everything was here that seemed to be scattered elsewhere. Ventry, Dingle and Valencia were amazing in the au-

tumn light, St. Finan's Bay and the Skelligs were hauntingly beautiful and Killarney, with its marvellous mountain gaps and silken
lakes, was resplendent. The mountains around the Gap of Dunloe
were ancient and bare, the curving lacquered water opened like a
garment and the ochre of the bog slept in the sleeping sun. The
light effects swept across structures like a wave washing over rocks
or a veil gently drawn across a beautiful face. I tried to catch this
effect as vision percolated to the brush. The Gap of Dunloe was
my last image of Kerry in a December day. The low noon sun had
melted the clouds over the Gap and a sweet perfume whispered its
sad forecast of transience. Such a heart-rending display of purple
and gold I'd rarely seen anywhere. There was sorrow in it too,
the sorrow of parting. We know how music can move us so that it
almost becomes unbearable. This scene became so intense I had to
turn away--for a while. The hills around remained hushed as they
grew darker and drained the complexion from the sky. And the
scene faded, the harmony dropped an octave and the colour was
dragged into the earth. The sky became pale, hills went dark, and
water silvered and was at peace. The light, that wonderful light of
the west, was gone. I had just experienced the almost indescribable
eeriness of a place that could be a foretaste of Heaven ...

... The journey was completed southwards through Kenmare,
Glengarriff and Bantry. Local history became almost palpable along
the five-mile road beside the Cloonee Loughs up to the wonderful
waterfall at Glaninchiquin--more a torrential cascade falling over
600 feet to the ground. Then over to Lauragh, the Healy Pass, down
to Ardrigole and the opulence of Bantry House. And on through
Durrus, Toormore, Goleen reaching lovely Barley Cove at the base
of Mizen Head--the southern most point of the country. The mountain, beach and cliff scenery of the southwest was so exquisite it

would've made angels blind with weeping …

… Some say that time goes by, but there are places where time stays and we must go. Before leaving I sat on the grass at Barley Cove facing Mizen Head with the taste of salt on my lips. A feeling of aloneness descended that brought great peace. In a place like this, days could merge into months and years without notice …

He stopped at this point wondering how to proceed. Illustrations were to be included and each required an accompanying explanation, some only a brief history and others a longer legend.

He called for Ruth to help.

'Ruth, what's your favourite painting in the show?'

She'd no hesitation in answering.

'The striking picture of Tommy the man from the west.'

'That's interesting. He was a fascinating character. Perhaps I could include a potted history of the work to explain how it came about. A little of the background and the trouble involved. But I can't do it for every painting.'

'Let's have lunch first Tom and you can tackle it later.'

'Yes all right. I need a break.'

After lunch and a brief walk he settled down again to write about Tommy, the man from the west.

… One day I was walking on a road beyond Cleggan--out towards Inishbofin. The day was grey and the wind was up. Few people were about and the area looked damp and depressed. There was little inspiration so I went over to Claddadhduff and entered Sweeney's all-purpose store for something to eat …

… It was late afternoon and the light was fading. I noticed a striking old man sitting in the corner looking out the window. He was alone and quite still so I'd a good opportunity to study the face in profile. Here was a face that could have been carved by Michelangelo, a long aquiline nose and a proud chin from which a white beard flowed straight down to his chest. His clothes were amazing, the hat defied description, the overlarge coat could have been worn with pride at the best race meeting in the country, the corduroy trousers, even though antique, now had a stamp of good breeding and the boots looked as if they suffered from the endless ache of miles …

… I approached him. He said little except the weather was bad and life was hard and beer expensive. I offered him another beer. Gradually a transformation came about and now he became a true saint. This was the picture I wanted to paint. I asked his permission and he agreed provided I would supply him with beer …

… A bargain was struck and we got down to work. As we talked there was a strong sense of decayed aristocracy about him. He'd many fascinating stories and a whole library at the tip of his tongue. This is what I've tried to capture in the painting …

That was enough for now. Probably more than enough. Ruth would tell him.

That night the Nolan family gathered around the fire and Ruth read what Tom had written. She liked the Introduction and the brief descriptions of paintings and loved the piece about Tommy, the man from the west.

'What can I do to shorten it? It would become pointless.'

'I don't know. Leave it until you've finished the rest. What's next?'

'Conclusions and Epilogue. There are certain issues I want to get across,'

'Of course you do Tom and you will. But the issues will become apparent from the paintings themselves. Some say that good books shed their meanings like trees shed leaves. Your ability is to communicate in paint Tom. Meaning is obvious and forces itself on the viewer with great impact.'

'Thanks Ruth. You're too kind. Is all this writing necessary then?'

'It is if the gallery has asked you to do it.'

Tomorrow came and Tom sat down again to finish his work.

Conclusions

... Some say landscape painting has run out of things to say. This cannot be true because never before has nature been under such attack; pollution, ozone layer damage and global warming are increasing. The landscape tells of this threat and therefore painting of the countryside has a great urgency to it. There is a last chance sense that artists have not experienced in the past ...

... In Ireland we still have a unique, yet shrinking, wilderness especially in the west, but the enemy is at the gate! Humans, by their reckless mechanical abuse of nature, now contribute the latest and, perhaps, the most dangerous of all threats. Extensive new forests have appeared in rows of Sitka spruce, geometric in outline and fast growing. They are alien to the landscape and its wildlife. Other factors include careless farming and fertilisers, fish-farms, wind-farms in scenic areas, the greed of the JCB and uglification by developers, mining with the scent of minerals and gold, power lines on the horizon, sheep stripping mountainsides, ubiquitous barbed wire fencing, together with flooding and gravel extraction devastating the countryside. In addition to polluting our atmosphere, our land, lakes and rivers, exploiting the bogs, we are conveying more people in more traffic on more roads and airports to have this same landscape 'explained' to them in interpretive centres located in scenic areas that should remain unspoiled ...

Epilogue

...The roads through the west revealed the most evocative sights including mountains ribbed with gleaming waterfalls, ever-changing hues in valleys and the heaving chest of the ocean against dark rocks. They had a seductive quality, standing there for all time, enticing, compelling with a fundamental curiosity. They possessed not just geological forces beyond understanding but something more sublime, an inner power that could, if one let them, have a profound influence on our lives. In the process we become aware of an essential reality, of the universal in the particular, of that which lies behind the surface of things. If this awareness is the origin of that glorious emotion--a passion to express--which is the lifeblood of artists, it is also reasonable to assume that others can experience a similar emotion by travelling a different road. It is within everyone's power to respond to the natural world at the most basic level, but sometimes the struggles and achievements of artist can help ...

... Today, some forms of experimental art are incomprehensible, so complex as to seem untouchable by reason and often made worse by the pretentious jargon of experts. For years an epidemic of ugliness has infected our world leaving some with an attitude of defeatist awe. Others, however, are demanding a return to realistic art--including painting--so that they can genuinely share in the process of creating something of beauty. This process may have taken years to achieve, but its effect is immediate. Perfect form can be seen with a glance--everything fits together and there is a balance of line and structure, light and colour. Great works of art do not easily reveal their secrets; we just surrender to their magic without question. The formal mechanisms are lost in the statement, in the effect. Yet, beauty can be heightened by simplicity and unity like the ravishing of the soul by sustained chords of a Beethoven quartet ...

... Having considered subjective beauty, as in the western landscape, can we find out what is required in its distillation into a work of art? The evolution of a visual image can be difficult to define and must include asking why the artist paints. The way we think and feel is not the result of present events alone but also of our past and our reactions reflect the kind of mental order--or disorder--we experience. Indeed, it is probably true to say that no activity reflects more accurately the state of mind of a person as painting. Some would call this state--inspiration, a state of mind that probably belongs to a world outside common time when, for a while, something exceptional and extraordinary is drawn out of us by the sheer grandeur of the landscape. The great blue expanse of the Mayo Mountains, the elegance of Croagh Patrick at dawn, the marvellous profile of the Twelve Bens grow, not darker, but more distinct with memory ...

... This has been a journey through spaces and places, searching for those mindscapes that no one has seen, in landscapes everyone has seen, and resulting in memories intended to implant an awareness of the deep interdependence of the world without and the world within for, surely, it is through art that our world is made visible ...

Several hundred guests along with the press arrived on the night of the private view. Great thought had been put into the organisation of the show. A drinks reception on the ground floor was the first to greet people. The main galleries were on the first floor and a lot of red stickers were seen in the first half-hour. The more one tried to circulate the more difficult it was to see the paintings. Some were disappointed that they hadn't time before the attack of the red sticker brigade. That's the way it went. The illustrious speaker, a school friend of Tom's, spoke of the works in glowing terms and quoted from Tom's booklet to emphasise various points.

It was a great evening for Tom, Ruth and Annette. The show was almost a complete sell-out and was scheduled to continue for two weeks. The gallery owner suggested another show in two years time.

'What would I paint?' Tom asked.

'You could go down to Mizen Head to begin with, turn around and travel north to Malin. I'm sure it would be a completely different experience.'

'I think we've enough journeys for the moment Mr. Osborne.' Ruth replied for him. 'One at a time. I think we should go home now Tom. Annette is looking pale and is completely exhausted.'

Tom looked at Annette. She did look more than exhausted. She looked terrible. She'd have to see Dr. Sutton again tomorrow morning.

2 5

John Nicholson was tired of university residence and determined to move house. He preferred the open countryside. He bought a cottage north of the city near the A 10 and not far from the towpath that winds ten miles to Ely. Mists rising from surrounding marshes have always plagued the area. He planned visits to King's Lynn and the coast around Brancaster. Furnishing the cottage was distracting and he could put his imprint on layout and décor.

As he approached the cottage the road was covered in mud and wind weaved a clammy haze across fields and trees. His old MG saloon was splashed as he parked in the driveway. A mixture of freedom and isolation came over him. He inspected the garden extending to about an acre. Piles of leaves covered the patio paths and lawn. Further down long grass strangled a cluster of gooseberry bushes. Weeds were everywhere; even the pool at the end was choked and plumb trees nailed to walls with some branches escaping their cruel fate. All a far cry from the smooth elegance of Cambridge gardens.

Then darkness created its spell. He went indoors, lit a fire and left the curtains open. Sitting beside the window he tried to get things straight in his head. Had he done the right thing coming here? Peace there certainly was, maybe too much and wretched mists were rising again wreathing the house and garden like ghosts embracing each other.

Enough of this sentimentality. He drew the curtains, threw logs on the fire and put on Mozart's Jupiter. The music could be as loud as he liked. He mixed himself a stiff drink, went into the well-stocked kitchen and made one of his favourite meals. After all he deserved it.

He returned to the sitting room feeling better. Doubt and uncertainty were dispelled as he sat back on the recliner. Certain things can happen at times like this, hovering between day and night, neither absolute between waking and sleeping. There's a magic that takes one over with imaginings of diverse proportions. The balance between wakefulness and sleep tipped towards the latter helped by the glowing fire and he drifted into blissful oblivion.

2 6

Each morning the old MG made its slow journey on bumpy lanes to reach the A 10 for Cambridge and became a familiar sight. Neighbours gradually thawed to the charms of the young doctor who worked in research in the city. Doing great work by all accounts and long may it last. The word spread and Dr. Nicholson became a figure of respect.

For too long winter lay prostrate on the land--only for the locals. John had seen far worse in Sweden. Eventually she gathered her garments and drifted north to be replaced by snowdrops, crocuses and daffodils.

Spring burst out and the landscape was filled with enchantment. Even the city changed character; for longer periods a deep purple lingered around the arc lamps as they flickered on the streets. A mixture of natural and arc light poured over the river in golden patches penetrating the darkness and lending a transient character to the town.

John drove past St Albans, Witney and on to Oxford the day be-fore the Union debate. The countryside gave space to prepare his thoughts and a warm wind blew in from the west causing blue and grey reflections to change places.

Approaching the city he stopped on one of the hills. The sun was sinking making the spires turrets and towers a backdrop to a medieval fairy story--the 'sweet city with her dreaming spires.' Town and gown merged with high street stores and mingled with elegant honey-coloured buildings.

After checking into the hotel he strolled around Deer Park and Addison's Walk. The wind became a breeze that moaned at its cap-tivity in trees along the water. The stroll by the river's edge was enough. Papers and books in his room demanded attention.

The debate was scheduled to take place in the Gallery. He in-spected it the following afternoon. It turned out to be a fine lofty red brick building with an ecclesiastical flavour, the high arched stained glass windows, long wooden benches, gallery seating and on the high alter rested the President's Chair. Immediately below him were two dispatch boxes for speakers.

Students and members arrived for minor debates from six o'clock onwards. The debate proper was due to start at 7.30 p.m.

Two speakers from the home team--one for and one against the motion--took their seats beside the dispatch box on the right side of the President and the two from Cambridge on the left. The Gallery filled to capacity well before 7.30. Excitement throbbed through the hall and reverberated from the hight ceiling. Each speaker was briefed on the sequence; the home team would start with speaker A in favour followed by speaker B opposing.

Then speaker C from the visitors' team would speak in favour. Finally speaker D would end opposing the motion--John Nicholson would be the last speaker. Although he'd misgivings about this arrangement there could be some advantages. A bell rang for proceedings to begin. The President stood and addressed the assembled.

'Ladies and Gentlemen, tonight we are fortunate to have four eminent scientists engaged in medical research in our two universities. Each is a leading expert and has achieved success in his respective field. We thought we should bring them together to tell us a little of their work and how it would support or disagree with our proposal, which I assure you has been carefully worded to allow maximum scope for everyone. To remind you again the proposal in front of us reads. "This house agrees that the benefit from animal research outweighs the harm." You will all have the opportunity to vote in the usual manner at the end of the meeting in accordance with true democratic principles. I would now ask for silence so that our first speaker, Dr. Rushford, from the home team can come forward and convince us to accept the motion. Dr. Rushford please take the floor.'

Dr. Rushford stood up slowly, placed his notes on the dispatch box, took a sip of water and bowed gently towards the President.

'Thank you Mr. President. I'm honoured to be asked to speak on an issue that's vitally important throughout the field of medical research--and is increasingly so. I could give an hour to the benefits in the past, great benefits in the present and most importantly the potential benefits in the future such as the prevention of heart disease and stroke, the treatment of cancer and other killing diseases. All these accrue from knowledge obtained from animal research. So far the benefits have been enormous, are increasing all the time and in future will yield results we cannot imagine today, but there are clues.'

He illustrated his work and produced some startling results. He finished.

'We've achieved much so far, and the benefits are there for all to see and, if left unhindered, you've seen nothing yet! However there're forces in our midst that would do anything to prevent us achieving these benefits and this must be a warning to us all.'

As he sat down he waved to the applause; yet somewhere there were voices of dissent.

The President called on the second speaker, Dr. Power, from the home team to approach the dispatch box.

Dr. Power turned to the President and thanked him for the invitation. His voice was loud as he launched into a tirade against the first speaker. The benefits obtained were essentially going to help one species--ourselves--but the harm and damage being inflicted was over a wide range of living creatures from all over the world. What gave one species the right to inflict torture cruelty and death?

He continued in a passionate voice.

'Harm is a word I loosely associate with contempt. It is merely a euphemism for words like pain, suffering, torture and murder of our fellow beings. And I ask, amongst all this mayhem, Mr. President, where is the benefit to them? If we scientifically measure the totality of benefit and relate that total to the enormous damage to all living creatures I have no doubt that the harm data collected would outweigh the benefit data a thousand times. I rest my case Mr. President.'

Whispered approval from certain parts of the hall was followed by enthusiastic applause.

The President again thanked the speaker and then turned to his left to face the visiting team. Dr. Juniper, who was to speak for the motion, was a good friend of John Nicholson's. The task ahead was going to be difficult.

As Dr. Juniper stood up he was quite apprehensive. Approaching the dispatch box papers fell on the floor. He bent down to collect them and took time to put them in order.

He turned to the President.

'Apologies Mr. President. A minor mishap. Again thank you for your invitation to speak on an important issue that has, and will have a profound effect on our lives, our families and on the lives of most people in the world. I speak of our demanding need for better and more sophisticated medical treatments. I won't dwell on the past as our two learned colleagues opposite have done so eloquently already. I will only speak of the future. I put two options to you tonight about that future and ask you to make up your own minds on which one you would like to see happen.'

'The first is to continue as we are using animals models and getting, yes getting, phenomenal results on how to cure some cancers such as breast cancer, leukaemia, bowel cancer and many others that a decade or two ago were certain killers. Now we have drugs to control and even cure them and expansion of our knowledge is growing at an amazing rate.'

'The second option is this. Say we stop all animal work--and as you know there are many who would dearly love this to happen and stop at nothing to achieve it. If we stop our current work we wouldn't just stand still, we'd go back to a time when serious illness would be treated by potions, mixtures, and nettle grass and maybe patients would be bled to death or poisoned with mercury and lots of other dreadful concoctions, which claimed miraculous properties. I don't think I would like to live in such a world. Would you be willing to accept such a situation? Would you welcome that kind of medicine for your loved one or your sick child? I think not!'

Dr. Juniper bowed to the President and sat down. The President called Dr. John Nicholson to come forward.

'And now, Ladies and Gentlemen, we have our last speaker of the evening, Dr. John Nicholson, who works with Sir Kenneth Richardson in Cambridge. Dr. Nicholson has had a distinguished career in Trinity College Dublin, the Helmuth Institute in Sweden and now is Senior Lecturer in the Genetics Department in Cambridge. He has a rather new approach to things I understand. But enough from me, would you please welcome Dr. John Nicholson.'

John confidently placed his notes in order on the dispatch box, removed a small photograph from his left breast pocket and carefully put it to one side of the notes. He stood his full six foot four inches and looked around the packed gallery. His words rang out in a clear and demanding manner.

'Thank you so much for your kind words Mr. President. They are much appreciated.' He turned to face the audience. 'But Ladies and Gentlemen I do not wish to treat you to kind words tonight. In the little time allocated I intend to shock you out of a sense of complacency because that same complacency condones cruelty of the most odious and heinous kind. Believe me. I've been through it, seen it at first hand and the effect would make the most hardened criminal curl up in shame.'

He paused and then raised his voice.

'There has been much cover-up all over the world by businesses motivated by one thing and that is greed. As a previous speaker said there are forces attempting to stop animal research. I believe there are even greater forces backed by huge financial resources that would go to any length to gag people like me, people who want to tell the truth.'

He sipped a glass of water.

'And what is truth? Yes, there are benefits from research on animals yet little accrues to them. These are only beneficial to one small species. The resulting harm is incalculable and the suffering is appalling. There are other ways being developed.'

'My main argument tonight starts with us. Some years ago the United Nations General Assembly ratified the Universal Declaration of Human Rights. It stated that humans could no longer be treated in law or public policy as mere tools by governments or states. Humans possess an inherent value and must be allowed live their lives according to the priorities they themselves identify.'

'This marked the beginning of an era in our morality in which justice, compassion and the rights of the individual finally took precedence over all other concerns.'

'There are still places on this planet where human rights are denied, but thankfully they are shrinking. I would ask you to consider the future while paying tribute to those who framed the Declaration in the United Nations in 1948.'

'I believe the future should not only consider the consolidation of these rights but also their extension. Surely the time has come to recognise the moral need to include non-human creatures within the sphere of protection of this same Declaration. Humans have long recognised that animals are not merely instruments or machines, or an assortment of instincts and reflexes; we know they flourish in freedom and languish under oppression just as we humans do. Their capacity to experience pain and pleasure, suffering and happiness must compel us to accept the need for moral limits in the treatment of non-humans as well as humans.'

'The argument that animals cannot have rights because we have not given them rights belongs to the past--like in times of slavery. Some say that animals should be refused rights because they do not share our intelligence, our emotional capacity and high sense of morality. I do not deny that most humans have a higher intellectual capacity than animals but why this should deny them protection from exploitation or harm has never been properly explained. Many humans also lack intellectual capacity either through illness, injury or inherited disorder. Today we correctly agree that these individuals deserve more protection and not less, not the relinquishing of their rights but the reinforcement of them. We accept responsibility for those who cannot fully participate in society and reap the advantages. The application of entirely opposite principles to non-human creatures is an unjustifiable discrimination and in my view is wrong and wicked.'

'I believe in the evolutionary and moral kinship of all animals and that every sentient creature has rights to life, liberty and natural enjoyment. With open minds we should search out the truth and be conscious that the future belongs to those with the intelligence and courage to question the perceived wisdom of the day.'

'The assumption that human affairs exist in isolation from all other living creatures on our planet is a charade. The lesson to be learnt from evolution is not arrogance but humility; the natural world is not only ours but belongs to others too. And the exclusion of those others from the benefits of compassion and justice is indefensible. Power and privilege should no longer be the measure of moral rectitude.'

He paused and took a deep breath.

'Finally let me remind you of a quotation from Bronowski in 1956. "Those who think science is ethically neutral confuse the findings of science with the activity of science." '

He took another sip of water, replaced the glass and gently bowed to the President. He then turned to his left and faced the main body of the audience.

'And.'

He raised his right hand in a gesture of pleading mixed with defiance.

'And Dante told us that the hottest places in Hell are reserved for those who in time of great moral crises maintain neutrality. I therefore implore you to abandon your neutrality and reject the motion before the house tonight.'

He sat down to tumultuous applause.

The electronic voting system was then activated and the President asked members of the audience to respond. John sat quietly staring into space having no inclination to speak to anyone. He'd said enough, perhaps too much. He would soon find out.

The bell went off and the President stood up.

'The motion is carried by 260 to 245 votes. Therefore this house agrees that the benefit obtained from animal research outweighs the harm.'

The place erupted into a mixture of applause and booing. A lot of people were unhappy with the result. John slowly collected his papers, placed then in his briefcase and prepared to leave the hall.

2 7

The volume of conversation increased as John Nicholson made his way to the back of the hall. Several times he said: 'Please, may I pass?' A way was cleared and he continued until a tall gentleman with a neatly trimmed beard said.

'Excuse me Dr. Nicholson. Could I have a quick word with you?'

'A quick word, yes.' John replied looking at his watch.

'My name is Challacombe. I'm in the philosophy department in Magdalene and I was impressed with what you said tonight. Most impressed.'

'Thank you but not good enough apparently.'

'Nonsense. The other speakers trotted out well-worn clichés and there was very little new. I suppose it made people relax and feel safe.'

'That's a pity,' John said, 'and should not be the purpose of a debate like this.'

'I agree entirely Dr. Nicholson. What you said was unusual and, if you don't mind me saying so, perhaps a little disturbing. You made people uncomfortable about the status quo. People don't appreciate that, you know. They prefer to be reassured and don't like change.'

'Progress is all about change. We'll have to change if we're to make progress.'

'Well said Dr. Nicholson. I agree. You implied changes are possible and they are coming. Yet you were vague about them. However I realise this is not the forum to go into the science of change.'

'One has to convince people on moral issues,' John replied, 'and the rights and wrongs of society.'

Dr. Challacombe held out a hand.

'Thanks for your lecture doctor. It was brilliant. You're a man before your time.'

'I'll take that as a compliment what you've said. Living in the present is a hard thing to do Dr. Challacombe. Now if you'll excuse me I'll have to go.'

'Very good. It was nice meeting you.'

John walked back to the hotel in the city centre. His feelings were confused, with not a little anger. Even though there was a reception organised by the Union he wanted to be alone. As he lay on the bed he analysed the faces in the audience as each speaker presented his paper. A lot probably had preconceived ideas, nodding agreement and whispering to each other. He sensed a difference when his turn came. People were quieter, motionless and perhaps uneasy. They stared at him as if--oh he didn't know--as if they didn't like hearing the truth, the unpleasant truth. The speaker was trying to rock the boat! Why didn't he leave things alone--we'd be far better off? And he couldn't say much of the other way--yet.

Enough of this post-mortem! He got up and prepared for bed. Distracting reading material rested on the table. He'd switch off and drifted into the strange field of someone else's fiction.

Next morning he bought a local paper to see if there was a report on the Union debate. There was, but it was a bland affair and gave the result as a good indication of the mood of the audience.

The journey back to Cambridge was tedious. Colours were flat with the sun behind him, the road was crowded with bad drivers and most traffic lights had the annoying habit of turning red. Even shadows were longer. It didn't matter anyway. He was in no hurry. There would be lots of questions and he'd few answers.

He went straight to Sir Kenneth and gave an account of proceedings. Sir Kenneth smiled and said he expected the meeting to go the way it did. People liked reassurance and resented challenges. Perhaps John upset them. That would be a good thing in the long term. This result must not be a barrier to progress and John had to continue his specialised work. No doubt whatsoever.

John drove out of the college car park, through the town and headed north along the A 10--the road to Ely--and home. The evening was pleasant pink and translucent, birds were singing sharply and preparing for night and earth was quickening get into full growth. Everything abundant with new creation reminded him of work in the garden.

Several times he noticed a grey car in the mirror; it kept a safe distance, disappeared and reappeared, yet never made an attempt to overtake even though John was driving slowly. Probably an elderly gentleman on a country run admiring the scenery. It was dark when he arrived so he parked in the driveway leading to the garage, took out his briefcase and entered the house.

Next morning he got up early to inspect the garden, and to make an inventory of all the must dos. Peace everywhere as he walked the paths in the warm sunshine, his mind finding refuge in such a place. A pleasant drowsy promenade, his footsteps soft on the cobble. The pond at the end of the garden was transformed; the chain of weeds he'd cleared away revealed a perfect sky reflection. This would become his hideaway from tension and stress.

Entering the kitchen he locked the door, grabbed his briefcase, car keys and jacket. The clock showed there was plenty of time to get to college. No need to worry.

An envelope lay on the floor inside the front door. No name or address. He opened it and removed a piece of paper with a message made out of letters from newspaper cuttings, which read: 'Thanks for your lecture in Oxford.' That was all. No signature. No stamp. Must have been delivered by hand. But why? And by whom? It was a mistake. He put it in his pocket and went out to the car.

The door was open. That was unusual. He was sure he locked it last night. Oh well, maybe he forgot. He sat in and inserted the key in the ignition. There was no response. He tried again. This time there was a sharp sizzle like a firecracker igniting. He jumped out of the car, banged the door and stepped back.

Then the bomb went off. An explosion engulfed the engine and spread rapidly to the petrol tank. He was thrown about twenty-feet across the lawn and ended up on his back unconscious.

Several hundred miles away Karita Isselherg sat down to breakfast in Kungsangen House. Excitement filled her as she inspected the table. Everything was prepared impeccably, the toast wrapped in white napkins and silver like a wedding gift, the butter rolled and juice sitting in crushed ice. The mail and morning papers arrived as soon as she was seated and were delivered to her along with the coffee. Afterwards she went to the library. The task ahead demanded concentration. The large gracious room with its sumptuous décor, peacock patterned wallpaper, cabinets full of rare china and porcelain looked over her, yet all she saw were great cliffs, foaming sea and sharp mountains where fierce and passionate people lived and died in another time and place.

2 8

In Greystones, south of Dublin, Dr. Peter Sutton woke early.
Another busy day and he welcomed it. The practice took off quickly
when he moved from Westport. Some regrets on leaving but he'd
never have peace from his wife, Maud, until the move was made.
A year had passed and yet she was not satisfied.

They were having breakfast; it was surprising she was up early.
Unlike her. There was something in the air.

'You might clear those dishes off the table and put them in the
cupboard,' she said brusquely, 'not any old way. You always leave
things lying around and I don't like it.'

'Maud I don't have time,' he pleaded. 'There's a busy surgery
this morning.'

'Don't care. Let them wait. Can't be expected to do everything
myself and this is Mrs. Prescott's day off. Everything's left to me.
It's not fair.'

Over coffee he glared at the obese individual ironing clothes with a look of a suffering saint; the kind of woman whose mission in life was to make a man miserable. At times he was tempted to go his own way though it never worked.

Friends advised him she'd only hold him back--like putting one's head in a noose. Unfortunately, being stubborn he took the plunge. The water had been icy cold ever since and as time went by it became more difficult to tolerate.

This morning he had enough. Dishes would be ignored. Her voice followed him into the hall as a steady prattle like old newspapers blowing in the wind.

'And don't come back with a bundle of worries and troubles. Many times I have warned you, but no you wouldn't listen. Don't expect any sympathy.'

He looked at the clock and mumbled he'd have to be off. She was left sulking. There was no other way; she enjoyed being the perfect martyr.

His mood wasn't helped by her disapproval as he arrived at the surgery. Work was an escape even though it meant listening to sick people. Yet they didn't have cutting tongues; their words were made of better things like thanks and please and other pleasantries. He saw a few old faithfuls who only needed reassurance. A number of repeat prescriptions and words of advice. Towards the end of the morning Ruth and Annette Nolan arrived. He was pleased to see them.

Tom's exhibition was a marvellous event, a magnificent show he told them, and he'd even made a purchase of a scene of Croagh Patrick from Old Head--a place he loved. He got carried away about Westport and Mayo when he glanced at Annette.

'Annette what brings you here this morning?'

'Well, doctor it maybe nothing.' Ruth answered for her. 'Nothing at all. Maybe all the excitement of the exhibition. But she's lost her appetite, not completely, and she complains of tiredness. We hope its just the 'flu or something simple.'

'That's right,' he turned to Annette. 'In spite of that, Annette, we'd better do an examination. Just pop behind the screen and let me listen to your chest. Mum will help.'

He took out Annette's folder and revised the history though it wasn't really necessary. The background was familiar. For at least a year she'd been in remission and doing well.

'May I come in now?'

'We're ready.'

He was extra careful and thorough. It was not a simple cold or 'flu. There was something else going on that didn't fit into the diagnosis of a transient illness; diffuse mild skin rash, weak muscle tone, sluggish movements, underweight, slow reflexes and pale skin. An immediate blood test was required and further investigations were needed.

'Do you think it's the old problem back again?' Ruth asked.

'I don't know. I hope not but we can't be too careful. The results should be back in three to four day's time. Can you come along next Thursday morning Mrs. Nolan?'

'We'll be here. Don't worry.'

He was worried but didn't show it. The rest of the day was filled with routine cases. No major problems. He'd become fond of the Nolan family. They were complete individuals, apparently happy. Tom aggressive and knew what he wanted, Annette full of potential--an intelligent girl who reminded him of his daughter, Diane, who died aged twenty-five years. Then there was Ruth, an attractive mother who knew how to behave in every way and had the utmost respect for her husband whom she adored.

Confused thoughts about his own life filled him, about the contemptuous Maud, about the loss of Diane, and now he sensed Annette Nolan was probably heading for a relapse of acute leukae-mia. How cruel life can be.

2 9

A sudden thought. Why not take a stroll along the beach? Just what Dr. Peter Sutton would advise others to do under the circumstances. She'd be sitting at home, waiting in silence. He'd always tried to be patient, yet her hostility concerned--even frightened him. Perhaps she couldn't help it. Some women were like that. Their feelings could take on an inexplicable turn, even against themselves. Still it was hideous to live with such a woman,ground down and helpless under the millstone of her misery. There must be a better way.

When he arrived home silence hung in the air. No barrage of why? What kept you? There was something on her mind. At table she watched him closely, his expressionless face, straight grey hair, perfect table manners and obvious moderation in eating and drinking. He glanced at her under his dark brows. All she could see was the cold grey eyes of an animal that had been held too long in captivity, having little to say for himself or guts to fight back when the need arose. She used to love her husband, except now she could not live with him anymore.

Even though life was a battle he had been attracted to her in a sadistic way, yet he could not live with her anymore.

They were both over forty-five years. Yet they could not live together anymore.

She had a plan. To go away to the sun. So it was agreed, planned and accomplished. A cruise was arranged to the south.

'These partings are no good,' he said surprising himself as she left, 'I don't like them but so be it.'

She agreed but remembered how bitterly each wanted to get away from the other. The distress of parting only made her more determined. Their ways of life were hostile, his and hers, like two engines running in disharmony; they were destroying each other.

Now it was to be. A thousand miles apart. When he sat in the greyness of the empty house with a certain grim fidelity in his mind, he was aware of his wife also, with a reluctant yearning to be loyal and faithful, but maybe having some gallant affairs in the sun in the south.

And she, smoking her constant cigarettes and gulping martinis and looking into the heavy dark eyes of an admirer, she was really preoccupied with the clean-cut features of her husband. Also realising he'd be asking his little secretary to do something, in that natural way of his, the commanding voice of a man who knows that his slightest request would be only too gladly accepted and processed.

Miss Murphy, the secretary, adored Dr. Sutton. She couldn't do enough for him and was very competent. She was also young and attractive. Yes, she really did adore him. Moreover all his staff did, particularly the women. Now when your husband had an adoring secretary, and you are his wife, what can be done? Should be

done? Of course there was nothing wrong going on between them.
Nothing at all. No. They were merely the perfect working team-
-the leader and master and his secretary. He dictated lots of work
to her, she slaved for him and adored him and the whole thing ran
smoothly without the slightest hint of impropriety.

He didn't adore her. He accepted her as his secretary. And a
man doesn't need to adore his secretary to work efficiently. But he
did depend on her. He told everyone he relied on Miss Murphy.
And there was a thing he could never do--depend on his wife, rely
on her. The one certain thing he found out early about Maud was
that she didn't intend to be relied on.

So they tried to remain friends of sorts, in the awful intimacy of
the once married. Each had a kind of bitterness towards each other.
The separation was a good thing--a solution to a developing crisis,
except it remained to be seen if the solution was the correct one. It
seemed built on rocky ground. Before Maud left she felt that Peter
had changed, even developed a streak of vanity. But then a handsome, clean-cut mature man like that couldn't help being vain. The
women made him so. Life could be complicated with too many
men and too many women knowing each other.

For Maud it was all very well having gallant affairs in the southern sun, when you are aware of your husband dictating to a secretary whom you know you are too scornful to hate, nevertheless you
despise; although you also know she has her good points--some-
where north in the place that should be your home.

What should be done now? Peter did not send his wife away.
She decided she had enough and went away of her own volition.
He had his work and his secretary and there was no room for her.
And that's the way it was. The way it had been for a long time and
she had enough. A change was needed.

So she went south for the winter and she had his blessing. He settled into his practice, working harder than ever and there was a sense of relief in his daily activities. The winter months rolled on. For Maud it had been difficult to get through, there were strange faces with strange intentions to cope with, but the cigarettes and icy martinis helped to cover over her worries. There, constantly in the background, was a picture of her husband working away and that persistent, confident but common secretary constantly at his side taking down notes and doing his bidding. Constantly.

He, of course, had to work hard. He'd debts and lots of expenses that had to be paid. And the secretary was so able to help clear the paperwork descending on him from the ever-increasing workforce of bureaucrats who demanded more and more useless information. And his wonderful secretary knew exactly what had to be done. She was so able and he could rely on her. Maud, of course was the wife, who said she loved her husband, but willingly helped him into debt. Such an expensive item a wife could be, especially away in the south cruising around in the sun.

After months of relaxing she decided to visit home, her home. She got a great welcome and an over emphasis on deference espe-cially from the secretary. However a haunting feeling remained, perhaps they'd be rid of her again. Things could run smoother without her. She was asked so many questions about how she'd like to run the house, the practice and the daily routine of ev-eryone's lives. It was claustrophobic. Everything was running as smoothly as it was. There was no room for improvement. It was intolerable. How could an extravagant wife interfere where everything was so well organised and too complicated for her now? She asked her husband was he pleased how things turned out.

'Things have worked out very well and I'm comfortable to leave things to others now. I can rely on them.'

'I know you're content. I can see that. You're less anxious and stressed. Are you sure all this efficiency is not bad for you?'

'It's not. I don't feel it is and hope I don't look it.'

He was the picture of contentment and this disturbed her. He'd nobody to argue with him, to contradict him and irritate him. The secretary, trying to be helpful, added she liked to think he'd nothing to aggravate him.

This remark angered Maud. But what was she to do? Late into the night she'd heard his voice dictating to his secretary, who scribbled away at anything he said. What did Maud want for herself? She certainly wanted no part of this dictating, secretarial business. It was beneath her. Yet why had she such a concern for him and his welfare? She was his wife.

Awful. That's what people call married.

She went away for a while and returned again. Even he treated her like a super-guest in her own home. And the secretary devoted her life to him. There were many uncomfortable pauses in their conversations. The secretary was unusually silent.

'I see you're very busy, as usual,' Maud said to them.

'There's so much to do. As you well know,' he replied a little impatiently.

There was a pause with its hidden message for Maud to leave them alone.

'I'm interrupting you' she said pointedly. 'So I'll leave you to get on with it.'

'Please don't go,' he said nonchalantly. 'I don't think it's right, all this work.'

'Then why did you attempt it?'

'Miss Murphy said we try it. I don't think it helps. Do you Miss Murphy?'

'I'm so sorry,' replied the little secretary.

'Why should you be sorry?' Said the overpowering wife looking down on her with obvious contempt. 'You only suggested it for his own good.'

'I thought it would help,' she meekly admitted.

Maud glared at her intensely.

'Why do people like you never think of themselves?' She asked.

The secretary looked puzzled and hurt. 'I suppose we do but differently.'

'Why don't you make him think about you?' Maud asked slowly and deliberately. 'On a lovely afternoon like this, he should be dictating poems to you about birds and happiness.'

Then the wife sauntered away having delivered her damage. The little secretary hung her head in silence.

'Where were we?' Peter asked.

The little secretary was unable to speak, feeling indignant, their beautiful relationship, his and hers, had been so insulted.

3 0

Maud Sutton decided the situation was bad for her husband and something had to be done. How could she make an attack on that devoted, efficient secretary? She'd love to wipe her into oblivion. Of course the girl was spoiling him, running his work, ruining his reputation as an individual who should think for himself, destroying him with her slavish devotion.

Maud tried to imagine him bereft of the super efficient secretary and she shuddered. She couldn't. Yet something should be done. She felt it had to be. She was, in a strange way, tempted to increase her mounting debts and send all the bills to him--as she usually did.

No. Not enough. Something more was needed. This was spring. She felt there was too much nonsense about spring, showy and stagy, a chorus girl flowers unless there was some reflection of them inside--which there wasn't.

Then she discovered them dictating in the garden, behind an array of bushes. This relentless distraction was becoming too much.

She approached and quietly listened. The secretary continued to take it down. It was too much for her to bear.

Most exquisitely dressed Maud appeared in front of them. The little secretary got a fright at the sight of the elegant rotund wife. Maud studied the secretary and then him with a predator look about her. He made some bland remarks about the beautiful spring day. No response from her.

Miss Murphy was invited to tea that evening. Many searching questions came from Maud and, at times, they were difficult or impossible to answer. Yet Maud insisted on getting clear accounts of her work.

'Oh. Go on. Tell us what you've really been doing.'

Miss Murphy sat dumb and angry. She was being ambushed and looked at everything except Maud.

'I'm afraid I'm not at liberty to tell,' she said.

'Are you afraid? You're so very confident. It should be no bother at all. I expect you do a lot of his writing for him.'

It was a cruel thing to say and they all knew it.

'I should be flattered, if I didn't know you're only trying to make me out a fool.'

'Nonsense child. You're much cleverer than me and so competent. I've the greatest admiration for you. I wouldn't do what you do for all the gold in Africa.'

Miss Murphy looked away and remained silent.

The husband tried to rescue the situation--but in vain. Eventually Miss Murphy turned on her with blazing eyes. 'You deliberately wish to spoil what there is between him and me. I can see that.'

She was obviously bitter.

'My dear, what is there between you and him?' Maud asked innocently.

'I was happy working for him, coping as best I could often in difficult situations.'

'But, my dear, go on working for him and be happy. Do you think I'd be so cruel to take it away from you--working with him? I can't do dictation and typing. I'm utterly incompetent. I never can do anything. I'm a parasite.' She looked down at her expensive dress. 'Although I'd have some criticism of you, Peter Sutton, for taking so much from her and giving her nothing.'

'But that is not true,' Miss Murphy cried. 'He gives me every-thing, everything.'

Maud turned on her angrily.

'What do you mean everything?'

Miss Murphy pulled up short. A sudden increase in tension in the air.

'I mean nothing that you need worry about,' said the little secre-tary, proudly. 'I never made myself a cheap person or a cheat.'

'I just can't believe what you say,' the wife said vigorously. 'You poor innocent girl. You don't call what you've done is cheap? Why, I'd say you got nothing out of him at all, the skinflint, you only gave. And if you don't call that making yourself cheap--I'm just at a loss for words.'

'There's the contrast, Mrs. Sutton. We see things differently,' said the secretary. 'Our values are not the same.'

With a booming voice meant to end proceedings Maud said.

'I must say they most certainly are not. And thank God for that.'

Peter asked with more than a hint of cynicism.

'Tell both of us on whose behalf are you thanking God?'

Maud was in complete high dudgeon as she blazed at them.

'On behalf of everyone. Yours because you are getting everything for next to nothing and Miss Murphy's because she says she likes it, and most importantly for me because I'm well out of it.'

Miss Murphy objected to the last remark attempting to save the situation.

'You don't have to be out of it at all,' she protested with a reluctant smile, 'if you don't wish to exclude yourself.'

'Thank you, my dear child, for your kind offer,' said Maud rising. 'But I'm afraid no man can accept two contrasting and combating forces of happiness fluttering at his feet and, perhaps, in the process tearing each other apart.'

With this final retort she walked away.

Miss Murphy, in a tense and desperate state turned to Peter Sutton.

'And truly need any woman be jealous of poor me?'

'Quite,' he said.

And that was the end of the matter.

John Nicholson sat in a heap in the darkened room as storm clouds staggered across the sky. He hardly moved except for recurrent clenching of the right hand. The expression was sombre and head-aches persistent.

Normally the view from the third floor of Addenbrooke's was a fine one, with rolling countryside and small farms if one was lucky to have a private room facing south. He had all this, yet when he looked he saw other things. All confused. And the headaches made the confusion worse. Pain seemed to shift about, as if there was motion inside his head, starting at the back and crawling to focus in the centre of the forehead. Not pulsating, just steady and nagging. Movement made it worse so he stared straight ahead. He would have to go away, definitely. He could not stand it any more.

Rattling teacups on a trolley outside made the headaches worse and the last two weeks were a blur; for the first week in Intensive Care consciousness was intermittent. Burns on his back were dressed daily but thankfully no bones were broken. The worst damage was to the nervous system--severe and delayed shock; great blocks of memory were missing, terrifying sounds were either imagined or noises from closing doors were like explosions, and the trembling could only be masked by hand clenching. Holding a cup of tea was torture.

Amidst the confusion visits from friends and colleagues including Sir Kenneth were vague and the chief inspector and his assistant stayed for ages asking hundreds of questions. The registrar asked them to leave, as John was exhausted.

'Don't worry, Dr. Nicholson. We've a few important lines of inquiry, which we are actively pursuing. We're determined to find those who did this dreadful thing.'

'Thanks chief inspector. I've told you all I can.'

'Of course. You rest and make a full recovery. Then we can talk again.'

John looked over the rural landscape of south Cambridgeshire. If all went well he'd be able to return home in a week or two. He saw the clouds, more depressing than ever, floating towards him, as an ominous threat. These things would not trouble him before; now he felt fear dejection and failure. I'm going away, I must get away.

It was necessary for John Nicholson to remain in hospital for a further two weeks. The back wound was slow to heal and needed daily dressings. Also the consultant was concerned about his ability to cope at home. Other considerations were not openly discussed--such as special investigations, press harassment and even a return of violence; and steps were put in place by police to intercept trouble when they heard Dr. Nicholson was being discharged.

Hospital transport left him home and waiting on the driveway was his new car. Letters from friends and people he did not know were piled up inside the hall door. They would be dealt with later. Everything seemed in order--just as he'd left it on that fateful day.

It was late afternoon. A lie down would help. He slept two hours because dusk had fallen and shadows were growing in the garden. A look outside again. Had it changed much? The last clear memory he had that bright morning before he left for ... Enough!

The sound of his shoes on damp grass was like soft hands been rubbed together. The air was cool and sebaceous borders full of promise. A full moon was rising over the fence behind the pool at the end of the garden. He threw a stone into the middle. The reflection swayed and a sound exploded as the stone hit the water. The image was shattered shooting out splashes of brilliant light. The moon cracked in the water and went flying in all directions; the furthest waves clambering at the edge of the pool trying to fight the darker ones on their return.

Shattering of the light shocked him unexpectedly and an irrational fear gripped him. He could stay no longer to watch the mayhem and returned to the security of the house. After locking the back door he sat motionless in front of the log fire, staring at nothing. The trembling had returned. If only he'd waited. Within a few minutes the scene returned to normal. The moon on the water was getting stronger, reinserting herself and took full possession of the pool shining in a triumphant glow. A Mozart symphony was the only distraction. The music poured out and he melted into its magic. Then it was time to retire.

He forgot to close the curtains and was overcome by a deep sleep. A surprise awaited him next morning. A blinding glow on his face pulled him back to consciousness. The heat alone was enough to waken him and the light was so strong that it was difficult to open his eyes. He crossed the room and pulled the blinds. At least that would soften the impact. It was another day--hopefully of recovery. The blast of heavenly light, his natural alarm clock, seemed to elevate his mood. This was another day. A new day. And he was determined to do something different.

The doorbell pierced the air. It was the postman.

'Parcel for you Dr. Nicholson. Also could you sign for it?'

An alarm went off inside him. He'd been warned to be wary of parcels and advised to check them thoroughly.

'Jim. Is there an indication who the sender is? Does it give a name on the back?'

'I think it does.' Jim turned the parcel around and read out the clear printing.

'Well, the stamp is from Sweden and the sender is Karita Isselherg.'

'Thank goodness. I know the sender. I'll sign for it.'

'Very good sir. Please sign here.'

As he took the parcel he noticed a constable from the local station standing at the entrance to the cottage. Poor fellow--must have been there all night. That's life.

About 100 pages of typed manuscript were inside the package. On the top was written First Draft Only. Celtic Mythology and Legends Revealed by Karita Isselherg. A covering letter from Karita was also enclosed. Obviously she hadn't heard of the assassination attempt. Just as well. She hoped he was well and working hard. She'd the courage, this time, to send a draft copy of the first four chapters of Part Two. There were probably a number of mistakes and she needed help. Remember his promise? She'd written about 100 pages so far but unfortunately had come up against a block. She knew the locations in Part One when she went as far as Aranmore. Now she was at a disadvantage. Part Two dealt with the south-west yet she'd never been there and it was hard to write about places one hadn't seen. Did John agree? There were so many questions he put the letter down and looked at the manuscript.

Immediately he was drawn into its potent and half repulsive style. It gripped. It hooked. A world of powerful characters, men and women who spent most of their time in conflict and darkness was revealed. In their voices he heard the voluptuous resonance of mystery and magic, of plotting scheming and conquering, the excitement of adventure against foes in a dangerous underworld that could not be imagined. They sounded like strange and terrifying machines.

Even though the writing was bizarre and beautiful, it was also compelling, yet there was a poverty of description. The action could be anywhere--in Eastern Europe or Transylvania but certainly not Ireland.

3 2

Chief Inspector Jordan and Detective Inspector Browne called to see Nicholson. Jordan observed a new red MG Saloon parked in the driveway. Strange thing that! Nicholson choosing the same make and colour of car. Must be bloody foolhardy. Didn't quite know what to make of it. He noticed things like that and pointed out his observation before ringing the doorbell.

'Courageous chap this Nicholson I must say.' He nodded to-wards the car.

'See what you mean chief.'

Jordan stabbed the doorbell and waited. John took his time in answering, which made Jordan impatient. In his circle he emanated energy and power and made others aware of it.

John opened the door. 'Chief inspector please come in. I was expecting you.'

'Good of you to see us so quickly doctor. May I introduce my assistant Browne?'

John nodded and led the way into the sitting room.

'Please be seated.'

An aroma of coffee from the kitchen and a glowing fire greeted them.

'Coffee?' John asked quietly.

'That would be very welcome.'

John left the room. Jordan continued his inspection, indicating things with his eyes. He liked taking mental notes of everything. The general ambiance was cool in colour, warm in appointment. Magnolia coloured plain walls, lightly stained polished wooden floors with thick ivory coloured rugs, pale amber suite of chairs, a large television and exquisite black hi-fi music system. Titles of the cassettes and CDs did not escape him--the majority classical.

It was the fireplace that took his attention. The white marble mantelpiece was fascinating with its floral carvings and Greek columns. Over the mantel an immense mirror, framed in ornate gilt, rose almost to the ceiling and gave the room an added dimension. Two marble statues, classical in style, rested on the mantel and several photographs were strategically placed. He nodded to Browne to take it all in. No words were exchanged.

John approached with a tray.

'Coffee is ready,' he said softly, 'will you help yourselves to milk and sugar.'

Jordan took charge of the coffee, pretending to help, but observing the tremor.

'Now Dr. Nicholson. We hope you're recovering well from your ordeal.'

John's expression altered as he replied.

'Yes. Physically. I'm well on the mend. Although the whole episode was a terrible shock. I can't understand … '

'Precisely.' The inspector said seriously. 'That's the main reason for our visit.'

Jordan sat back in his chair noting the slackness in John, slow movements as if he were extra careful not to make a mistake.

'As you know doctor no one has admitted responsibility for the incident. It leaves us open to pursue several lines of inquiry. Firstly we've had the report from the forensic people about the nature of the device used. It was a crude affair. Badly put together. The intention was to have the ignition linked to a fuse line, which connected to the engine and the fuel tank. There were no explosives involved. A simple but potentially fatal combination. It appears someone tried to kill you doctor.'

'And nearly succeeded too,' John said a little startled. 'It was lucky I jumped out of the car before it exploded and also the petrol tank was almost empty.'

Jordan held his cup out for more coffee.

'We know how it was done. We know where, when, but we do not know why? Is there any way you could help us answer that question Dr. Nicholson?'

'No immediate answer, although you're probably aware I took part in a debate on animals in research at the Oxford Union and the letter was posted just before the blast.'

'The letter of thanks for the lecture. Somebody being sarcastic.'

'Sounds like it but really sinister.'

'Are you suggesting someone knew you were speaking at the debate, didn't like what you said and tried to take revenge?'

John answered with a hint of bitterness.

'That could be one interpretation.'

'It certainly has been speculated on. Considerable coverage of the incident was in the local and national press. Browne has brought a number of copies for you to go through and see if you can get anything useful from them. Maybe you could spot some angle that we've missed, although we've gone through them with a fine tooth comb.'

'I'm grateful. I suspect there'll be some weird innuendos and hurtful things.'

'Don't worry if you find something like that Dr. Nicholson.' The inspector replied confidently. 'This attempt on your life had no hallmarks of a professional or paramilitary background. They know exactly what they're doing and do a clean effective job. And don't mind me saying, doctor, we've also checked with our security people about you. Nothing has come up.'

John smiled and nodded as if he understood what was not said.

'Inspector.' He looked at Jordan seriously and again said in a slow deliberate voice. 'You seem to imply some hothead group such as the ALF didn't like the idea of the Oxford Union debating the use of animals in research and decided to hit out.'

'Yes. That's our tentative conclusion.'

'But it doesn't make sense. Let me explain. The proposal for debate was. "This house agrees that the benefit from animal research outweighs the harm." '

'That's what I heard. And what's more the motion was passed by a majority. That would certainly make the ALF and their associates very angry. No wonder they wanted to hit out.'

'Agreed,' John said although still puzzled. 'But why select me for the attack? This is confusing. I made an impassioned plea that the motion be totally rejected and gave what I thought were powerful reasons why the research should be stopped.'

'I didn't realise that Dr. Nicholson,' Jordan said cautiously. 'What you now say throws a different light on our understanding.

You're the last person they should attack as you were trying to help their cause.'

Jordan looked at his assistant and mumbled something.

'Browne it's not so cut and dried as we thought. No one has claimed responsibility. That's strange for the ALF. They have boasted their exploits in the past. It suggests there could be another force in the land that didn't like what Dr. Nicholson said and would like to eliminate the source of irritation. Is that possible doctor?'

'It's remotely possible inspector that somebody, or some agency even acting for big business with investment interests could be angry with what I said.'

John stared into space with a frown and fear in his eyes.

'If that were the case,' he continued carefully, 'the issue becomes more sinister. It would imply something rotten is going on and then I would not know who to trust in my work. It could make research almost impossible if sabotage is the order of the day.'

John stopped talking. His expression suddenly altered. He might have gone too far and should say no more.

The inspector lifted his head taking in the implied meaning.

'Yes, well, doctor. We will continue with our inquiries and will let you know if we have any further developments. Browne, I think we have kept the good doctor long enough. We should be going. Thank you for the coffee Dr. Nicholson.'

'Anytime.' He tried to affect indifference. 'Anytime at all inspector.'

Jordan and Browne took their leave and drove away.

'Well, Browne, what did you think of that?'

'He was telling the truth,' the other replied modestly, 'he was completely unostentatious and still in shock. He was willing to lis-

ten to everything we said. And yet, and yet, he was also complacent and sure of his position.'

Jordan nodded and added.

'Although he's a handsome man he was very anxious and had
a way of looking at you as if determined to hold his own at all
costs. His eyes were the most striking part of him as if struggling
with some grave emotional crisis. I also got the feeling he's holding
something back. I only wish I could have heard him speak at the
Oxford Union. It probably was electrifying.'

Browne surmised the feeling.

'This probably goes deeper than we first realised. It may take
time.'

John felt a cloud of despair descend. Perhaps he'd said too much.
Yet he was compelled to tell the truth. Was it a can of worms he'd
opened and caused more trouble than it was worth? Tomorrow he
was due back at work and the officers had stayed longer than expected. Already a touch of pink and red in the sky and the evening
clouds were gathering. How time flies! He returned to the sitting
room. It was cold again so more logs were required for the fire.
Darkness coming in the window was reflected in the mirror.

As he walked though the hall the floor assumed a cracking
sound, which struck a chill note. And then into the kitchen, his
pride and joy, where his meals and other enjoyments were focused--
a solitude he'd enjoyed. The greatest bonus was the freedom. Now
there was a change. He returned to the sitting room. Everything as
it should be. The music, a huge legacy of Linda, the television, the
lovely mirror and marble mantelpiece glowing with heat.

Now a cell would be more acceptable! The glorious stained
wood and the thick carpet were almost an anachronism. He didn't

deserve them. And as for the mirror it was an abomination. It showed too much truth and who cared about truth? The plain walls, were hard to look at--especially the emptiness. There was nothing there. That couldn't be right. Everything was dull to his senses.

Friday was the first day back to work for John Nicholson leaving the weekend to recover. It was also Dining-In night, though he was reluctant to go because of questions.

Despite walking with a slight limp--partly self-consciousness-- his outward appearance was impeccable. Others noticed unease as he struggled at being ordinary, his old self. And he did it well, succeeding in taking all the duties and surroundings as familiar. Pleasantly he spoke with staff and students and a social smile came easily. A large amount of mail would be dealt with later when the dust had settled. Midmorning Sir Kenneth invited him for coffee.

'Great to see you again.' Sir Kenneth handed a mug of steaming coffee--just the way he liked it. 'A little thinner but that's expected. How does it feel to be back?'

'Fine,' he lied. 'Everything's the same. A great welcome from everyone.'

'Good. Although you mustn't feel any pressure to get into the swing of things until you're ready. You understand that?'

'How kind.' John smiled. A tremor was obvious as he drank the coffee. He described the visit from Jordan and the forensic report on the device under the car. A hesitation came into his sentences. Sir Kenneth remained silent. He listened and observed; any comments were bland, non-committal and for the first time John sensed an air of detachment, not only in words. Maybe it was his imagination.

Sir Kenneth ended the discussion with a gesture.

'Hope you'll come to Dining-In tonight John. You need to relax and let your hair down. It'll probably do you good.'

'I'll be there. It'll bring me back to earth and discover life must go on.'

'That's the attitude I like to hear. Now please excuse me. See you tonight.'

Everyone in college took Dining-In night seriously. Staff assembled in the great hall properly gowned and guests were advised on appropriate eveningwear. The formalities and ceremonies went back several hundred years and were sacrosanct. John found the atmosphere potent and a little threatening. Why was this college so different from others he'd been to?   Here one lived in a world of coded word meanings and gestures, a world of power, a place where if you were not in, you were out and an underworld that could be dangerous, mindless and even cruel. Some people sounded remote cold and efficient.

He mixed with staff in the quadrangle and in some areas a suffocating atmosphere of callousness was there. Academics moved with a distorted dignity, an aloofness, which had an old fashioned beauty--even pomposity. Some had a look of abstraction, others resignation in their pale drawn faces, serious with burdens untold.

They belonged to another domain of well-oiled machinery that moved relentlessly onward letting nothing, nothing whatsoever stop its progress.

The bell sounded to assemble in the dining hall. John processed with the crowd and found himself sitting beside an old gentleman from the philosophy department who was full of words. As he listened the words did not always convey a great deal of meaning; they were merely words. The man was a roomful of old echoes.

John was on an emotional tightrope and was glad to leave early. He collapsed into his favourite chair and let gentle music calm him. The first day back was difficult and things were seen in a different light. He needed to think--to think in solitude. So far his career had wrestled with powerful forces and his scientific methods were unconventional, yet he felt compelled to continue.

He studied the photographs on the mantelpiece and talked to them. A side-glance in the mirror caught him unawares and he was confronted with reality. An inexplicable person with passionate desires was looking back at him, along with powerful inhibitions, as unresolved in this thirty-five year old as they were in the twenties.

He slept late next morning. It was Saturday. A relief. With a good breakfast he returned to his favourite chair beside the fire and found Karita's envelope on the table. With the excitement of the past few days, the garden, the police visit, the first day of work and the unpleasant Dining-In he'd forgotten about her manuscript and letter. What a shame because he'd intended replying immediately. She would be waiting everyday. And he'd promised.

Only one thing to do now and that was to read it more carefully. He made coffee, gathered a pile of pencils, blank paper and surrounded himself with cushions and started work. He spent the rest of the morning spellbound. With a wider vision he saw things differently. From his first impression when he hurried through the writing, his mind was on other things. The second reading shifted his perspective and revealed a richness of shape, colour and rhythm. This was different. Karita had the gift of changing reality into fiction and making it more real than life and more convincing than fact. The flow, tension and cleverness of character interaction were phenomenal.

Yet again there was no feeling of location--as before. No sense of place. There was only one thing to do--to tell her the truth. He'd promised and knew what to do.

John Nicholson arranged to meet Karita Isselherg in the lobby of McCormack's Hotel near Shannon Airport on a Monday in late March. He'd asked for two weeks leave and Sir Kenneth readily agreed.

'Going anywhere special John? The sun perhaps?'

'Special to me, though the sun may be rationed and changeable like a woman. I'm touring the Kerry coast and west Cork. Can be spectacular at this time of year.'

'Something like Scotland but a little warmer I suppose. You mentioned "woman." Is she metaphysical or real?'

'That's a good question!' John laughed. 'She's real enough but is full of metaphor and is turning out to be a brilliant author mainly for young adults. She writes a kind of ancient Celtic fiction based on legends and some facts. I've read parts of it. Truly remarkable. Her first book was accepted and is located in the Midwest, Achill and The Aran Islands. She travelled there extensively. But doesn't know the south-west.'

'So you're going to show her the way?'

'Only as guide and driver, with some knowledge of places to see and to avoid.'

'Who's this lucky lady, or perhaps I shouldn't ask?'

'Not at all. It's Karita Isselherg, Gustav's eldest daughter. She graduated with a First in ancient history and Celtic studies in Stockholm University. She's hoping to use her knowledge in this way.'

'Sounds intriguing. Have a great time and trust more than the weather will be kind to you. You deserve it.'

He went no further.

John sat reading in the hotel lobby. A flight from Sweden via London was due in at one o'clock and Karita was to make her way to the hotel. Their rooms were booked, the car was hired and a rough itinerary prepared.

Time went by. No sign of her. One o'clock, two o'clock. He had lunch. Three o'clock came and went. Still he waited. Then at three-thirty she ran into the main entrance followed by the taxi driver carrying her luggage. She spotted John, rushed over and embraced him.

'Sorry for the delay. Got held up in transfer in London. It's great to arrive.'

' 'Tis. Now you can relax. Perhaps you'd like to go up and unpack.'

'Good idea. I couldn't sleep last night. This trip means so much to me.'

'Let's start the right way. You need a good rest. Then, if you agree, we could meet here at six-thirty and I'll explain the itinerary.'

*

Karita waited at a table beside a window overlooking the Shannon Estuary. The sun was dying and darkness weaving. Lights were already on when John appeared with books notebooks and maps.

'Karita, a drink before dinner?'

'No thanks. This is top priority. Perhaps later.'

'Good. I'll begin by asking a simple question. What do you hope to gain most out of this trip?'

'I've come to a country, your country, that's had guts and strength to get through a terrible war of independence, that pulled its blood stained way through nine centuries of conflict, which must be the longest struggle in the history of the world.'

Her response surprised him.

'And lots of terrible things happened before that time, back in prehistory. There are 40,000 dolmens, wedge shaped graves, ring forts, including the 4,000-year-old site at Tara that records the passing of the Stone Age, Neolithic and Bronze Age. There are ancient hill forts and Ogham Stones incised with runic script reflecting the Iron Age. The whole collection spans a history of 6,000 to 8,000 years in a manner not found elsewhere.'

'Karita you know more than me. Please go on.'

'The greatest achievements are at Newgrange and other sites along the Boyne. For centuries they were probably the burial places for kings of Tara and this predates Stonehenge by a millenium, predates the pyramids and the hieroglyphics. Newgrange stood complete when Babylon was in preparation.'

He took a deep breath. Karita knew her stuff. These were the facts but they were not enough. She wanted more than the written words of others, which were a kind of second hand language. She wanted experience and something more. There was an enthusiasm for something more than facts.

'Armed with that knowledge what else do you want? What do you really want?'

'First hand knowledge of this extraordinary place.' She gave a knowing smile. 'To see massive cliffs, which battle with the ocean, mountains that change from hour to hour, ruins that can speak if you listen, Ogham stones, forts, burial grounds and the great valleys. I could go on. I want to see everything. Is that too complicated? Can't get those images from books. One has to breathe life into them.'

'You must be careful whom you speak to. Locals do a great trade in imagination.'

'Don't worry John. I've got my own. At times it becomes too powerful to handle. It can even be frightening.'

'Both the gift and the curse of writers,' he said sympathetically.

'It's what we live by. J M Synge said about these places: "One wonders … why anyone is left in Dublin, London or Paris where it would be better, one would think, to live in a tent or hut with this magnificent sea and sky and to breathe this wonderful air which is like wine in one's teeth." '

John laughed. 'That's not my cup of tea Karita. We'll do it in more comfort and cover some distance as long as the weather is kind.'

'No time will be wasted if we get bad days. Paper has to be filled with images and immediate memories before they're lost. Let's have a mixture of good and bad.'

'That's all right by me. How about some dinner?'

John and Karita were prepared to get started early next morning. Each had an agenda but said little. The Tarbert ferry crossed the Shannon and delivered them into north Kerry.

'John please regard me as a human tape recorder.' She said when they landed. 'I'll hang on to anything you say and store it. You've been here before. I haven't. Also my eyes may not see what you see. Sometimes I say--this is not the way it was but the way I want it to be.'

'Let's stick to those rules. Let's head for Dingle first.'

Dingle had three major valleys, which enhanced the size of the great mountains. Karita's mind was working overtime along with her camera. Megaliths, sou terrains, Ogham stones and ruins were found on the slopes of Mount Eagle between Ventry and Slea Head and the sight of Mount Brandon thrilled her.

'Ireland's second highest mountain,' he informed her. 'I must show you the Connor Pass in the hills above Dingle.'

As they moved carefully on the narrow road through the Pass immense cliffs rose on the left and fell away rapidly on the right down to a stone-scattered valley.

Overnight they rested in Dingle town. At dinner he told her the exploits of Finn McCool and the Fianna. Next day they passed through Killarney and the lakes.

'The most beautiful spot on earth according to Bernard Shaw,' John said, 'although it's a bit spoilt by tourists today.'

'It's lovely here,' she replied, 'and there's a special kind of silence.'

'Your imagination's in top gear again,' he said. 'I'll show you my favourite.'

'What's it called?'

'The Gap of Dunloe.'

Horses were hired to explore the Gap, a restricted roadway through a mountain gorge. Great boulders, mountain streams and vertical cliffs rose on each side.

Then to Waterville on the western edge of the Iveragh Peninsula. She asked to see Staigue Fort as she was greatly impressed with Dun Angus on Aranmore. Dating from the Iron Age it was approached by a boreen and set in an amphitheatre of boulder-strewn mountains. The skill of the workers who built the vast fortress was evident in the eighteen-foot high and thirteen-foot thick inward sloping walls. She walked around it, touching the stones. This would be the site for the beginning of her second novel--as Dun Angus had worked so well in the first. She loved everything about the place and surroundings and said until more excavations were done the truth would not be known.

'Around here is part of the story of Oisin I'll tell you tonight. So let it soak in Karita. We've time to reach Ballaghbeama Gap about eight miles inland.'

Eastwards through a long valley they travelled. Towards the end, the road rose steeply framed by lush vegetation, rushing streams and waterfalls. Still the road zigzagged upwards to a height of 2,000 feet. At the top they were confronted with a view to the east, one of the best vantage points he knew. Another favourite. They saw MacGillycuddy's Reeks in ethereal light. Below the dark earth led in perspective to the purple-blue peeks of Ireland's highest mountain crowned by golden clouds like a scene from the beginning of time.

He pointed to something.

'Karita see those giant boulders on the side of the road?'

'They're enormous.'

'I'll tell you about them this evening. For now, this place called Ballaghbeama Gap is where Oisin returned to Erin on his white steed from Tir na nOg. I'll say no more.'

They booked into the beautiful Butler Arms Hotel, owned by the Huggard Family, in Waterville. The superb dinner was mainly occupied by the story of Oisin, son of Finn MacCool, and his wonderful adventures.

'I'm listening carefully John. You go straight ahead.'

John looked into the distance searching for the correct sequence.

'Difficult to know where to begin. Let's say about a 1,000 years before the concept of chivalry and when the medieval system of knighthood blossomed in England, there was a great hero Finn MacCool and his warriors called The Fianna who held power in most of Ireland. They took an oath to uphold including the protection of women, to maintain one's honour, to punish crime and wickedness and defend Ireland from her enemies.'

'Wonderful start John. This is precisely the task I've set myself. To find out what kind of people lived and worked here? How did they dress? How did a man indicate his love for a woman? Where did they live and sleep at night? What animals did they hunt and what were they afraid of? What made them cultivate imagination and even what made them laugh?'

He was anxious to continue.

'Well let's concentrate on Oisin, son of Finn. Finn married Saba in his young days and they were happy. Then Finn was called away to battle and Saba waited--and waited--for his return. One day she thought she heard his footsteps and hastened from Staigue Fort to greet him. Tragically it was a phantom from the underworld and with a hazel wand he maliciously changed her into a deer. A great common hound then noticed her and she was forced to flee. Finn was told the story on his return and ordered The Fianna to search for Saba for seven years throughout Ireland but to no avail. Then one day on the slopes of Ben Bulben ... '

'Ben Bulben in Sligo. I remember.' Her eyes brightened.

'Finn came across a truly handsome lad and The Fianna brought him home. In time he told his strange story. He'd existed in the wild, known no father or mother and lived in a pleasant valley shut in by cliffs that could not be climbed--like Shangri-La. Finn took the lad as his son and called him Oisin, which means little fawn, and he grew up to be a strong and courageous warrior. His greatest strengths were in songs and poetry--like you Karita he was a great writer and poet.'

'I would just loved to have met him.' She looked dreamily.

'I know that,Karita. Well he did meet the love of his life.'

'Now it does get interesting,' she smiled.

'It happened when Finn, Oisin and others were hunting on the shores of Lough Currane. It was a misty summer's morning when they saw a maiden of great beauty approaching on a white horse. She wore clothing fit for a queen, with a crown of gold and a long purple mantle of silk. The horse's hoofs were made of silver. She spoke to Finn. "I've come from far away and I have at last found you, Finn of The Fianna." Finn was intrigued. "What is your land and race? And what do you want of me?" "My name is Niamh daughter of the King of the Land of Youth or Tir na nOg. What has brought me here is the love of your son Oisin." She then asked Oisin in a voice no one could ever refuse. "Will you come with me Oisin to my father's land?"

Oisin replied. "I will and to the ends of the earth." The fairy spell left him in such a state that he cared no more for earthly things. She described the land of Tir na nOg. Then The Fianna watched as Oisin mounted the white steed and held the maiden in his arms and she struck the glinting bridle. Never again did Finn or The Fianna see Oisin on this earth.'

Karita looked disappointed.

'That's a sad ending.'

'No Karita,' he protested, 'that's not the end. There's the journey to Tir na nOg. And Oisin's return. I think we should have a break now and enjoy the rest of our meal. We could go for a walk along the beach. The moonlight can be lovely out there.'

It was bright when they crossed the road. A small pathway led to the beach.

Karita was first to speak. 'I adore the beaches around here. There's only a few at home and most face east. Here we've the fading sun for company.'

'And you get all day to prepare for the feast. Which reminds me there's more to the Oisin story.' Linking his arm they set off across the firm sand towards Ballingskelligs. 'Where was I? His end was strange because after he saw Tir na nOg he came back to tell what he'd seen.'

'All right John. That's too quick. Aren't you missing something?'

He looked at her in the half-light.

'The journey to Tir na nOg. Oisin was lost in this other world but he saw large towers and palaces, strangers cloaked in floating silk of many colours. Eventually they reached her father's palace and Oisin had wonderful adventures in this new land, including the rescue of an unhappy princess who was imprisoned by a Formonean giant.'

'John that could be my princess in the epic poem. So Oisin rescued her. How marvellous. Please go on.'

'So many things happened, yet he longed to return to his native land and see his old friends. Reluctantly Niamh agreed and made him promise to return. She gave him the great white steed, and warned him when he reached Erin he must not step down from the horse or touch the soil with his foot. If he did so his return to Tir na nOg would be barred forever. Confidently Oisin set out on his visit, crossing the mystic ocean and reached the western coast of Ireland. He searched high and low but there was no trace of The Fianna, his colleagues and friends. All the old familiar places were changed. His frustration turned to confusion. At one place, near here, at Ballagbeama Pass he saw men attempting to roll a great boulder obstructing the pathway. He rode towards them and asked about Finn and The Fianna.'

'As he approached they became afraid. He appeared different and presented an awesome spectacle like a messenger from another world or an angel from heaven. He was taller and stronger than them, the ice blue eyes, tanned skin and long bright hair issuing in great clusters from under his golden helmet.'

'He looked on them as weakened souls, exhausted from toil and care, and at the great stone they were trying to move. He took pity and stooped from the saddle to help. He placed his hand on the boulder and with one mighty heave sent it rolling down the hill. The men were thrilled and shouted approval and thanks.'

'But their joy changed to cries of horror and they ran away.

Oisin's saddle girth had broken as he gripped the stone and he fell to the ground. In an instant the white steed disappeared like a puff of mist, and what was left was a feeble man stricken with age, his white beard long and knotted, his hands stretched out and he moaned with weak and bitter cries.'

'The others returned and asked who he was and what had befallen him. He replied. "I was Oisin, the son of Finn, and I ask you to tell me where he lives." '

' "We know Finn MacCool and his generation are dead for three hundred years." '

Karita stopped walking and stared straight ahead.

'An amazing story. It'll be called the swan song of ancient literature.'

'It was all a matter of time,' he said almost to himself.

They reached the old stream that divides the Waterville and Reenroe strands. It was impossible to cross so they lingered in silence. A glow still hung over Ballingskelligs making a visual epilogue for John's account. The story helped to make the earlier sunset one of the most perfect she'd experienced. Pink clouds were lying in the sky over Bolus Head and further out on the Skellig Rocks. They caught fire and grew dull--so quickly.

The sea swept in half-moons in the weak light becoming silver, the sand was grey and the afterglow trembled overhead. Mists started to roll from the dunes reminding her of the golden mists of Tir na nOg. Cold began to engulf her. She turned to John and, for a moment, her heart missed a beat.

'You're getting cold Karita. Let's go back.'

'Wait John. Please,' she said sounding desperate.

She turned her face to him. Less than a second later they were in each other's arms. The embrace and kiss went on and on. When it ended he said simply. 'Karita.' She immediately stopped further talk by putting her hand behind his head and kissing him again. It was deep close and long. Words were no longer necessary. She wanted to hold him. And not let him go.

It felt like the first day of creation.

Dr. Peter Sutton continued to prosper in Greystones. His patients loved him, and nothing was too much trouble. Yet struggles remained at home. Maud was back from one of her cruises, on a visit to make sure everything was all right. She was not happy with the decor of the house. It had to be changed. An expensive oriental rug was fitted in the sitting room with a light stained wood surround, the mantelpiece was replaced with Italian marble, the baby grand stood with Beethoven sonatas open for all to see and hand painted watercolours were hung on walls with one expensive oil over the fireplace.

Logs were burning brightly in the grate one evening with the curtains drawn and trees shuddering in the wind outside. The room was cosy and comfortable as Peter Sutton concentrated on reports letters and journals. Maud looked at him with a strange malignant smile.

'What's all the secrecy about Peter? Are you going to share things with me?'

This woman was impossible! She'd informed him there was no way she'd be interested in his work. He was not to rely on her. What had come over her?

He replied with some irritation.

'I've a lot to catch up with and the only way is to bring work home.'

'I'm not good enough to share it then?' Her voice was plaintive and venomous. 'I see I'm not wanted. After all I've done for you, the sacrifices, hard work and the doing without. There's no end to the effort and planning I've had to undertake to make you a success and all the thanks I get is to be told--go and get lost. You're not needed anymore.'

Stiff with anger he sat through the tirade, but remained silent. Experience taught him it was more expedient.

And there they sat in cold detachment, he struggling with non-essential paper work from bureaucrats and she puffing furiously on a pile of cigarettes, which he dare not tell her to stop. Dire consequences would reverberate if he did. These conflicts were continuous when she visited. Never got used to them; they went on and on. The silence was not golden and his blue eyes were almost black with rage.

He'd to prepare for tomorrow's surgery. First the moderate problems. Then the Nolan family, Tom and Ruth, were due in at eleven o'clock to see the report from Professor Kennedy. Annette was admitted to hospital two weeks ago with a relapse of leukaemia. She'd undergone tests to assess how rapidly the disease was progressing and she was not responding to chemotherapy. She was getting worse. In spite of piercing glances from Maud sitting well padded among her mountain of cushions, he opened a recent letter from Professor Kennedy. The report was long and detailed.

On admission Annette was in poor condition, undernourished, neglected looking, exhausted and in a non-communicative state. She was still not responding to therapy and it was with the greatest regret that he and colleagues concluded the only way she could be saved would be to find a suitable donor to give a bone marrow transplant after marrow ablation. Peter Sutton knew the technique in the 1980's was in its infancy in Ireland. This would require a search for a donor who must be a hundred per cent compatible with Annette.

Kennedy wanted Dr. Sutton to explain the letter to the parents. He always liked to do things by letter. It was clearer to everyone and, of course, less emotional.

'Less emotional to Professor Kennedy,' Peter mumbled to himself. Maud overheard and put down her cigarette.

'You're mumbling again Peter. I don't like it. It just means trouble.'

'Don't worry Maud. It doesn't mean trouble for you. So relax. Please carry on with your martini and smokes. I didn't mean to interrupt your enjoyment.'

'That's kind of you Peter. The first kind words you've said to me today,' she replied in a mellowed voice.

He ignored her and returned to the letter. This was serious, very serious. If Annette were to survive she'd have to have total body irradiation. What an undertaking! The parents and relatives would have to be tested first. If that failed the search would go international. It got more complicated.

And tomorrow Maud was off again on one of her cruises to the sun.

3 8

The Nolans arrived at the surgery at ten-thirty next morning. As they waited they could have read magazines and newspapers. No. They weren't interested in glamour or world affairs. Only thoughts occupied them.

The previous night Tom visited Annette in hospital. He wanted to spare Ruth; she'd been overwrought. Annette's appearance filled him with dread--gaunt, with a deathly pallor and flushed cheeks. She was in a single room with barrier nursing and masks and gowns added to isolation. She was sleepy and reluctant to talk--only smiling and waving. Marks were on her hands and arms for I/V lines. These images were scars in his mind. He shrank with an agony that went unspoken and in spite of her suffering she felt sorry for him. Both were in torment; yet could only communicate through looks tears and touches. Words were useless. He crept from the room when she drifted off to sleep. She merely pretended.

For Ruth the doctor's waiting room was an opportunity to sit and do nothing; something she was unable to do at home. Not long ago she'd sought the bright notes in everything and life was good. Near where she lived she could hear water laughing in streams and beaches, birds singing in bushes, the call of the wood pigeon and loved the aspen leaves fluttering like drapery.

Now there was only indifference. The world was collapsing. She'd find out how far the collapse had gone. What the future held? Thoughts revolved like a prayer wheel, obsessive, tenacious and constant. Difficult to think of anything else, her head throbbing like waiting for a blow to fall the nearer time travelled to eleven o'clock.

Dr. Sutton invited them into the surgery. They sat but neither spoke. It was up to the doctor to get things started.

'I've had a letter from Professor Kennedy explaining the results of Annette's investigations. They're complicated with statistics and scientific names which I won't confuse you with, but he's asked me to explain the basic situation.'

Tom laughed nervously.

'Dr. Sutton, with respect why have you to do it? Should it not be Professor Kennedy's place to tell us?'

'Tom leave things be please.' Ruth pleaded.

'Professor Kennedy prefers writing letters. He tells me it's more precise, accurate, states the facts and that is the end of the matter.'

It was Tom again.

'Yes, for him. But what about us? And our worries, questions and what ifs?'

'He's asked me to deal with those as best I can.'

Tom gave an indignant chuckle, more out of frustration.

'I know. I know. He's a very busy man and he loves to delegate.

Takes the load off him for more important work. When I saw him some weeks ago he did say he'd be writing to you with all the facts. No need to bother him with questions. And most of the interview was conducted as he continuously looked at the floor. That was peculiar.'

'You know Tom, Professor Kennedy's a fine clinician and he seems to be in the forefront of advances, although I've heard his manner can be a little trying at times.'

'Bloody maddening,' Tom exploded.

'Quite,' Dr. Sutton said gently. 'Perhaps you'll let me continue with the letter.'

Ruth came to the rescue. 'Of course Dr. Sutton please tell us all.'

He took up the letter again and started to read.

'Thanks Ruth. There's no doubt Annette's had her first relapse. Chemotherapy has been intense and resulted in severe neutropenia or drop in white cells and platelets. The main drugs used include dauorubicin, cystine arabinoside and thioguanine. However the overall prognosis is 20% long-term survival. Bone marrow transplant, or BMT, may be indicated in first remission cases. The idea is to destroy the malignant cells and the entire immune system by cyclophosphamide and total body irradiation and then repopulate the marrow by plantation from a perfectly matched donor. With this technique, i.e. BMT, there is a 50% long-term survival as far as we know. So there you have it. Poor Annette is now having a slight remission but is still doing poorly. With BMT there is probably a 50% long-term survival. Professor Kennedy is putting the case quite clearly.'

Ruth was the first to react. 'Professor Kennedy is not giving us much of a choice. Long-term survival is the obvious aim.'

Tom immediately saw another problem.

'What about the donor? Who can be a donor and will they want to be?'

'We usually look for donors in the immediate family first.'

'That's just Tom and myself. We've no siblings and our parents are dead.'

'A pity. Professor Kennedy wants to test both of you, if you agree.'

'We'll agree,' Tom said, 'but what if we're unsuitable?'

'That makes it more complicated. Sometimes we can be lucky and get one soon.'

Ruth burst into tears. 'Only sometimes and Annette could die in the meantime.'

Dr. Sutton looked at his watch and said firmly.

'Please could you make an appointment with the haematology department for the specific tests and I'll give you a letter. We'll get the results as soon as possible. I'll mark it urgent and a copy will be sent to Professor Kennedy. I'll telephone him to say I've spoken to you today.'

Tom gave an angry laugh. 'You'll be lucky Dr. Sutton. You'll be lucky.'

'I know. But I'll keep trying. Now here's the letter. Take it with you to St. Mary's haematology when you make the appointment.'

They stood up and shook hands.

'And good luck to you both.'

Karita found The Beara the wildest, loneliest and least spoilt of the three great peninsulas. The red stone cliffs and mountains showed the results of amazing struggles in the earth aeons ago, especially marked at Hungry Hill. Then through Durrus, Toormore, Goleen to reach lovely Barley Cove Beach at the base of Mizen Head--the southern most point of Ireland.

They stopped the car on the hill overlooking the upper reaches of the golden beach. Three Castle Head had an eerie appearance and was located beside a lake that was said to be haunted. Further on was the entrance to Mizen Head Fog Station, built on a rocky island called Cloghane--a lump of rock, which is separated from the mainland by a long and shaky suspension footbridge; the bridge, almost 200 feet above the roaring Atlantic, would test the nerves of most people crossing it on a calm day.

Karita climbed down the few hundred steps to the bridge and led John across to the middle where she stopped. To the north the clearly marked layers of sandstone rocks piled into angular, tortured shapes rose about 800 feet.

'Let's stop for a while John,' she said. There was something special here for her; probably the end location of the second novel and she wanted to soak in the atmosphere.

He preferred the Fog Station.

'Right then. I'll stay on the bridge for the present and join you later.'

'That's fine. Are you sure you'll be all right?'

'Of course. Alone in a unique and wonderful place. I want to mentally photograph it because it'll be used in the book somehow, probably near the end.'

'Good. You've some thinking to do and this is the reason we're here.'

She looked at him sadly, wishing to say something, but kept silent.

'I'll be in the Light Station if you need me Karita. Enjoy yourself.'

'I will. See you soon.'

He threaded carefully to the end of the shaky bridge and disappeared. She stood still, looking north at the crazy contorted cliffs with the constant noise from the agitated water far below. Gazing at the rock formations she could make out images of faces here and there. She could do the same with clouds, which were easier, but there was something different here. Each time she looked back at an area it had changed. Maybe it was the shifting light.

She closed her eyes to memorise what she'd seen, and to get away from images that were grotesque. She gripped the ropes at chest height for stability as the bridge became unsteady and started to move. With eyes closed and feet trying to stay in one position things became difficult. The bridge swayed to and fro, horribly, although there was little wind blowing. It was scary.

Holding on to the rope that formed the upper support of the suspension she felt a strange pulsation going through it that had not been there before. Fear gripped her and she trembled, breathing deeply and rapidly, deeply and rapidly--many times. Her fingers tingled and she opened her eyes. To her horror the faces were much clearer and they moved with the bridge. In fact the cliffs were also moving and swaying--to and fro.

She screamed for John; the only response was an echo, the more she screamed the greater the echo and the more she breathed the dizzier she became. She collapsed on the floor in a heap, crying and attempting to crawl towards the Light House afraid to look around in case the awful faces pursued her. She was terrified. Where was John? Why didn't he hear her? She could go no further, and collapsed.

Several minutes later she came to with John bending over, hugging her and telling her not to worry. Everything was all right. She'd some kind of fright and fainted. She was taken to the Light House where the keeper made hot tea and toast and a miracle of revival occurred. It was one of the most eerie experiences in her life and she wouldn't forget it for a long time.

All she could say to herself was--ghosts need memories to survive. And it wasn't only the views that produced tears in her; there was another reason she knew only too well.

4 0

Karita had enough. Really enough. Mizen Head was the culmination of the tour. Rugged scenery, mixed with beauty, huge skies, changing weather and menacing silences on the shores of lakes told a myriad of stories. People could identify with them. After all there was little evidence what she produced was not correct; it could be fiction or fact. She longed to write a work of factual fantasy, as she put.

Plans were discussed on the way to Cork where they booked into the Metropole. The flight to London was next day. They arrived about five o'clock; both tired and anxious yet there was something John had to share with her. Things were moving in a direction that demanded no deception and truth was at a premium. A quiet corner in the lounge with oak panelled partitions was selected. She smiled at him as he brought drinks to the table.

'Firstly John. I must say thanks for an enthralling experience. I've seen and heard more in two weeks than I would have learned in libraries in two years. You've made it much easier and more pleasant. The holiday will always be something special in my life.'

'It's been great fun for me. You're very pleasant company you know.'

'Do you really think so?' Her tiredness suddenly left her.

'I do. But Karita there're things you and I should know. Something I didn't tell you until the end of the trip. And I had good reason.'

'You're not going to say you're too old for me, or something silly like that. There's only ten years between us and that's nothing.'

He made a gesture of helplessness.

'You're streets ahead of me in emotional stakes. That's not what I wanted to tell you.'

She was downhearted. 'What could be more important than what's happening between us?'

'Something serious has happened and I haven't told you because I didn't want to spoil things. The holiday has been a relief and a distraction to the event that occurred some weeks ago.' She put her hand over his and held it tightly.

'You remember I spoke at the Oxford Union.' She nodded. 'I used your wonderful words of consideration for animal research in medicine. The speech went well I'm told, but the motion was defeated. I was devastated; not only because of your help, but that my speech was electronically voted nine out of ten by the audience. Although not enough to turn the total vote. It was a bitter disappointment.'

'I'm sorry to hear it. It probably affected your work.'

'Not so much that. The real blow came two days later when someone tried to kill me with a bomb under my car. Fortunately I jumped from the car in time. I sustained burns to my back, but the psychological trauma was devastating.'

'Who did it? The ALF nutters.'

'The police are not convinced because I spoke strongly against the motion. Why kill me for that? And the ALF have remained silent--didn't claim responsibility. Unusual for them and so the case is still open.'

She touched him on the cheek.

'Poor John. And you never said a word. That was kind of you.'

'No sense in spoiling your tour. After all, this was not just a holiday it was a serious business of collecting material. And I had to keep my promise. I could have been a bit of a bore.'

'Never, never,' she scolded him. 'You were fantastic. This book is going to be twice as good as the first and all because of you. Remember I had nobody on my trip to Aranmore. I found that hard--exciting but lonely.'

She longed to say more. Tomorrow they had to say goodbye.

'John our time together is running out--fast. And I for one regret that greatly. I want to ask you a personal question, which I hope you won't mind.'

'Go ahead. I won't mind. I know you too well.'

'Can you tell me again what your greatest fear is?'

That was not new. The response came easily.

'My greatest fear is the fear of failure as you well know.'

'Still an honest answer. You're afraid of failure. Why? Is it because of competition from others--that they'll get there first and leave you behind?'

'I don't care a fig about competition. That's healthy. I fear my own failure. I mean a failure to meet goals. If I were an artist I'd have a vision of the end product, what it should be like and if I didn't achieve that, it would be a failure.'

'You've high principles. Most are content to live compromises. That's the commerce of business and even politics. You know, John, you're just a damned perfectionist. Everything must be perfect, otherwise it's rejected.'

She sounded a little angry.

'No Karita. You're too harsh.' Perhaps she was right. Maybe he was too rigid and unyielding. Could he change? 'Same question for you. What's your greatest fear?'

'Mine? May sound strange to you,' she said. 'It is the fear of un-reality. An admission like that from a writer is probably a contra-diction. Fiction is unreality surely, yet I don't want to get trapped in the world of unreality and have no way out. In a way unreality is closely related to loneliness. So that would be another fear, the fear of loneliness; true, stark, unrelenting loneliness from which there's no escape. I've experienced it in Sligo and at home and it's horrible. Don't confuse that with solitude, which can be a blessing and especially important for good work because we know we can escape from it at any time. As a writer one seeks solitude.'

'I understand. There is a difference.'

She longed to stay with him, to give in to anything he wanted. She tried to convey it without words in her intimate way. Soon she realised he was exhausted not just from the journey; no his exhaus-tion was deep-seated, more long standing. Tonight he'd given her a glimpse of the anguish he experienced before keeping his promise. She appreciated the demons that were raging inside him, his battle yet to be fought and hopefully overcome.

Was there a place for her, at a distance or even at his side? She wanted to know--desperately--but perhaps not now.

It would be a matter of time.

She had come to Ireland, first alone and now with him and found places full of drama, beauty and tragedy, unhappy things that shake the heart. Places lonely, remote and withdrawn. Memories poured in on her, images of sharp sunlight and deep shadow, the smell of burning turf, light throbbing in the sky, endless stone walls, crowded streams turning into waterfalls, heavy clouds pressing on mountains spilling over the edges in slow motion.

Was she right to come and stare at some inexplicable old ruin in these settings and wonder? To see the jagged old trees leaning with the wind like crowds of hands held in supplication. To wonder at what connection they had with centuries past, times past and beings past. She was right as ghosts need memories for them to exist.

It was John who suggested she see things because her imagination was in need of nourishment. She could have stayed at home. Not come. And just imagined. She knew then where home was. Now she was not sure. Now she'd to think of the long journey home. And did she want to make that journey? She had visited Tir na nOg and now faced a return to reality.

That night as she lay staring at the shadows, the sound of car on country roads from Shannon to Mizen drove deeper into her wakeful lucidity.

John was full of inhibitions. She'd love to give him a good shake and wake him up before life passed by. On the beach in Waterville she felt their pulses beat in unison, both, for a moment the excitement of an exhaustless future.

Years ago she felt life had a grudge against her. Her own father seemed to dominate every so-called freedom she pretended she had--until the time when John came to Kungsangen House and the country estate.

Then there was an extraordinary awakening in Karita, which developed into a singular longing for John. But at the time he was promised to another, a rival to her, but a lovely person, Linda Lindstrom. She was now gone! And John was alone. And Karita was alone. It wasn't fair. Where was the justice?

She desperately wanted to speak her mind, to say the truth. Her upbringing forbade it. As for John he dressed the truth in useful hopeful euphemisms. Everything was going to be all right. How maddening it was for her.

The searching had to continue.

4 1

Research continued in Cambridge. Outward appearances could be deceptive however. Memory of the bomb remained a catastrophe in John Nicholson's life. He went about his work methodically, his face a mask but occasionally a flash of anger could be seen. He had told Karita his greatest fear was failure. That was true until now. There was a greater fear, which he found difficult to express.

Even the police were not able to help. The case was being pursued and he was advised on security measures. These were carried out. It was suggested he consider moving back to university residence. He resisted this. Why should he? He loved the cottage and garden in the countryside where peace and solitude were precious to him.

Spring promised new life, and snowdrops, crocuses and narcissi were in abundance and the smell of the damp warm earth. He loved to sit on the patio by the hanging rose tree--a little world of its own looking across the lawn to the pond framed by ivy leaves and beyond to the open spaces of hedges trees and fields. A farmstead to the right with great barns and Friesian cattle; to the left the village among the trees, which partly hid the spire of the church. For hours he'd sit in the sunshine.

Some might label him selfish and non-caring. To others, to stand aside in the shadows, letting himself be obliterated by more forceful and ambitious academics in college was admirable. That was the impression he gave, of one standing back, half-hidden, half aloof, non-participating in social events. A man alone treasuring his solitude.

Yet they didn't realise the striving for something that might be obtainable, just beyond, always beyond. At times his life was an abyss of nothing. The more he reached for the fateful flower, trembling so blue up in a crevice just beyond reach, he'd become aware of a gulf below him into which he could plunge if he tried to reach. Nearer he had flowers to pick--many were easy--but it was never <u>the</u>flower.

And he constantly felt tired, like a child who fights against sleep, for sleep can make one defenceless, even a form of extinction. His nights were torture, which led to a restless impatience. An explosive rage came over him as he remembered the bomb, becoming violent and murderous. He wanted the perpetrators annihilated, swept away, locked away, so that the world, his world, would be a safer place.

For a moment sunshine blazed across the garden, there was a scent of rising sap or violets. White daisies were out in abundance, bright as angels and all around unfolding leaves were bravely coming into the world.

The doctors said John Nicholson was suffering from acute anxiety interspersed with a reactive depression and suggested a spell in hospital under supervision and appropriate medication would be helpful.

So he entered hospital for a period that was not specified. Nobody could tell how deep the damage was and what specific reserve, or even the will, was there to fight and resist it. As he sat by the window another hour fell like a petal from a hanging branch, the wall clock watched him silently with its red hand jerking around in an endless circle of seconds. With discovering fingers he touched the smooth surface of the hour glass in the same way he'd touched Karita's cheek. A great pleasure and intimacy was there. And it was his only way of controlling the flow of time.

He had the choice.

To stop or allow it to go on.

Karita Isselherg returned to Stockholm full of plans. Places came alive and her mind was teaming with ideas. She told her parents about the assassination attempt, which John kept to himself until the end. So strange because he spoke against the motion. Fortunately he was not badly injured.

She was torn by indecision. Two options were open; one was the work ahead, the other was concern for John. She decided to develop the second novel based on the journey with John. She'd the characters, locations and time to make this her best because she'd a real live hero throughout the journey to the ends of the earth. She'd fainted on the last crossing over the sea with laughing monsters threatening to overwhelm her. And who was the person to rescue her? John Nicholson taking her in his arms, and carrying her to safety in his castle or lighthouse, where servants gave her sustenance and reassurance that the monsters of the rock would do them no harm as long as they travelled back to the mainland together. The end to her story would be in some beautiful castle where everything worked perfectly in a time when horses reigned, when women were revered and protected on principle and where the land of fiction could make anything happen.

The time had come to start. Preparation took a couple of weeks and included riding horseback over weird landscapes in all sorts of weather, sometimes getting soaked imagining movements in the forests behind her and being pursued by ill-shaped monsters whose screams and claws almost grasped her mount but never quite reaching. All good for atmosphere though bad for dreams; at night they came like a wind through her soul, drifting with the seed dust of creative experience.

The time arrived to start covering blank pages. Again she selected the French windows overlooking the garden. Nature changed rapidly in this climate. She'd work with three candles on the writing desk. They had atmosphere, otherworldliness, and were surrounded with moving shadows into which she could project shapes and objects.

Smoke from the candles reminded her of the incense of Ireland, the scent of the turf fires. At first she cried like a child that doesn't want to but is forced from within. She was helpless. Then her mouth crumpled and an inner crash came from nowhere with blind weeping. She was alone; yet shadows were breathing in silence as they watched.

It was time to start.

PART THREE

1

Tom and Ruth Nolan sit in the lounge. The fire sends out a warm
glow and flowers--yellow flowers--rest in a vase beside Annette's
violin case.

There is silence. An uneasy silence. And the clock on the mantelpiece ticks loudly. Ruth is aware of her husband's the affection.
It's in his eyes--the quiet patience of a man who was tormented in
his youth and who's suffering now more than ever. Waves of regret
flow through her.

He makes gestures like a confused man; she's like a ghost in his
consciousness. Something is stuck inside him, something he's trying to resolve. He stares into space, far away, out of his reach, trying not to yield. His expression shows anxiety, horror and pain that
crumples his face.

They've returned from hospital and seen Professor Kennedy.
Results of the donor tests were available and Professor Kennedy
gave them out like a schoolmaster stating both parents were unsuit-

able almost implying it was their fault.

'What's the next step professor?' Ruth had inquired blatantly.

'We'll now have to start searching wider for a suitable donor,' he sighed. 'This could take time. And it's very tedious. There are lots of people out there who could be donors and suitable but they just refuse to help.'

'How sad,' Ruth said. 'But the search will go on professor?'

'It will. We have our ways and means.'

Tom stayed quiet, watching and observing carefully, leaving the initial questions to Ruth. She was clutching at straws. 'Do you think our daughter is going to die professor?'

Tom was suddenly startled.

'I don't know,' was the uneasy reply.

'Don't you really?'

'Nobody knows for certain.' He fiddled with a paper knife as a distraction. Suddenly he volunteered. 'Of course she may die.'

Ruth was persistent in a childlike way. 'But do you think she will die?'

It was like a question to a pupil; the professor resented the tone as well as the question. She was determined to force an honest answer out of him.

He slumped in his chair. There was no escape. This irritating woman was almost diabolical.

Tom caught Kennedy's eye knowing he well understood the drift of the question.

Kennedy was silent, and then nodded agreement.

'Do I think she will die?' He repeated. 'Yes. I do.'

This remark shocked beyond measure. The arrogant fellow with grey hair, hard eyes and twitching hands had elevated rudeness to an art form.

'I don't believe she will,' Ruth said mockingly.

Tom stood up quickly, holding a hand out to Ruth.

'We've heard enough. I do not wish to listen to any more of these gloomy predictions. Come Ruth. We'll go home.'

The words are imprinted in Tom's mind forever, beyond escape. He goes to the French window to look at the garden. There is still light, the lovely young flowers of early spring; his favourites for painting are in bloom, the gorgeous display of red roses, but now they could be the sprinkling of sacrificial blood.

Ruth tries to bear it. Courage possesses her and she's the stoical bearer of bad news. She comforts him holding his hand lovingly and protectively. As he returns her look, fire flickers in his eyes; his face is yellow as wax and his beard now streaked with grey. His changed appearance is lodged in her soul. His vacancy tells of a man who's defeated and knows it.

That night Ruth cries for hours. They're like people who've died. There's no hope. In the night she lies awake and trembles like a suffering animal. She feels the shivering could do her damage.

But she has no care.

2

The Nolans are engulfed in confusion. Routine chores are in chaos. Ruth cannot run the household and Tom sits in the studio in a stupor, each hurting from the Kennedy interview.

She goes over it again. The professor's discomfort at their probing was obvious. What kind of man was he, desperately trying to avoid questions? Was he a coward or was there an inner problem blocking natural sympathy for others' suffering? Some people are strange and difficult to understand. She could feel his discomfort growing like an advancing tide. She didn't blame herself for the questions that produced the outrageous response. She could've wilted under his stare. But no. She stood her ground and demanded an answer.

She got it and she denied it. But the shock of his words, cruel and unthinking, went deep into their psyche. Something had to be done.

She looks at her husband as she sips a cup of tea.

'Tom dear. There is no next week,' she says, 'there is only the present.'

Her eyes fill with tears.

He nods vigorously. 'We'll have to do something. Kennedy doesn't give a damn. And he's always too busy to get through to him. Bloody frustrating.'

'My God Tom. It's not frustrating; it's potentially fatal. We could lose our daughter from sheer neglect.'

'She's getting the correct treatment and Dr. Sutton says she should respond.'

'But even if she responds only 20% survive long-term. Remember? And 50% will probably survive donor transplant and Kennedy said they are working on it.'

'He did.'

'I don't believe him.' She says angrily. 'He sounds like a politician. I don't trust him. In fact I don't really like him at all. He's a hateful person.'

'That's a bit strong Ruth. He's the consultant in charge. If we are going to get any good out of him we'll have to be nice to him.'

'How could you Tom.' She screams at him. 'He's useless. He only thinks of himself, his image, his delegations, his golf and how important the managers in the hospital are to him. They're more important than patients. Well that's what I think. It's a woman's intuition.'

Tom is shocked by her directness. She's streets ahead of him in assessing relationships and attitudes; she can read people like a book. And she's usually right.

'You know something Tom. I've always regretted Dr. Nicholson leaving St. Mary's to go to Cambridge. I know he was offered a better position. But what a loss. Someone of his calibre. From the moment I met him he was the kindest and most sympathetic doctor I ever met. I could trust him. Annette really loved him and he started her off on treatment. Then this Kennedy character appeared out of nowhere and started throwing his weight around, abusing everyone including the children. Shouldn't be allowed get away with it. He even insulted us yesterday for daring to ask questions about our own daughter.'

'Everything you've said is true.'

He isn't as quick as Ruth on rhetoric, but once he gets going little will stop him.

'We'll tell Dr. Sutton what happened with Kennedy, the results of the donor tests, and ask him is there any way Annette could be transferred for marrow treatment in a specialist centre in England. Hopefully Dr. Nicholson could be approached for advice.'

'Tom. Would you ever do that for us? For Annette? It may be her last chance of a good life. You realise that?'

'I do. I'll see Dr. Sutton tomorrow.'

3

There's no difficulty in getting an appointment with Dr. Sutton. Instructions were left with reception to fit the Nolans in at the end of surgery--anytime. Tom appreciates this kindness. It's typical of the man. He enters the familiar surgery and is greeted in a pleasant manner though the doctor looks tired and troubled. Perhaps another domestic upheaval.

'Tom what brings you here today?'

'It's about Professor Kennedy doctor.'

'I've a letter from him stating both your results are incompatible for a donor transfer. A great pity. The search will have to be widened. We could be lucky.'

'According to Professor Kennedy Annette may not have much time left.'

Dr. Sutton frowned. 'Did he say that? How does he know? What did he say?'

It all comes out. Firstly Ruth's queries were put down with rising impatience, then hostility when the matter of treatment was raised and the final question from Ruth about Annette's future--she was brutally told that Annette was going to die. Dr. Sutton finds this incredible and asks was it as bad as that? Tom nods and adds a few more nasty details.

'What a pity there're people like Kennedy in positions of power who treat vulnerable people abominably. There's no place for this behaviour in a civilised society. The man is a menace. And I've heard other stories. It just goes on and on.'

Tom is hesitant to proceed.

'Doctor. Ruth and I are wondering would there be anyway Dr. Nicholson could be approached for advice on how to proceed and even, if possible, have him come in on the case. We'd be willing to take her to Cambridge.'

'I know what you're saying. But there're enormous problems administratively. One of the most difficult I can see is getting Professor Kennedy to agree.'

Tom bangs his fist on the table.

'To hell with Professor Kennedy and his precious feelings. Our daughter is more important than his feelings. She's dying and we have to do all we can to save her. The only way out of the impasse is to approach Dr. Nicholson. How best can we do that?'

'Well I could write to him. He's bound to reply saying Kennedy would have to give permission. I understand Kennedy and Nicholson are not on the best of terms. A lot of one sided jealousy is there and it takes little effort to guess on whose side that is.'

Tom nods. 'Tell you what Dr. Sutton. I'll write to Dr. Nicholson explaining the facts and follow up with a visit to Cambridge, if he'll agree. I think the direct approach is best and I'd be more than willing to do that. You could give me the medical records to take with me.'

'All right Tom. You're a brave man and I wish you well. I'll prepare a report on Annette's progress so far. That's the one good thing about Professor Kennedy; he gives all the relevant details in his letters including copies of laboratory reports. They'll be essential for Dr. Nicholson. In spite of that I can expect fireworks from St. Mary's with complaints about interference in professional integrity and all that guff.'

'To hell with it. We want to save our daughter. Perhaps it's the only way to keep our family together. Do you understand Dr. Sutton?'

'I understand perfectly well.'

'Did you ever have a family doctor?'

'We had one, Diane, a beautiful girl who had to leave home because her mother drove her out. She went to St. Mary's and qualified as a nurse. I believe she knew Dr. Nicholson when he was a junior doctor in St. Mary's, knew him quite well, but nothing came of it when he opted to go to Sweden for three years' research.'

'This Nicholson fellow has gone into cancer research in a big way.'

'He's one of the biggest names in cancer research although working in a most original way. He's abandoned the idea of animal models. Instead he's developed what's called in vitro techniques of measuring drug toxicity on cell cultures under varying laboratory conditions. He's probably the first to have promoted the technique and some pharmaceutical companies have criticised him, finding fault with his results. In spite of this he has persisted. I've followed his career assiduously as a fellow Irishman and I'm proud of him. He's a man before his time and people don't appreciate what he's trying to do.'

'Dr. Sutton. Some do appreciate what he's trying to do. He tries to avoid cruelty on experimental animals. He may make a break-through and save enormous amounts of suffering.'

'I didn't think you'd an interest in animal research Tom. You feel strongly about it.'

'I do doctor. But that's another day's story. I've now got my daughter to think about. And that's top priority.'

4

Maud Sutton is home--on a visit. She sits in the upholstered sofa with an air of superiority--waiting. In days gone by Peter Sutton had some attraction for her. What she did rebel against--bitterly--was his lack of ambition to get ahead. She had to plan various homes, various moves. He didn't care. He'd no initiative at all. It was infuriating. Spending as he went, not caring, but always working hard. Patients were asking for him and at all times. Ridiculous. No peace.

Yet he did not look happy. Something always seemed to be troubling him and he was not the best communicator. He'd sit there at dinner and hardly say a word. She ranted at the despair in him, the lack of incentive, the acceptance of things as they were. He seemed to be like that on purpose. Food and pleasure were not important to him. Although she did notice he'd a charm, particularly with other women, his way of making them feel they were special, a respect beyond the common place and this would drive her mad with rage.

Maud had tried to make their lives a world of somebodies, people who mattered, who were important and a force within the community. This was left up to her entirely. Little or no cooperation from him. She was essentially a snob who tried desperately to get her own way. All she could organise were gatherings of nobodies and a smaller number of somebodies; this only partially filled her ambitions. Life became boring. Eventually she did not even bother. Everything was turning into one great disappointment. And she blamed her husband.

Peter Sutton is upset after listening to the story about Annette.

'Anything exciting happen at your little practice today Dr. Sutton?' She asks in a tone intended to provoke.

'Nothing you'd be interested in dear.'

'That's not right Peter. You know I can keep a secret.'

Probably the greatest gossip around. He tells her about the Nolan's dilemma.

'Keep away from them Peter. They're common people and I don't like them. I can see trouble there if you try to help. Mark my words. Don't deserve to be helped.'

'There's a chance their daughter will die if she isn't given the right treatment.'

'Surely she has the right treatment now,' she says as if sitting on hot bricks.

Not the whole problem again especially with someone who's totally opposed to the Nolans. There's some kind of war going on, he knows nothing about, and wants to stay out of it. It's the only way he can manage to have a stable, balanced life, and a harmonious existence with mostly happy patients.

Maud has made her own life now. In the past it was nothing but friction against an uncooperative household, in which she was reluctantly immersed. Often she wished out but felt trapped. It was her own making. Gradually she began to abhor the house, the practice with a loathing and, yet, strangely she could not get away. She felt tied to the place and she made damn sure everyone knew about her revulsion. It was a kind of revenge she planned on her husband for all his miserable failings and disappointments.

Before descending into one of her moods of irritable silences she flings at him.

'How really awful this house is. I just hate it.'

He glances back at her. Experience taught him a lesson in holding his tongue even though he's now on the edge. All he sees is this obese woman, old before her time, sitting like some red-faced Buddha on crimson coloured cushions, wallowing in self-pity-- and no doubt enjoying it. Probably all the more because she'd been able to say her piece about those dreadful Nolan people.

Because of her antipathy to help he sees her in a worse light. The flushed round face subsumed into several chins replacing a visible neck. But it is the mouth and jaw that really tells her venomous nature. The lips disappear in a tight compression, the lower jaw pressed forward in an attitude of defiance.

'Do you hear me Peter? I just hate it.'

Thank goodness Maud is off again on another cruise to the sun tomorrow. He puts his head down and drafts the letter to Dr. John Nicholson in Cambridge.

Peter Sutton gets an urgent phone call informing him that Maud has collapsed and was rushed to hospital. Her condition is critical and can he come as soon as possible? He catches the next plane to the Canary Islands and decides to sit up all night as a kind of penance. Under the circumstances bed would be frivolous. Anything could happen as she's had a stroke.

He should be sitting at her bedside but she doesn't want him there, which only adds to his distress and hurt. He's always been a serious person, now seriousness overwhelms him. His dark handsome face, with sunken eyes, is dazed and confused. He rests a little, but does not sleep and still feels hopeless. Many tests are done and her condition remains critical. Days later he is shown into Mother Superior's room. She gives a courteous bow, looking at him along her nose.

'Dr. Sutton, I'm afraid your wife passed away this afternoon,' she says in faulty English.

He stands there in shock, unable to feel anything, gazing at nothing. Mother Superior reacts by placing her pale hand on his arm and stares into his eyes.

'Have courage my son,' her voice is reassuring. 'Courage.'

He steps back in fright when a woman like that approaches him especially in voluminous skirts. She is very matronly.

'Of course,' he says softly. 'May I see her?'

The Matron rings a bell and a young sister quickly appears. She has a naïve and mischievous look in her blue eyes. Something is mumbled between them and the young woman demurely makes a bow and becomes serious. Peter holds out a hand. The young sister unfolds her creamy hands and slides one into his, passive as a sleeping bird. Out of the depth of his gloom he thinks what a lovely hand.

She then invites him along a corridor at the end of which she taps on a door. He's aware of the fullness of the young woman's skirts, moving with a fluttering haste in front of him. He's apprehensive when the door opens and sees candles around a single bed. A sister kneels beside the bed, her face downcast and expressionless. When she notices the visitors she rises and makes a little bow. A black rosary is being twisted slowly against the rich blue-black of her bosom. The sisters in their black silky skirts move to the bedside. Mother Superior makes her entrance, leans forward and with great delicacy raises the veil from the face.

The peaceful composure of his dead wife is revealed and instantly something leaps inside him and a smile comes to his face. The three nuns are studying his reaction carefully, eyes full of compassion. At first there is fear, then puzzlement and wonder, later a strange involuntary smile also appears on their faces. The Mother Superior tries to resist. Yet he persists, so eventually she too responds with a reluctant smile.

There is mild consternation in the room. Suddenly Peter turns to the bed, just in case his wife might have observed him. It is a moment of fear.

Maud lies, in a strange pretty way with her sharp, dead little nose sticking up and her expression fixed in the final obstinacy of a child. Peter's smile disappears. He does not weep. He gazes blankly at her and knows a certain martyrdom is in store for him. He's numb and washed out. They were married twenty-one years. He was not perfect and he knew it. But Maud had always wanted her own way in everything and usually she got it.

She had loved him, but grew obstinate contemptuous and angry. Ten-times she left him and then came back. Now the eleventh-time and she was gone. Now she will never come back. Even as he thinks about the inevitability of the occasion he feels her urging him on, to make him smile, for some reason. Maybe now she realises he has something to smile about. No he is not going to smile as he looks down on the infinitely provocative dead woman.

'At it again Maud,' he mumbled to himself.

He turns to the three nuns who'd retreated behind the candles and are hovering. He suddenly feels he wants to leave. Mother Superior is saying the Pater Noster with clanging beads. The pale young woman fades further back.

He addresses them collectively.

'You must understand. I'm terribly upset. I really should go.'

The hovering shadows say nothing. He makes for the door. Even as he leaves the smile returns to his face and he secretly wishes he could hold the creamy hands that folded like sleeping birds, so sensitively. He is not interested in his own imperfections. It's my own fault, he inwardly groans. And even as he tears himself apart in guilt, he feels something whispering distinctly and clearly to him.

Smile now. It's all over. You can smile again.

6

After three weeks in hospital John Nicholson returns home. Days grow longer and warmer. He sits on the patio overlooking the garden; Cruickshank, the gardener, has done a marvellous job in tidying the place. A thick wand of sun spotlights trees at the back of the pond transforming them into a refulgent yellow and urges him to think of the joy of spring.

Yet he shrinks inside. Fear still lingers, driving, meeting people, going to the village or attempting country walks. Natural he was told and would gradually disappear.

He only feels safe at home. Adjust to a new concept of people and live a life will be an effort. It's useless to do otherwise--others keep up an appearance. Colleagues are courteous and understanding but then everyone is extra polite. College is a regime of permanent good manners and solicitude. Underneath this insouciance a fundamental hardness evolves in him, a coldness in attitude. Spontaneity to all things is lost. To others he appears normal, yet inwardly a detachment develops and lurking in the background is insidious revenge. Still he remains the same as always. It's the game everyone plays. It's what's expected of him.

The sun grows stronger as he pretends to read. All the time his fists are clenched and he holds himself in. Form and balance in life are lacking.

Karita Isselherg drifts back into his mind; he visualises her sitting beside the French windows writing furiously under candle-light--as she describes in her letters. The dim light falls on the long hair, with wisps of gold straggling down the nape of her neck doing exactly as she promised. She is away from him, beyond him. Out of reach in her exquisiteness and he's lost in himself.

Fits of yearning have become part of his nature, a certain place with somebody who meant home. That had been Linda. She's now gone, gone forever. This bright blue morning it's Karita who could make it home. It slowly dawns on him. Is she aware of him? The way she'd kissed comes back--something he couldn't forget. One of those special moments.

Once he had thought he'd everything in this house in Cambridge, everything a man could need. True. He had, except a woman. He now accepts his need, and desires this woman, Karita Isselherg-- tall, blonde, handsome--supremely confident and intelligent.

Clouds disappear and the sun shines on every open space. The sky in these parts can be amazing--wide expanses of wonder--with incredible blue and golden clouds. Blue is his favourite colour es-pecially the skies. Today reminds him of the blues around Achill and Aranmore, a colour so intense yet soft and changing.

The doorbell shakes him out of his daydream. The postman smiles with a large parcel stamped in Sweden with a name on the back.

The following day John Nicholson returns to his overcrowded office. A large volume of mail waits on his desk; its content he can tell at a glance. Two letters, however, stand out, both from Ireland and marked <u>Urgent.</u> Posted by recorded delivery and signed for by his secretary Gillian.

'Like a cup of tea, Dr. Nicholson, while you face that lot?' She asks pleasantly.

'Would be very welcome.'

He opens the large envelope from Dr. Peter Sutton. The letter is a masterpiece of detailed construction of his (Dr. Nicholson's) original patient in St. Mary's. Her name is Annette Nolan. John cringes but continues. Dr. Sutton vividly describes the progression of her illness under the care of one of the consultants. He's been kept informed by detailed letters from the hospital and he is in a position to send them to Dr. Nicholson.

One of the most important considerations, and a delicate one, is the appalling treatment the parents received from the consultant, who gave the impression they were just a nuisance and when asked by the mother was Annette going to die the answer was plainly put: 'Yes. I think she's going to die.' The letter continues: 'The parents are well informed on current medical practice and know that the survival rates in bone marrow transplant are higher than medical treatment alone. No donors have been found here as yet so could I ask you to carry out a UK search for a suitable donor for Annette before it's too late? She has responded a little to current chemotherapy but all the experts here agree her best chance of survival is a direct donor transplant. So I appeal to you, not just as the Nolan's general practitioner, but also as a close friend and one who has experienced the frictions and egos of those involved in medical politics in this town. I cannot name names, or quote individual cases, but I think you've sufficient knowledge of the system here to know that personal egos are sometimes more important than patients' welfare. This is probably going to be the most difficult problem to overcome. It boils down to the saving of a young and beautiful life.'

'There will be difficulties, hurt feelings and recriminations but please, Dr. Nicholson, the whole family have faith in you. If they are left without hope or help I can see them rapidly disintegrating. Please help if you can. Sincerely, Peter Sutton. MD. LRCP&SI.'

'PS. I believe Tom Nolan is also writing to you. I think he'd like to travel to Cambridge to talk to you. I hope you'll welcome him. He's a fine but impetuous man.'

The second letter was from Tom Nolan. John read it carefully.

7

Tom Nolan is one of the first passengers to disembark from the Aer Lingus morning flight to London Heathrow. The Piccadilly Tube takes him to King's Cross where he boards the train for Cambridge. An hour later he arrives at the station in the south of the city and walks up Hills Road where he books a room in a comfortable hotel.

It's late afternoon. A few hours daylight are left to relish a beautiful city. He visits the Fitzwilliam Museum in Trumpinton Street opposite the site of the old Addenbrooke's Hospital, then explores other buildings including King's College Chapel and strolls along 'the Backs' as far as the Bridge of Sighs.

The day is beautiful with a pale blue sky--a 'growing day' some would call it--with the silence of the swelling sap especially evident as he walks down Queen's Road and into Silver Street to reach his hotel. Imagination breathes life into the history of the city, but he's not a tourist on this occasion. He has serious business to discuss.

The appointment is at ten o'clock tomorrow morning.

An early evening meal precedes a visit to the lounge just to observe others at a distance--one of his favourite pastimes--and hoping not to be seen. The room is about half-full. He orders a soft drink and retreats to a dark corner with a good view. A novel sits beside him and notebook full of questions for tomorrow morning. He reads the questions several times and then looks at the steady trickle of customers coming and going. Most know each other so Tom Nolan--a casual guest--feels an extraneous nuisance, like someone in a club while his own is being renovated.

It is too early for bed so he remains. Customers become louder and more boisterous. A debauched looking mahogany upright piano with old-fashioned candleholders stands among ornate gilded chairs. It looks like a wise old gent in the company of fools. More empty glasses rest on its yellow keys giving an air of tiredness to the pathetic instrument.

Before he retires the lounge wears an expression of potential nefariousness. Two businessmen, whose wives and works mates would not approve, sit drinking with two young women who are obviously not local to the town and are attractive in an over obvious way. Even the fatherly old man with the white hair and whiskers in another corner, thinks the same as Tom, as he pretends not to look over his newspaper. A harassed pageboy is asked for more whiskey as he gathers empty glasses and wearily disappears. Visitors begin to thin out leaving behind a pall of foul smoke, dirty dishes, crumpled newspapers, an apparently dead person in a chair and a strong feeling that this is no place like home.

Tom Nolan arrives at the hospital in good time and reports to the receptionist who contacts the pathology department. Yes. Mr. Nolan is expected and Gillian will come down to the main hall. A few minutes later a tall dark girl approaches and introduces herself as Gillian Gilchrist, Dr. Nicholson's secretary. She suggests they go straight to the department and will lead the way

Tension rises as he approaches; animosities come back although are tempered by facts he'd learned about Dr. Nicholson's work.

Gillian knocks on a door marked <u>Private</u>.

'Come in.'

She opens it and invites Tom to enter. John stands and comes forward to meet his visitor. She offers to take Tom's coat and asks if he'd like tea or coffee.

'Coffee please. Milk no sugar.'

John is silent as he looks at the other, memories flooding back of their first meeting. A major row developed. John was younger and totally committed to saving lives in St. Mary's. Is this going to be another confrontation? As ever he's prepared to defend himself.

Tom is shocked at how Dr. Nicholson has changed. He was much thinner, more cautious and anxious and greyer at the temples. An awkward moment occurs as Tom puts out a hand hoping it will be accepted. It is and John speaks first.

'I'd a letter from Dr. Sutton about Annette. Most detailed and helpful.'

'Glad to hear it. He's an excellent doctor. He will do anything for his patients even causing trouble with bureaucrats and colleagues if necessary.'

'He gave a clear picture of what's happening to Annette. There're hurdles to overcome if she's to survive.'

'Doctor what are her chances?'

'On this evidence she needs radiotherapy ablation and a suitable donor transplant.'

'What we were told, obliquely by Professor Kennedy and openly by Dr. Sutton.'

'Please sit down Mr. Nolan. We need to talk about what can and can't be done.'

Gillian appears holding a tray laden with cups and biscuits.

Tom begins to relax. He was afraid of a hostile reception or even rejection. 'Dr. Nicholson before we go any further I'd like to say my wife and I, and I'm sure a lot of the staff in St. Mary's, were shocked to learn you were leaving. You left behind a legacy of caring politeness and kindness--something that's sadly missing now.'

John smiles for the first time that morning.

'Dr. Sutton has filled me in with a few picturesque details. If anything is to be done for Annette I can see a fight coming from that Kennedy block. He may cause blue murder, citing interference in clinical practice and even use his bureaucratic friends.'

'There may be a battle on our hands?'

'Could be a right royal battle I'm afraid.'

John feels a certain congeniality for his old adversary. Tom Nolan was the antithesis of what he was trying to achieve. Things changed. Attitudes changed. Now it's the task in hand and how to overcome it. Congeniality drives away others emotions. Only in his heart is worry, a tightness like conscience.

'I'll discuss details of Annette's case with Sir Kenneth. We need advice on protocol between the two jurisdictions and how it should be handled. Other overseas patients have been treated here with no real problems.'

'Sounds encouraging, Dr. Nicholson.'

John frowns holding up a hand.

'One word of advice about Kennedy. From your end it'll be you and Mrs. Nolan who must insist that Annette is transferred to a suitable unit in the UK such as Addenbrooke's. Then we'll take over from there.'

'One thing worries me doctor. Professor Kennedy says he's going to set up a search for a suitable donor for Annette. Just suppose he finds one quickly. What then?'

'That'd be a problem. I can't anticipate what would happen. Still we must set up our own search--the sooner the better.'

'I agree. It's a kind of race now. Isn't it?'

'Yes but Mr. Nolan. I'm confident, no matter what; we're going to win that race.'

'Kind of you to say so.' Tom hesitates a moment. 'To change the subject before I go. Do you still hold your views on animal research you postulated in St. Mary's?'

'I don't. There must be a better way. I've changed my views

radically and working exclusively on an <u>in vitro</u> technique, which bypasses animal research. I cannot tell you too much about it but it looks promising.'

'I know and am delighted.' Tom says with a broad grin.

He continues in a serious vein. 'I was at an Oxford Union debate and spoke strongly against the motion on the table. You probably don't know that.'

'Of course I do.' Tom smiles. 'I was there and applauded your speech. You scored nine out of ten. You were the best speaker by far. It was a masterpiece of delivery and deserved far more recognition.'

John gives a sigh of regret.

'Well, it <u>was</u> recognised some days later. A letter was posted to my home thanking me for the Oxford lecture and a bomb placed under my car. I'd a lucky escape.'

Tom's face drops. He's obviously shaken.

'I never knew. How dreadful.'

'So it wasn't the ALF then?'

'My God, they wouldn't do such a thing after the Union debate. There must be some other motive. Perhaps a motive opposite to ours.'

'The police are baffled. Glad to hear your people were probably not involved.'

'I'm damn sure of it.'

*

Tom Nolan arrives back at the hotel about twelve o'clock, collects his luggage and settles the account. There's time for lunch before catching the train to London and he chooses the same seat in

the corner as last night. The room, which then had the appearance
of a profligate rake, is transformed into a magical palace. Wands
of light beam through windows and settle on the gilded chairs now
proudly shining like servants in livery. Even the debauched mahogany piano has regained its elegance and dignity.

That evening John Nicholson arrives home feeling he'd achieved
something--detailed information and planning to be put into action
for Annette. Next is Karita's letter and manuscript. She reminds
him of his promise. He makes himself comfortable with soft lights
curtains closed in his favourite recliner and the first page on his
lap. The opening is dramatic cliff-hanging stuff; the story develops
rapidly, with unexpected twists and builds from one small crisis to
a moderate one then the big crisis and total dilemma. Where is the
way out? Where is the resolution? There are several options. It
sustains the suspense. The greatest revelation, which no one would
have guessed, happens and resolution occurs. Surprise is achieved
with great impact.

He stares at the fire. The story definitely is aimed at young
adults. He feels humbled and unable to suggest improvements or
criticisms, yet he'd been asked to say something! Karita eagerly
awaits. He tries to formulate a response. He congratulates her on
a truly gripping piece. It would be acceptable as it is. However,
she'd asked for additions, perhaps some of his experiences he'd encountered or read about that might--that just might--improve overall impact of Part Two or even Part Three, when it comes. Other
things are mentioned about life in Cambridge, including the visit
from Annette's father and his current research. Finally, he asks her
to look at suggestions attached to the letter and hopes they'll be
taken from someone who'd a rich childhood in the countryside and

his clumsy efforts needed refinement and adjustments.

Energy infuses him and ideas impressions and images from long ago form like flames in the fire. To his surprise words flow and papers pile up beside him.

9

John Nicholson writes quickly and easily:

... During our trip I brought you to Ballaghbeama Pass, where Oisin returned from Tir na nOg. Looking east the mountain ranges are the most beautiful anywhere. An unearthly quality exists, a dreamlike elegance, which is found in all high places. I've a kinship with this region, a sense of belonging, of possession and being possessed...

... Similar areas you were shown such as the Connor Pass but we didn't climb any summits. In words may I take you to the highest peak in Ireland, Carrauntoohil and describe my experiencesthere. Some may be useful, like heather the colour of spilt claret, wind that comes from all directions, rocks that might be enchanted men or misshapen monsters pretending to move ...

... To start with imagine the sun is shining and there's a glow in the spring air. Bushes and trees are bursting with leaves and your path curves and twists beside an excited stream. There's no one about. Foothills are laden with swaths of heather rich with purple and mauve and interspersed with yellow gorse and shoulder the clouds above. Bleating lambs, rushing water and cry of the lark are the only company at the beginning of the journey. All is peace ...

... Onwards and upwards with the Ordnance Survey Map for guidance. Resting at a certain height to view the opening land-scape is a blessing. The path becomes a mere line between postage stamp fields and cottages are like toys far below ...

... At this stage one should turn away and face the excitement ahead, the loneliness of great hills and a solitude that cannot give sustenance or shelter for long. With the elation of the unknown, certain hostility may also be present. In this area it's almost as if the lower hills move together shouldering one another and attempt to cut one off from familiar places. You've to continue compelled by a force that's hard to resist...

... Clouds loom nearer. When seen from earth they're usually in-nocent puffy things; now they assume a different texture and move around in spirals like ghosts, the larger are misty and menacing and threaten rain, grass gradually disappears, rocks and boulders are numerous and wind becomes stronger and colder ...

... Continuing on against a strengthening wind and swirling mist I reach the edge of a precipice that looks down 1,000 feet into a dark valley known as the Devil's Punch Bowel. The dark water below is like a witch's cauldron boiling and bubbling away. The rocky bed is deep and full of caverns. Far into the fathomless water I imagine unspeakable thoughts depth beyond depth. Even when feet lacerate and bleed and the head feels faint for more than one reason, and muscles make their presence felt--a clean cold stream is a blissful relief and a kind of temporary anaesthetic ...

... After a well needed rest the path grows steeper, criss-crosses more frequently and the surface gets rougher. Air is light and like wine making one's head dizzy. As I look west across the valley the Atlantic is a dazzling strip of silver. In front another valley now filled with its own crop of clouds, which for a change are below me, slowly crawling along like a serpent over the edge of the valley …

… Even though I'm far above ground level and the sunlight glares intensely it does not have the same warmth. And the behaviour of clouds is less benign than elsewhere …

… The same golden clouds that sail placidly over fields now obliterate a person and he can be lost in seconds. In these circumstances one is nowhere so alone as high up on the mountainside. Yet I tramp on with aching feet, rapid heart and bursting lungs. According to my map the summit cannot be far away …

… Then the sun dies suddenly. A mist descends cold and clinging. Nothing can be seen. There can be few experiences more frightening than being imprisoned high up on a mountain in mist and rain. As I struggle on mist grows thicker and rain falls in that persistent way it almost seems to come up out of the ground. Above is a grey wall, in front and behind the same, only the rocks under foot are real. There are no sounds except falling water somewhere and the few dislodged stones rolling down the path …

… There is something terrifying being lost like this, it cuts a person off from the world and even in daytime from the sight of the sky. It's like been struck by blindness and there is no way out. To be lost this way is to experience horror and panic to the highest degree …

… I press onwards on what appears to be the semblance of a path. The mist thickens further. Snow appears. It gets colder. I appear to have come into a spell of winter. An icy wind, sleet and snow dance around me. The only thing is to find shelter among the rocks. And stay put--hoping …

… Then another torment comes. All the fiends of the air have combined to produce the most hideous noise on earth, the whistling and moaning of wind coming up over the summit of the Reek. I listen with chilled blood to an evil dreadful sound. I am drawn towards it to the edge of the highest peak. The snow is rising with it and not falling, merely whirling about madly …

… I stand on the edge chilled to the bone, watching the eerie display, blowing shapes to reveal dim, craggy, boulders like moving monsters, alien men or ancient beasts. All the time the dreadful whistle of the wind over the precipice, offering an evil invitation to follow, moaning almost with a suggestion of human mirth, and make me face the precipice as if something might come out of it, which would have to be confronted in battle …

… I can stay there no longer and turn back. On my way down a great rent in the clouds occurs, and I see a magnificent panorama of mountains with sun on them; the evening blueness spreading amongst them, peak calling peak, and the Atlantic beyond--a silver streak that dances in the light. Out there--somewhere beyond--is Tir na nOg …

… I reach the lower hills and ground level as the sun prepares to leave this earthly paradise for another day. Its exit drama unfolds as I sit there with a mixture of exhilaration and exhaustion. Only the cricket, chirping monotonously, fills the universe with shrillness. Even to this day I still feel that if the Gods ever thought of revealing themselves it would probably be in these western jagged hills and mountains at the dying of the day, perhaps the last day, when the hushed world around these magical places is tense with extreme beauty and the earth waits….

… For a while I sit on a wall by the little stream that greeted me that morning, sitting in the shadow of the mystery of time, which has puzzled and saddened human kind since the beginning of history ...

John finishes his letter as carefully as he can, aware that his reply is anxiously awaited--probably on a daily basis. He concludes:

... Well, my dear Karita, this is one story I am unable to illustrate to you in person. I couldn't ask you to go through it with me, but I did take you as far as <u>base camp</u>, as it were, that is the Gap of Dunloe, which is itself a place of beauty. I have now given you a first hand experience of what it's like to climb the highest peak in Ireland and encounter only some of the dangers and horrors--there are many, many more--but at least these may be useful to fill in gaps and locations when you are fine-tuning your truly brilliant manuscript....

Lots of love and luck,

John.

Meanwhile Karita Isselherg wakes early each morning and breakfasts before anyone else in Kunsangan House. She is waiting for something. She goes into the library and sits at her desk, cleaning and polishing, laying and rearranging things. Then the extensive bookshelves and manuscripts are refiled all the while listening and waiting. The same routine is carried out every morning. Others can't understand what has got into her. Rachel worries whether she is afflicted by some disorder such as writer's block, which is rapidly denied with a gesture and a laugh. She is waiting. Simply waiting.

One morning a ring comes to the front door. It is the postman with a parcel stamped in the UK. She is thrilled as she grabs it, signs the docket, shuts the door and hurries to her desk. Even though it's morning, she lights three candles.

The letter is read first quickly then more slowly and she kisses the signature. Then the corrected manuscript. Lots of blue lines together with footnotes are present. Instead some notes in red ink with suggestions like expand, more detail on location, local colour to make it convincing and please remember our journey at such and such or were you asleep? A question mark--is this really true? She laughs. Of course it's not true. She made it up but it had to be that way because fiction lets you do what you like, you can fantasize, you can even fall in love with the person you want to love and you can make it all come true--in fiction. That's its beauty. If only life could be this way then everything would be perfect. Everything would work out fulfilled for everyone. Wouldn't that be wonderful? But life is not fiction.

She settles at her desk and rereads his comments carefully. On mature reflection he does have many valuable points. She will act on them.

Another intensive week or two passes as she puts the final touches to Part Two of The Trilogy. It is sent to London for appraisal. The agents are more than delighted and insist she travels to London to sign the deal for the complete Trilogy. As an incentive a generous advance is offered to temp her to complete. How can she refuse?

About the same time a letter arrives at Addenbrooke's for Dr. John Nicholson. It's from Professor Kennedy agreeing to allow Annette Nolan to travel to Cambridge when a suitable donor has been found. He would continue the search in Dublin.

1 0

It isn't the burden of years that sets the pace of Ruth Nolan's walk it is grief. Tom told her the news from Cambridge, the good and bad, good because they'd agreed to accept Annette and bad because Annette would have to travel there--with the possibility of not coming back. Tom says of course she will come back and the best of treatment will be available.

Ruth is not convinced. She wants to know more and yet is frightened to talk to Professor Kennedy. The only person they can approach is Dr. Sutton who agrees to see them any time. The waiting room is so warm this morning. Nobody else seems to notice as she struggles to take her coat off with trembling hands. What does it matter?

'Ruth Tom. Please come in.' Dr. Sutton appears from his room and holds out a hand. He notices Ruth's flushed face. Maybe she's been crying. 'I hope you are both bearing up all right.'

'We're fine.' Tom replies. Ruth says nothing as she sits down.

Tom continues. 'Been to the UK and had discussions with Dr. Nicholson.'

'So I hear.' Dr. Sutton reaches for a file.

'I've had a copy of a letter he sent to Professor Kennedy. He's a real diplomat. In essence he told Kennedy you'd been to see him and asked if Annette could be transferred to his unit. He went on to say, if Kennedy agreed, he and his colleagues would be prepared to accept Annette firstly for assessment and, if necessary they would be prepared to carry out a donor marrow transplant.'

He produces another letter.

'I also got a copy of Professor Kennedy's reply. Surprisingly he's willing to cooperate and would be glad to see Annette getting the best treatment.'

Tom smiles.

'That's an interesting way of putting it. His tone has mellowed, but I think he may even welcome this as a way out. Or am I judging him too harshly?'

'Let's give him the benefit of the doubt and say his heart's in the right place.' Dr. Sutton's remark is typical of the man. Always prepared to forgive.

Suddenly Ruth, gripping her chair, looks past Tom and straight at Dr. Sutton.

'Enough of politics and man-talk,' she says pleadingly. 'I want to know what exactly is going on. Really going on. I'm in the dark.'

Dr. Sutton smiles at her apologetically. 'Dear Ruth. Sorry you feel that way. Anything in particular you would like you know?'

'I want to know everything Dr. Sutton,' she says and bursts into tears. 'All along I've been told bits of things like Annette is ill, she has a blood disorder, she needs medicines and that's about it. Please Dr. Sutton, could you explain to us--both of us--what exactly is wrong with our daughter?'

Dr. Sutton nods and reaches for another folder, which has grown in the last six months.

'Ruth I'll try my best. Annette has leukaemia or cancer of the blood. It's a serious condition in which marrow inside bones produces abnormal cells. The healthy cells have less space to develop normally, which means less white cells and platelets are produced. There're several types of leukaemia and each acute or chronic.'

'And Annette has the acute form?' Ruth asks.

'Yes. Acute leukaemia usually attacks immature bone marrow cells and unfortunately is most common in children.'

'What causes leukaemia doctor?'

'Simple answer is we don't know, yet. There may be genetic factors, radiation exposure, drugs and chemicals such as benzene from traffic pollution. I believe future genetic research may help clarify the origins of the disease and that's why we're fortunate to have John Nicholson in on the case. His work on genetics and computer technology is making progress and his unit is one of the world leaders in the field.'

'Thank God for that. I'm so glad for Annette then.'

'It looks more hopeful than the present set up. We have Tom to thank for travelling to Cambridge to put the case to the right person.'

Tom tries to intervene.

'It's the least I could do for Annette especially after the snub from Kennedy.'

Dr. Sutton feels there's enough of the blame game. 'Let's leave that behind.'

'Dr. Sutton I still want to know more.' It is Ruth again demanding to be heard. 'How can leukaemia be treated?'

'It's difficult to treat because the main aim is to prevent the body's ability to produce new cancer cells. This can only be done in a highly specialised unit. The first line of treatment is chemotherapy. Each course lasts a few days and attacks healthy bone marrow cells as well as cancer cells and in so doing reduces the patient's ability to fight infection.'

Ruth is impatient and perplexed.

'But doctor, Annette has had all this chemotherapy and she's not better.'

'I'm aware of that. She's known as an unstable and progressive case.'

'What's that?'

'Well radiotherapy may have to be given, and in certain cases the leukaemia may require a bone marrow transplant.'

Ruth looks distressed. 'Oh no. That sounds like a kidney or heart transplant.'

'In many ways you're right. If transplant is decided we have to find a suitable donor. Both of you are unsuitable and Annette has no brothers or sisters so we must look further afield. Professor Kennedy has already set up a search in this country but that could take some time.'

'Annette may not have much time left.' Ruth sounds desperate.

'That's where Dr. Nicholson and his team have a much greater advantage over us. A bone marrow transplant registry has been set up internationally. We might be lucky here in getting someone suitable but the UK has a huge pool of potential donors to choose from. They seem to be better organised over there.'

'So the search is on,' Tom says in a loud voice, 'blood and marrow samples from Annette have been sent to Cambridge. So we'll have to wait and see.'

'That's right Tom,' agrees Dr. Sutton. 'Annette can continue with chemotherapy here but it appears to be only having a limited effect. She definitely needs more aggressive treatment in addition to chemotherapy, such as radiotherapy and a suitable matched unrelated donor--known as MUD for short.'

'MUD for short. That's a good one,' Tom laughs.

Ruth glares at him. 'How could you Tom? With Annette so ill!'

Dr. Sutton looks at them and tries to end on a note of encouragement.

'The international registry is growing rapidly and many volunteers are coming forward. Also the outlook for leukaemia is getting better in recent years due to advances in refining drugs for use in humans.'

Tom says nothing further, but thanks Dr. Sutton with a light handshake and helps Ruth out of the surgery and back home to wait. And wait.

1 1

Time races by for John Nicholson. The day is gone before it's time to go home. He's been working hard on a special project refining agents for chemotherapy. The in vitro technique is, at last, showing the results he's been searching for. Pieces are falling together like a jigsaw puzzle and are almost complete.

This morning the ultimate result comes through. It's one of those rare moments in science, which can be described as a genuine breakthrough. Everything that blurred and puzzled is now sharper as he trembles on the threshold of discovery. Such events are rare- -outside normal daily experience. It's almost as if the spirit has crossed a boundary. This work could possibly replace current research methods in major pharmaceutical companies and may have considerable effects on many work practices.

Such things could only be hinted at during the Oxford Union debate. Now there's far more certainty. The results are discussed with Sir Kenneth who asks John to prepare a report for the research committee. Registration and patents will have to be gone into before publication. This is strange as he's anxious to publish as soon as possible. However these are the rules of the university. No question whatsoever.

Later in the morning Dr. Winter from haematology telephones to inform him that four possible marrow donors for Annette Nolan have been identified from the registry. John asks for details. He'd like to interview each separately.

And Chief Inspector Jordan also telephones. Everything seems to be happening together--all in one day! The inspector would like to call over to the department to discuss some outstanding issues.

'Of course. Can you make it three-thirty?' John asks.

'That would be fine.'

The inspector arrives on time and Gillian shows him into the office. Detective Inspector Browne is also present.

'Good afternoon Dr. Nicholson. You've already met my assistant DI Browne.'

'Indeed. Please take a seat.'

The inspector glances around the room as if he's looking for clues to some mystery he's working on, his usual way of coming round to any problem.

'I'm afraid doctor we haven't got very far on your case. I'm referring to the incident that took place outside your home. The main suspects were the ALF people. We've interviewed some of their members, not only locally but also in several hot spots throughout the country and consistently come up against a brick wall.'

'I see.' John says nodding agreement. Not surprised but keeps his silence.

'I've carried out a number of interviews myself,' continues the inspector. 'My impression is they seem to have respect for you and it would be most unlikely any of their groups would wish you harm.'

'That's a welcome change for me,' John replies with a sigh.

Jordan is determined to press ahead.

'Of course they were obvious suspects. Look at the title of the debate in the Oxford Union. Bloody stupid thing to do, if you ask me. Just looking for trouble they were. Although they're only students who run it. But they should know better.'

'Especially when the motion was carried,' Browne interjected. 'That could have made the ALF see red and force them show their annoyance in some way.'

'Like a bomb you mean?' Jordan says. 'But the stupidest thing of all was to pick on Dr. Nicholson. From what I hear it was you doctor that spoke most vehemently against the motion and, incidentally, I believe yours was by far the best presentation of the entire evening. I only wish I'd been present. You didn't deserve to be attacked by the ALF. On the contrary you should have been congratulated. And some of their leaders have come out and said so.'

Browne adds. 'So they have no motive. Unless it was a mindless mistake.'

'No it was no mistake,' Jordan says slowly. 'It was well planned, address known, timing almost perfect, except for your quick action doctor.'

'I shudder to think what could have happened.'

The inspector gives a gentle cough indicating he wishes to move on.

'Which brings us to the next point. Perhaps there are other possibilities. One would be some kind of paramilitary incident carried out by say republicans who are active in certain parts of your country. I've to ask is there any connection, or reason why these people would want to harm you?'

'No reason. I've never been involved in politics or paramilitary issues and would never wish to be. My life is taken up with research for cancer treatment.'

Jordan rubs his chin and looks straight at John.

'Now then. There's the final option and probably a remote one. I'm not a scientist and know little about research but can I ask does your work differ from current work in other universities and drug companies?'

The inspector has put his finger on a raw nerve and John senses the question could be a loaded one. He'll have to be careful and not give too much away.

'To a certain extent it's different. What we're trying to do is to replace current techniques with tissue cultures and genes in testing the efficiency of drugs. It's an uphill struggle but we're beginning to show encouraging results.'

The inspector is persistent.

'Are you implying, Dr. Nicholson, your methods could replace current procedures for producing drugs? I want you to concentrate on the word "replace." '

'I wouldn't use the word replace. I'd prefer to say complement other methods. But some day--who knows? Science is unpredictable and can lead to discoveries unheard of a few years ago. And knowledge is growing at a phenomenal rate.'

'If that is so doctor then competition would also be growing at a phenomenal rate and could call for measures contemplated by unscrupulous people.'

For the first time that afternoon John looks worried.

'Thank you for that last remark. I get the drift of what you're saying and will be careful in more ways than one.'

Jordan stands up and prepares to leave.

'Thank you doctor. It has been most instructive talking again. We won't keep you any longer. We know you've important work to do. And we will broaden our field of inquiries, but don't worry--we have our own way of approaching matters and are best left to us. They won't involve you.'

He holds his hand out and smiles pleasantly.

'Carry on your great work doctor. I hear you are doing marvellous things here and Sir Kenneth and staff are very proud of you.'

They leave John with the impression they know more than they let on. It's a little nerve racking but he soon forgets about it.

Interviews of potential donors for Annette Nolan are scheduled for tomorrow morning.

The potential donors arrive at Addenbrooke's. Blood samples had been processed by Dr. Winter and results showed a close tissue type with Annette Nolan. Exciting news for Nicholson although the problem of persuasion has now to be tackled. Like asking a healthy person to donate a kidney to a stranger and not everyone is full with altruism.

The first interview is with Karen Kelly; a pleasant twenty-one year old medical student who'd volunteered to become registered. She walks into John's office and sits with pen and notebook in hand.

She speaks first. 'Dr Winter has kindly explained the principles about marrow unrelated donor. Apparently it's not as simple as giving a pint of blood.'

'Of course Karen. And thanks for coming.'

'Dr. Nicholson I'd like to help my fellow human beings in any way. That's why I chose medicine. Yet there are dangers not only for the patient but also for me. I want to find out what they are before any decision. Please treat me as a layperson as I've only started medicine.'

John smiles and appears relaxed.

'Karen, I understand your dilemma. I'd be the same.'

She speaks with her notebook at the ready. 'May I ask you a few questions?'

'Fire ahead.'

'Who requires marrow transplant?'

'It's an option for patients with certain types of leukaemia or aplastic anaemia.'

'What exactly is a marrow transplant?'

'The process of transferring healthy marrow into a person to re-place diseased marrow. Before this happens the patient's original marrow is obliterated by chemotherapy and or radiation.'

'Sounds radical.'

'It is in bad cases.'

'Maybe a silly question but why are donors needed?'

'Matched unrelated donors are an alternative for patients with no family donors and an increasing number of such transplants are carried. Matching is done by tissue typing patients and donors-- like you and our patient waiting each day in hope. We have four good matches so far.'

'And the procedure itself?'

'As you already know about forty mls of blood is taken from each potential donor. Some is used to check the donors blood health and the rest is for tissue typing to see how close the match you are to the patient. The donor with the closest match will be asked to donate marrow.'

'What will happen to me if I donate?' She asks apprehensively.

'Marrow extraction, sometimes called "harvesting" of marrow, is performed in a specialised unit. If you're asked to be a donor and you agree you'll be supplied with full information. You'll be given a number of weeks to decide about continuing. However, although all donations, including bone marrow, are voluntary, there comes a point of no return. Once a patient is started on treatment to destroy their bone marrow, that is between two and ten days before transplant, the process is <u>irreversible</u>. If the donor pulls out it will most likely lead to the death of the patient.'

Karen looks down and thinks a while.

'I see the seriousness of what you say. I could never do that once committed. It's making the initial decision that frightens me.'

'I see that. The technique's relatively new and we're learning all the time.'

Alarm bells ring inside Karen as she says hastily. 'You mean learning on us?'

'Yes.'

An idea comes to her. 'Why not use animals to perfect the technique first?'

'I'd be against that. Other ways are better.'

Karen quietens suddenly and looks at him.

'I've heard about your ways. You've quite a reputation, Dr. Nicholson, in cancer research with lots of original views and unconventional approaches.'

'That's a compliment. But we're straying from the point. Any further questions?'

Karen is jolted back to the present. 'How about the harvesting of marrow?'

'A general aesthetic is given to the donor in an operating theatre. A biopsy needle is used to remove marrow from several bones and takes about two hours. Approximately a litre of blood is taken. If all goes well donors are free to leave hospital after two days. It's recommended they take two weeks off work to convalesce.'

'I see. I could miss a lot of lectures then.'

He ignores her comments as he continues. 'One last thing, which is important.'

'What's that?'

'The procedure is anonymous. The donor is not given any information about the patient. There are good reasons for this. However, there's a policy that may allow the donor to meet the recipient after two years if both parties agree.'

Karen Kelly stands up, holds out a hand and barely smiles.

'Dr. Nicholson you've been very explicit. I understand what would be involved and am grateful for the information.'

John also stands and holds her hand.

'Karen I'd urge you to think carefully about what we've discussed and you would be doing a wonderful thing if you agree. What I mean you'd almost certainly be saving a young person's life. I've no doubt about that.'

Tears well up in her large eyes. 'And risking my own to an unknown degree.'

He nods agreement and shrugs.

'Life is a risk. It's good to share what's given to us with those less fortunate.'

'Thanks again doctor. I'll let you know my decision as soon as I can.'

She walks away with no indication what direction she's heading in.

1 3

$\mathbf{K}$arita tells John by phone about the invitation to London. He's thrilled but also saddened to hear about Gustav. Probably been working too hard.

'So you'll be coming alone then?' He asks.

'I don't mind.' Really she does.

'Karita may I make a suggestion and please say no if you've any doubts.'

Excitement goes through her. 'Go on John. What is it?'

'Why not visit Cambridge? You can stay with me and you'd be more than welcome. I've plenty of room and you'd be free to do as you please. We could spend time planning the final part of your work and I might take you on a mystery tour to gather more locations. Could even be a little holiday.'

'That'd be wonderful. Just wonderful. You're so kind to think of it.'

'Karita. I've much to thank you and your family for during my time in Sweden.'

'A great pleasure for all of us.'

'That's settled. When you get to London call me. After you've completed your business deal you can get a train from King's Cross to Cambridge every half-hour. The journey takes one hour. And I'll meet you.'

She's so excited. 'I'll be pleased to see you and catch up on all the news.'

'Remember bring good walking shoes and a tough raincoat. You may need them.'

'Intriguing. For the mystery tour I presume?'

'Right. But it must remain a mystery for the present.'

'See you soon John.'

The evening before departure Karita sits in her library--thinking. It's such a change to listen to the silence and let her thoughts wander. The old grandfather clock that rests in the corner facing her desk was company through those long weeks and months, keeping time but now she appreciates how it ticks methodically with a simple swing pendulum, the second hand jerking relentlessly onwards in endless circles. She looks at it as if some greater meaning can be extracted from its movements. Time is running out! She's finished a major task and faces a journey alone. Her father's ill and yet she's successful. And the trip to Cambridge is an unknown entity. Swinging to and fro the pendulum tells her things; some she doesn't want to hear such as how unhappy she is to be leaving--in the midst of her happiness, how unhappy. It doesn't seem right!

At night she lies awake consciousness reluctant to leave her. She stares at the shadows on the ceiling. Waves are crashing on a shore, landing on an island where rocks and mountains are so eerie she has never seen their likes before and they frighten her. The waves brake with a rhythm of fate; a fate that's waiting for her. There are no details--only blurred vision.

Maybe she's suffering the effects of too much writing in a short time. She's on the edge and a change is needed. There's a thirst for something in every human heart, something that will satisfy our longings. Often we search in the wrong places; we try to draw water from the well of praise to quench self-esteem, water of success to quench importance and water of pleasure to quench joy. Yet we remain thirsty. She's thirsty with a longing. Now she's time to think, to think for herself. Insight is far more complex than eyesight. All this she cannot know. She longs to be made much of, she longs to be adored. But how to achieve it is beyond her. The night passes restlessly. Her wondering and dilemma remain, but softens with the dawn.

Eriksson leaves her to the airport; it's a silent journey. She prefers it that way, and he knows it keeping his distance and silence. He knows the family well and senses Karita's heart is probably broken, with a child's anguish. She's uncertain of what's ahead, or what's taking place. Deep down she weeps--is it hopelessness or a premonition? The great curse of an imagination is where everything is possible and fiction and fact can so easily merge.

She calms down with one of her favourite sayings: Hope always begins with hoping. She is going to work on that one.

In the empty library the old clock ticks away doing its work unobserved.

1 4

The London publishing scene is an eye-opener for Karita Isselherg. Two full day meetings are scheduled with editorial staff, marketing people, design teams, legal experts and financial advisors. Others are called in marketing her as a valuable investment. Yes, she's even spoken of as an investment where good planning could yield fortunes--talk she finds hard to believe. Maybe it's only talk.

This commercialism is impressive because the UK publishing machine controls the majority of worldwide rights. At the close of the second day she suspects it may be an act put on by some people--probably by a few who get through the net to an inner circle.

Perhaps she's wrong. It could be genuine. She doesn't know. She's glad it's all over as she sits in the lonely hotel room near King's Cross.

Next morning she's in good time for the train to Cambridge via Hatfield and Stevenage. Cambridge Bridge Station is a typical Victorian shambles. The train is on perfect time stopping precisely at eleven o'clock at the BR station south of the city and close to Addenbrooke's Hospital. John doesn't have far to travel and he's on the platform fifteen minutes early. The train pulls into platform one full of importance. It is from London--no less! Passengers rush through the ticket points. No sign of Karita.

He checks his watch. Five past eleven. No Karita. Perhaps she missed the train. Then a tall figure dressed in black, with long blonde hair--it used to be short--descends the steps of the last carriage and pulls a suitcase towards the exit point. An old-fashioned black hat is pulled down over her eyes and a long black cape descends to the ankles--the epitome of one of the ladies travelling in the Himalayas and not the lawns of Cambridge. His heart misses a beat when he spots her. A lot has happened since they last met. She's been living in a world of imagination at home, which was magical and terrifying.

He embraces her and quickly releases her. 'Have a good trip?'

'Very comfortable. Though the scenery wasn't inspiring. Too flat for me.' She smiles. 'I prefer a roller coaster ride.'

'Maybe we can see more of your kind of landscape in the coming days.'

'The mystery tour?' She enthuses.

'Tell you about it later. For now you must relax. I'd like you to see a bit of Cambridge and maybe have lunch.'

'That would be lovely John.'

The Fitzwilliam Museum is visited before lunch. Isn't time to see it all as he'd booked lunch at the Garden House Hotel around the corner of Trumpington Street. A table is reserved for one o'clock. The dining room is about half-full when they arrive and conversation fills the air. Their window table overlooks the river and lawns.

As they settle he says: 'Karita you look lovelier than ever. You've changed. Let your hair grow and taller, more mature and self-confident.'

'Thanks John. Things have changed and I'll tell you about them later.'

The waiter gives them menus.

'First things first Karita. How's your father?'

'Stable at present. His has cardiac insufficiency but they're doing wonderful things like bypass operations. He'll probably have to undergo one of those, but he's a terrible patient. Wants to know everything and very demanding.'

'I'm sure he'll do well.'

A young waitress in black and white uniform takes their orders. Karita makes mental notes of happenings around her. The first course arrives and there's still hesitancy in the air; he has always found it difficult to overcome, especially when faced with an attractive young lady.

'How did the publishing deal go? Congratulations on your success so far.'

'It's so exciting. I still can't believe it. Even though Parts One and Two were hard work the basic story lines were written a long time ago.'

'I remember rambling on about Celts and mythology, epic battles and love stories and lots more.'

'Which started me off. I got down to work and never stopped since.'

'You've produced a huge amount of material and what I saw was amazing although in places there was a feeling things were happening in a vacuum. Please don't take it critically. I wanted to help. You know that?'

She puts her hand on his.

'I know that and what a help! The second trip to the south-west was magical and weird and eerie and unforgettable. It made a huge difference to the quality of the narrative and the agent's one remark was it seemed so real and believable.'

'I would like to think those things you wrote about really did happen. What a different time we live in now. Because of you, people will want to discover more about the powerful events that probably did happen, not so long ago, before history could be written and recorded accurately. Your version of events is so credible and the nice thing is there are few people who can contradict you.'

'You say the nicest things and I love listening. Now what'll we have for dessert?'

1 5

Karita looks worried as she puts her coffee down.

'The last part is ahead. It's the one that's proving most difficult. It's when the final crisis takes place resolution is achieved and the dust settles over battlegrounds. When good finally triumphs over evil.'

'Lovely thought.' John says simply. 'Does good always triumph over evil?'

'In fiction it should and nearly always does. But in real life-- well.' She shrugs her shoulders. 'I don't know. But I'm anxious to find out.'

He doesn't know how to take it. What does she mean? In real life does good triumph over evil? It'll remain unanswered for the moment. Time is pressing on, other things have to be settled and plans made.

'Karita. May I ask some questions?'

'By all means. I'm all yours.' She smiles mischievously.

'I didn't mean that.' He blushes slightly. 'Could you spare about a week or ten days' touring? There're places I've never seen but believe they could be fantastic locations for your type of fiction.'

'Where's that for heaven's sake?' She asks a little breathless.

'It's the west coast of Scotland and especially the marvellous Isle of Skye where mountains, gorges and lakes are said to be extraordinary.'

'It'd be a lovely experience--a voyage of discovery. I was hoping something like this would happen. There was an empty feeling about Part Three. I didn't know what to put into it except vague references to Tara. And now Skye. What a finale! It'll be different to Parts One and Two. I'm getting excited thinking about it. I know little of Scotland. You must tell me more.'

For a moment he recalls the interviews with Tom Nolan and Karen Kelly--and the associated problems. 'Even though there're things happening in the hospital I can take ten days off and still keep in touch. And you can telephone home when you please. '

'This mystery tour is going to be inspiring,' she says huskily, 'I'm dying to get started. I've to bring strong boots.'

'The weather can be unpredictable. But we're still in Cambridge; it's a glorious afternoon and if you're not too tired perhaps a gentle stroll around the Botanic Gardens, some of the colleges, along the Backs and then I'll drive you home.'

She melts under his gaze.

'You lead the way Prince Charming. I'll follow obediently although I'll be all eyes and ears. This is one of the most remarkable cities, perhaps almost as beautiful as Stockholm although that would be hard to believe.'

'It would. But the weather's kinder here. Not so much snow.'

She says softly. 'Snow can have its own kind of beauty.'

She likes to have the last word--especially when it concerns home, her home.

Outside abreeze is gentle and sun shines kindly. Since most of central Cambridge is pedestrianised they walk to several colleges including Trinity on St. John's Street, Magdalene beyond Bridge Street, then left into the Bridge of Sighs and along the Backs beside the River Cam and finish at the hotel in Mill Lane.

It's time to set off home; his guest is wilting after her London trip and journey to this strange environment. She needs time to herself--peace and quiet and he knows just the place. He brings the car to the front of the hotel and loads her belongings into the back. Bach music accompanies them as they head out of Victoria Avenue and on to the Ely Road. Throughout the journey she remains quiet. Both weary and excited she lets tiredness get the better of her and gives in to the gentle movement of the car, gentle undulating countryside and gentle music.

Not a word passes between them on the twelve-mile trip to the cottage. A profusion of wisteria hangs over the hall door. It appears to own the area and inspects everyone who passes beneath its arches.

Once inside Karita wakes up instantly. The place is a gem, the kitchen sparkling with every conceivable accoutrement a cook would require, the library with a new personal computer and the sitting room a masterpiece of planned comfort.

She mumbles. 'You've got almost everything a man could need.'

He fails to respond.

And the dining room, although complete and beautiful, looks as if it is rarely used. Apparently the kitchen and sitting room are sole areas of activity.

After the downstairs tour he suggests going upstairs. He takes her suitcase in a firm grip. She's hesitant and doesn't know what to expect. She follows slowly. At the top he turns left and opens a bedroom door overlooking the front of the house with panoramic windows.

'Karita. This is your bedroom,' he says triumphantly, 'double bed and en suite attachment. It has the best view in the house and I hope you have every comfort here. The en suite has recently been decorated.'

She's puzzled and yet pleased at the sheer luxury. After inspecting the room she asks. 'And where is your room John?'

'Don't worry. I'm far away at the back of the house facing the garden. Incidentally the garden is lovely this time of year.'

'I'm sure it is.' She mumbles again.

'Karita.' He looks at his watch. 'It's five o'clock now. Perhaps you'd like a rest for an hour or so. I'll prepare a light meal for around seven and we can discuss our future plans over the next few days. That's the best way forward. You should relax awhile.'

'I will. Thanks John.'

He gently closes the door and is gone.

At seven o'clock Karita comes downstairs rested and refreshed. He's busy in the kitchen; a table has been set with candles and silver and gentle music wafts in from the background. Far better than any hotel, real cosy. He suddenly notices her.

'Please sit over there Karita and leave me to jump up and down when necessary.'

She laughs nervously. 'Need any help?'

'No thanks. Everything's ready. May I pour the wine? White to start with OK?'

'Lovely.'

He says dreamily. 'Better approve or we'll send it back.'

She samples it. 'No need. It's delicious.'

'So we can start.'

'A toast to happy times ahead and successful hunting for striking locations.'

She suddenly remembers. 'On that point John you're going to tell me about our mystery tour--a different place to the others but also in keeping with them.'

He replies. 'The trip to the Isle of Skye especially to see the Black Cuillin.'

'The black what?' She recalls her dream the night before.

'The Black Cuillin is a range of unique mountains. Let me start at the beginning.'

He looks into her eyes and takes a long draft of wine and commences his story.

'The Black Cuillin. According to my research this great mountain range when first seen is one of the most extraordinary sights anywhere. It covers the skyline like a huge castellated fortress--someone called it a glimpse of the Promised Land. Their grandeur is all their own and straight out of the sea. It's actually one enormous mountain massive formed by the folding and buckling of the earth's crust, then a cataclysmic crumpling of the crust allowed the inner contents to protrude upwards to over 10,000 feet. Erosion carved weird patterns of rocks. The raw appearance it has now--it only lasted five million years--started about seventy million years ago. This is relatively recent because the Cuillin hadn't formed until after the age of the dinosaurs. The ice-age then came and produced what we see today.'

Karita cannot contain her excitement.

'The perfect place to finish the battles and struggles and bring resolution and peace.'

A smile appears on his face.

'John let me tell you in as few words what I want to find. It's a place where one can experience adventure in physical and psychological terms, where reality can merge with the imagined, rational feeling with instinct, the clever with the crazy, the impending decision and timelessness side by side. A mixture of fear and excitement and testing each to the limits.'

He laughs over his coffee.

'Karita you're sure to find what you're looking for. I've never known anyone so sure of herself. You certainly know what you want and you'll find it.'

'Do you really think so John?' She asks flatly.

'I'm sure you will. I've no doubt. We should have an early night. Tomorrow we fly to Inverness and get the train to Kyle for the ferry.'

1 6

After spending the afternoon on Skye hill walking in Brittle Gorge it's time for John and Karita to head back to Kinlock. Beyond Sligachen he stops the car facing the sharp features of Glamaig. Déjà vu runs though him as he gazes at the mountain rising 2,500 feet from the ground; it could be Croagh Patrick in Mayo. Grey-white streaks converge towards the cone, and with the afternoon sun they're like golden veins on the back of a giant's hand. The mist on the other mountains grows orange as the minutes race by producing a spellbinding rainbow, which moves gently across its volcanic face.

They watch the colours unfolding. Karita recognises this as a fitting climax to their last day on Skye. A place like no other. Glamaig mesmerises her, no better volcanic cone could she imagine. At any time it could erupt with a blinding explosion like Pompeii centuries ago. Yet it keeps its silence in the intensifying colours of the mellowing sun.

John takes her hand. It's cold and she holds on tightly. They walk along the road and become aware of something vast and immense on the right--out to the west. The awesome sight of the Black Cuillin before sunset is one of the most thrilling experiences. Never so much raw spectacle of dark blue ragged and jagged peaks, of every contortion and convolution, has she seen. Her expression is total amazement and imagination runs riot. All that can be terrible on mountains and high places; scarred ravines leading to towering spires of rock, splinters striking at the sky along their summits, constantly changing but shrouded in mystery and terror. It takes time to adjust, if at all, because of the continual changes.

They walk some way up the Sligachen Glen. It's dark and grim in the hollow of the enclosing mountains and her hand tightens. The sun sets fire to clouds above the jagged spires. This must be the weirdest place anywhere, she says to him. Hallucinations could be commonplace here; it's certainly outside normal experience--similar to Aranmore off Galway yet different. It's surely one of Nature's greatest experiments in atmosphere. There's a feeling of being watched and they hear a rumble of activity underground. The air sobs ghost's stories and legends.

'The fascination of the Cuillin is, I think,' Karita says deliberately, 'something mysterious can be seen everywhere, approached even touched, but never understood. We examine the volcanic rock, follow the glacier lines, we visualise the mighty eruptions, which flung them up from the centre of the earth. Now they appear settled, wrapped in wonder, imagination has covered them in an enigma as thick as mists that can hide them from view. We climb them, pretend to conquer them, knowing they are as far from been conquered as the mountains on Mars.'

They stop in their tracks. They shouldn't go any further. A stream gurgles beside some rocks and she pulls him toward it.

'Let's sit here and absorb the uniqueness of this other world. We'll never have this experience again.'

'You're right Karita. This place is different. It has a terrible beauty all its own. I have no talent for contemplation. But Karita …'

'Are you all right?'

'I'm all right. Never felt better even though I'm sad at leaving tomorrow.'

'Glad you took me here. I thought I was going to shatter a dream by coming here. Instead it has enhanced it a hundred times.'

'That's lovely Karita,' he says, his eyes full of memories. 'There is something else I'd like to say to you.'

She finds her interest quickening. 'Are you worried about something?'

'Not worried,' he chuckles, 'I invited you here so that you could collect material.'

'It's been enormously helpful. I couldn't have done it alone.'

He gives a nervous cough. 'Karita there's another reason for inviting you to Skye.'

She laughs and shakes her head. 'Another reason? What can that be?'

He tries to find the right words. It's an effort.

'I suppose this is as good a place to bring it up. I'll be as open as I can. For some time I've struggled and fought, resisting a longing, an attraction for you. I've fallen in love with you months ago but tried to suppress it for many reasons.'

'Oh poor John.' She kisses him on the cheek. 'I can guess some of the reasons. Perhaps, too soon after Linda, age difference and maybe something you haven't told me.'

He concedes the point, smiling.

'You're right on the first two counts, but there's nothing else I haven't told you.'

She persists stubbornly. 'John I too have feelings; strong feelings and I've always been open with you--never holding back. I have no hesitation in saying I love you deeply, deeply, deeply.'

They kiss and hug closely and tightly.

Then he fumbles in his pocket, takes out a small box and gives it to her. She opens it and beholds a large solitaire diamond ring that sparkles in the sunset.

Her shrill voice surprises him.

'It's lovely John.'

He lifts his head, kneels beside her and looks straight into her eyes.

'Karita in spite of everything I'd like to ask you to be my wife. You don't have to give an immediate answer. Take your time and let me know in due course.'

She laughs with complete abandon, flings her arms around him and kisses him.

A smile lightens her classic face. 'I do not need time. My answer is yes. Completely wholly yes. No dithering, no thinking. Just, yes, yes.'

He's overcome with emotion. The roller coaster of the last few days with this wonderful human being has reinforced his determination to ask the question. And selecting the last night of the holiday is probably the best one he could think of. He considered a climb but anno Domini shook her head implying he should have more sense.

Tomorrow is another day. They have their last night together on this magical island before returning to the real world. As the light fades they return to the hotel; this time Kinlock Lodge in Sleat, the early sixteenth century home of Lord and Lady MacDonald. They are in time for predinner drinks in the beautiful drawing room. He orders a large gin and tonic and a chardonnay for Karita. They are the only guests and choose to sit on the large sofa beside the glowing fire in the white marble fireplace. A young waitress places their drinks on a small oak table and smiles as she glimpses the sparkle from Karita's left hand. The striking red wallpaper over the mantelpiece, the circular gilt mirror with two sentinel lights on each side, the gold inlaid curtains and the light blue plain carpet are all taken in by Karita's photographic memory.

Time for the evening meal.

Next morning the sunlight is reluctant to let them go. They look back from the ferry to a mixture of cloud, sky, shadow, mist and rain. The island has its own peculiar weather system. In front as the ferry docks the smoke of a railway engine beckons them. A slight shiver goes through the vessel when it docks. As they set foot on dry land they are back in the real world again.

Ruth Nolan remains at home as Tom drives Annette back to hospital in Dublin. She is uneasy staying in the house alone. The day is uncertain and changeable--warm in the morning with the sun racing among the clouds. Later cloud rolls in from the east and there is a mutter of thunder. Then sun and shadow again.

A messenger of the storm moves menacingly across the sky. Nevertheless she'll decide to take Patsie for a walk; they're blessed with walks nearby all full of nature. Next door the geese cry as a strong gust of wind wanders about, disturbing them and make their annoyance heard near and far. A grey squirrel darts in front of Ruth, daring her to follow, though not for long. Suddenly he disappears up a willow tree, lies on an outstretched branch and freezes. Patsie barks and it takes time to calm him down.

They walk a mile along the shore. Clouds reappear and stretch in long projections overhead. Raindrops begin to hit her face. She hurries back hoping it will ease off quickly. Thunder explodes above and a shower of hailstones attacks. They make for shelter under the willow tree in a nearby field. The shower passes away and evening puts on a dazzling display of moving light.

They return home a different way. Hedges glisten and glow in the wet evening. Temperatures drop and a mist develops; from a distant sanctuary comes the mournful cry of waterfowl. A splatter of cold water sinks deep, chilling her to the bone when she attempts to break off a branch from a tree.

The porch light is on when they reach home. Fumbling for keys she thinks there's a ghost in front. She glances around and sees a reflection in the window under the porch light. With relief she recognises who the author of the ghost is but the episode adds to her anxiety. She lets herself in and dries her face. The familiar sound of a motorcar grows louder. She frets as she removes wet clothing trying to make herself presentable. He's pale when he enters, the paleness shining through the tan making him sickly. He looks at her with dark eyes full of misery and a kind of childlike despair. Tired and exhausted he says Annette was quite resigned to going back to St. Mary's. The young doctor emphasised chemotherapy was the only way of keeping her stabilised until a suitable donor could be found.

' "and when do you think that might be?" I asked.'

' "Impossible to say, " he replied, ' "it's a waiting game hoping a volunteer will turn up. Appeals are being made all the time. Lots do come forward but nothing suitable for Annette. Not so far. We must keep hoping." '

'We must keep hoping.' Ruth echoes the words almost wondering what they mean. Annette cannot go on forever with repeated courses of chemotherapy. The only real option is marrow transplantation and radiotherapy.

They have to wait. And wait. It is torture. Strange thoughts pass through her mind. The pathetic picture of the dying tree on her walk with Patsie comes back. After the storm she noticed it, examined it covered with ivy, that suave smooth ivy, with its strong fingers around its throat. Trees know how to die and half mentioned it to Patsie.

Tom sits in his chair staring absently into the flames. These weeks and months were also hard on him. Annette's illness is slowly destroying something inside. He's finding it difficult to produce paintings for the gallery and their earnings are not in a healthy state. They're eating into the funds achieved from the one-man show. Won't last forever. Something will have to give.

Annette lies quietly in her isolation unit in St. Mary's. She's trying to get used to this ordeal but each time it gets more difficult. Her parents are good to her and try to visit when possible. Yet it is becoming an increasing strain on them--especially her mother. Before leaving home it was obvious her mother had been crying although she tried to hide it. Such things are hard to hide from those we dearly love. And her father was crumpled up inside when he left the ward. Even Sister Agnes was nice to her, and attentive, but one word lurked in the background to everything they did, everything they felt, and everything they hoped for.

The word nobody used but everybody knew.

Sitting beside the fire Tom and Ruth talk quietly of the past and speculate on the future. As the evening grows older she tells him about her walk, the geese, the squirrel and the icy shower. She says nothing of the dying tree, strangled by the ivy. Life is too full of anxiety.

When she goes to bed she leaves the curtains open and looks out towards the lights on the harbour swaying in the wind, sending their own message back through the mist. The stars convey their torment in trembling shimmers of brightness. But they're too far away to trouble with us. All the great vastness above means nothing, it just roars ahead in its own way, unconcerned about mere mortals and their suffering. It's the here and now must listen, the earth, the people must listen and do something. It is here on earth are sympathy, compassion and hope; the heavens have nothing to offer but distance. Tom says good-night. She replies in resigned sadness.

1 8

John Nicholson returns to Cambridge. Many problems have landed on his desk and most are marked <u>urgent</u>. Karita asks if she could stay a few days more to get her thoughts together and, perhaps, see the city on her own. She can look after herself and even enjoy it more, she suggests impishly, without been told what to do and where to go. She can't stay too long because of her father's illness. She urges him to travel to Stockholm to meet the family and friends again. Who knows--have a wonderful party like only the Isselhergs know how to do?

He promises he will, although there's work, life saving work and he's to act quickly.

He's dumbfounded at the letter from Karen Kelly, the medical student he spent most of a morning explaining transplantation. She'd listened carefully and he hoped he'd convinced her. She seemed enthusiastic but wanted time.

Now the bombshell. She'd thought it over and decided not to

proceed on personal grounds. <u>Personal grounds</u>are underlined, which intrigues John. Such a setback. She was identified as a perfect match for Annette, the same tissue type and genetic make up. What could have gone wrong? Was it his fault he didn't explain the process fully? Was there something she didn't understand? All perplexing questions and with no answers. He'd explained everything as clearly as he could.

Or maybe, just maybe, there's something more sinister. Maybe something on the agenda that remains hidden. He's determined not to give up on a life that easily. He'll ask Karen Kelly, gently and politely, to explain herself and the devastating decision. There must be something happening that goes deeper than a simple refusal or mere whim.

And more's the pity. The three other possible donors are, unfortunately, not close in tissue typing and it would be a risky business to undertake transplantation if the exact marrow donor is already available--but not cooperative.

Something has to give. A resolution has to be found.

Karen Kelly sits glumly in Dr. Nicholson's office. She knew she was going to be sent for and was well prepared. After all he'd explained the procedure clearly and she understood what was involved. With her limited medical knowledge perhaps she understood too well; understood the dangers, the complications and because it was a recent technique the long-term consequences to the donor were unknown. Someone mentioned it was like a kidney transplant. What would she be left with? Possibly a defective bone marrow leading to a defective immune system. Her friends were full of predictions about unforeseen horrors and bridges to be crossed. Even her professor of physiology shook his head; his body language was enough. Answers to her questions were loud and clear. There were other reasons.

'Miss Kelly. How good of you to come and see me again.' John Nicholson rushes in and shakes her hand. He sits beside her and smiles.

'I came as soon as I could because I know it's important to you,' she says gently.

'Yes. And it's more important to our patient. I got your letter and felt that maybe I hadn't explained everything clearly to you.'

'You have Dr. Nicholson. You have indeed. I think I know as much as anyone can tell me. I would love to help … '

'Save a life,' he interrupts.

'Well I'd love to help you--but you see--I'm too frightened to go ahead. Perhaps being a medical student is a disadvantage. You know when reading pathology some imagine they've every disease in the book. I exaggerate, of course, but as they say a little knowledge is a dangerous thing.'

'I see where you are coming from. A lay person would just trust the profession.'

Karen Kelly looks at him trying to communicate her misery.

'Doctor surely there is another donor that can take my place.'

'So far there are three others but none is as perfect a match as you.'

'I see. That's just my bad luck then.'

'Don't put it that way. Some would argue it's good luck that gives them the chance to save another's life. And that's the truth of the matter. So once again I appeal to your inner goodness, your humanity, to let us go ahead.'

Karen Kelly sits straight up and is gripped by fire.

'Dr. Nicholson. I am no saint. You said this is an entirely voluntary procedure.'

'I did and it is.'

She starts crying. 'I'm being coerced into it and made ashamed. I feel awful.'

He remains silent wondering is she a good actor or is this genuine fear. To test the situation further he gives her time to recover.

'Please don't upset yourself Miss Kelly. I understand completely. We'll just have to continue the registry searches.'

'Do please. That would be best,' she agrees enthusiastically and tears disappear dramatically.

She stands up and prepares to leave.

'Before you go, Miss Kelly, may I ask were there any other reasons why you might have refused to go ahead with our request?'

She hesitates and struggles for an answer.

'I had hoped you wouldn't ask that question. I'd prefer not to answer it.'

His is intrigued and presses the issue.

'Please do tell me Miss Kelly. Even though you're reluctant I'd prefer to know everything behind your decision.'

The words come out impulsively. 'All right doctor. I was at the Oxford Union debate on animal research. It was a wonderful evening and the motion was carried. I voted for the motion and I still would today. Your speech condemning this kind of research really did upset me, a very great deal. You had some strong arguments and were able to convince some people, but I'm afraid I'm a traditionalist and can see the best progress is made by research centres doing what they are doing. Your way seemed to me a cop-out, a soft option that a sentimentalist would take.'

He stands aghast at this young but eloquent student. He has many answers for her at his finger tips but feels under the circumstances it would be futile to attempt a conversion. He's reached the end of the road. They both know it.

He puts his hand out and smiles.

'I won't keep you any longer Miss Kelly. You can forget about the situation now and not let it concern you any longer. Just go ahead with your studies and some day I'm sure you'll make a fine doctor.'

'Thank you Dr. Nicholson. It's kind of you to say so. I'll do my best.'

He steps forward and opens the door. 'And Miss Kelly.'

She stops and looks up at him.

'It's almost certain our twelve-year old girl is going to die.'

The search for a suitable donor continues. Dr. Nicholson contacts every registry in the UK again stressing the importance of time. It's running out and this is made obvious in a pleading letter from Professor Kennedy who suggests the Cambridge team might take a risk with a less suitable donor. A dilemma for Nicholson. A huge compromise.

Dr. Winter in haematology reviews the situation and shares the compromise.

'So your prize donor refused to cooperate with you John.' Dr. Winter looks disappointed. 'You know, I'm not surprised. I've little faith in the rectitude of human beings. I've seen it happen all too often. They withdraw almost at the last moment but of course it's their choice. Must be hard to live with one's conscience. I tell students it's like seeing a man drown and deciding to reach out your hand, or not, to save him. Of course there are dangers if you reach out--and it's much easier to run away and let him drown.'

'A good analogy for the man in the street. But I can see Miss Kelly's point of view. This is more involved than giving a pint of blood. One litre of precious marrow fluid is considerable. She's asked around and didn't like the answers.'

Dr. Winter nods. 'The dangers are there and we're only a few years into the technique. Yet there're some very good results. Mustn't forget that.'

'Good results when we use perfectly matched donors, not partially matched. We'll have to continue searching.'

Dr. Winter points a finger and says with a smile.

'Ever thought of submitting yourself John?'

'No. Why?'

'What blood group are you?'

'AB negative.'

'I see.' Dr. Winter sounds interested. He straightens in his chair and colour creeps into his cheeks.

'So is Annette Nolan. She's AB negative. Would you be prepared to have blood taken for tissue typing and matching and a small marrow biopsy? I know it's a long shot but who knows?'

John is taken aback. Looking at other options he has to say.

'I'll do it. Please go ahead and arrange it.'

'Get things rolling straight away, John. Like today--if that's all right with you?'

'Please go ahead. I'll do what I'm told. If unsuitable there's nothing lost. And there's an outside chance we might be lucky.'

Tests are carried out that afternoon and are more extensive than he imagined. Now he's on the receiving end and gets an insight into a patient's anxiety. Blood and marrow samples, bone scans, ECG together with full systems' examination are ordered. Dr. Winter is known to be a thorough physician and he's proving it now. John feels knocked out when it's time to go home. It's for a good cause and he hopes for the best. Karita welcomes him home. She'll be able to stay on a few days.

She gives him a long searching look. 'You look as if you've seen a ghost.'

'No ghost.' He tries to smile and she notices a slight limp in his right leg.

'Did you have an accident or something?'

'No accident.' He collapses into his favourite recliner with a sigh.

'What then? I know something's happened. Is it bad news?'

'No bad news.' He gives a wintry smile.

'Oh John you're exasperating. You really are. You arrive home as pale as a sheet limping your way into the house and collapsing into the first chair you see and you imply nothing has happened. What on earth am I to think?'

He explains, eloquently and at length. She's upset because of the joy in his voice, his eyes, and his every gesture as he tells the sequence of events.

'Karita please forgive me. It's been a most gruelling time since we got back from Scotland. I told you about the tragic twelve-tear old girl who's waiting for a donor transplant. We thought we'd the perfect match but the donor withdrew support ostensibly because she was afraid for herself--that something might go wrong. On further questioning I found there were other reasons. She didn't like what I said at the Oxford Union debate implying I wanted to destroy the best way medicine could progress to find cures for cancer and other diseases. It sounded like a prepared speech and, somehow, I felt her words were not her own--someone else's. It was obvious she supported animal research. My methods, which are still being developed, are quote "a cop-out" and what a sentimentalist would try to think of as a means of getting out of the rat race. All hurtful stuff. And I felt it was intended to hurt.'

Karita stares in shocked surprise. This is an appeal for help from a proud man.

'Poor John. You've been through the wars. Why so?'

He runs a hand through his hair. It's an effort to keep his thoughts in order.

'Dr. Winter came up with the suggestion that because my blood group's AB negative and Annette Nolan is also AB negative there might be a match. So he asked if I'd submit to full testing as a donor. I obviously said yes.'

For a moment she weighs the information and then shrugs.

'Oh John darling. I don't like the sound of this. Not one bit. You may be sacrificing your life for someone who is already dying. Is it worth it? I'd be so worried about you. Something might go wrong.'

'Dr. Winter is a perfectionist. He'll do all the tests as thoroughly as anyone. And I can trust him emphatically.'

Her voice is a masterpiece of understatement.

'John. I am still worried.'

Karita doesn't know what to think. Every time she's troubled she has to keep busy; she lights candles in the sitting room. They usually relax her and have a calming effect. John sits there motionless, watches her lighting matches and holding them to the candles. Light rises quickly in the dimness and then sinks back but not quite. This is repeated around the room.

'Now.' She smiles. 'That's better? The shadows will hypnotise us if we let them.'

'They're lovely Karita but it makes reading difficult.'

'Relax John. Don't bother reading. You've had enough in the last few days. Let's drift and talk while I get a meal together. How about that?'

'Fine. Mozart would also help.'

'I'll switch it on and you close your eyes.'

In the kitchen she tries to work. In the candlelight his profile is visible, head back and eyes closed. The attractiveness of his dark face, which is still a wonder to her, casts a spell. Tenderness over-whelms her; he's vulnerable and needs protection. Underlying it is fear and jealousy. He's going to give part of himself to someone--if the tests are positive--that almost produces a feeling of hatred for the other person. She must not let it happen. He's too precious. He's been promised to her and her alone.

She busies with the meal as best she can but agitation gets the better of her. She drops the saltcellar and spills the milk--twice. He relaxes in a dream world. The meal is enjoyed yet she feels it's a di-saster. Neither makes any comment. They talk about her writing, her plans and her family.

'You must visit us John. My parents would love to see you again. They'll be anxious to see all the arrangements are made for their el-dest daughter.'

'A splendid event.'

'You can be sure of it.'

'Oh dear. I prefer a quiet time.'

'I know you would John. But you're marrying into a family that could help your career go in any direction you want it to go.'

His tiredness lifts. She is carried away with enthusiasm. She's acutely aware of everything, her childhood with the excitement of half growing up in a large country estate, her adolescence and the numerous suitors who had only one thing in common--to annoy and irritate her immensely. She hadn't understood the family as her interest in literature became all absorbing. A full time occupa-tion. Then three years ago John Nicholson entered her life and she was devastated. A lot had happened in that time, sadness, tragedy, loss and release.

Now she's achieved John for herself--a final and complete achievement--and no one is going to take that prize away. No young girl, whoever she is, has priority over her and John. She will not let it happen.

But how is she going to stop him?

Anyway, nothing is certain. It'll take another three days for the results on tissue typing and matching to be completed and she'll be back with her family. So for the time being they're in a state of suspended animation. No options yet, no decisions. She whiles away time playing with the old hourglass, watching the minutes flow by and thinking lots of contingency plans.

The next couple of days are hectic for John but he makes time to leave Karita to the airport for the flight to Stockholm. He has to travel this far with her. It is an emotional goodbye.

He returns home and waits.

The Nolans also wait; Ruth, Tom and Annette and the waiting is unbearable.

'Can nothing be done to hurry them up?' Tom asks Dr. Sutton one day.

'I understand everything possible is being done. I had a telephone call from Dr. Nicholson yesterday. I don't know why he calls me rather than Professor Kennedy.'

'Maybe he can never get Kennedy--always too busy. He probably only gets an obnoxious secretary who takes messages and tells people to write letters.'

'I know. Nicholson says they have found four possible donors so far, but for one reason or other each is not able to proceed.'

'If it is money Dr. Sutton we'd mortgage the house if necessary.'

'It's not money at all. This is an entirely voluntary procedure and because it's voluntary no coercion must enter into it. It is the guideline set down in the transplant registry that works internationally. There cannot be a financial consideration. In other parts of the world certain things do happen that are appalling such as selling kidneys for profit. It's just criminal. And cannot be allowed here.'

'Sorry Dr. Sutton. I shouldn't have mentioned it. Annette is disappearing before our eyes and we're powerless to do anything about it.'

'Perhaps I shouldn't say this but Dr. Nicholson did mention, confidentially, that there's one line of inquiry in Cambridge they are investigating thoroughly. He could not give details and didn't want to raise hopes but it's an indication he's desperately trying to pull out all stops to help Annette. He said so in as many words. He should know in about four days. Then it could be all go. Who knows?'

Tom puts his head in his hands and mumbles something like--if not then it's curtains for the lot of us. Poor Ruth is going downhill with the strain and my work is suffering although that's not important.

'Tom I know what your family is going through. I'm doing everything I can and pushing others that need pushing even though they don't realise it.'

'Dr. Sutton.' Tom takes the doctor's hand and says slowly. 'No matter what the outcome of this, we will never forget your kindness, your humanity and your--I'm lost for words.'

He breaks down in tears. 'Tom. You go home to your wife now. She needs you and you need her. Now go along like a good man.'

2 1

A telephone rings in John Nicholson's office.

'May I speak to Dr. Nicholson please?'

'Speaking.'

'Oh John. That's good. Simon Winter here. The results of the marrow profile have come back. I thought you'd like to see them.'

'I would. How did they match up? Good or bad news?'

Winter hesitates. Why is he evasive?

'It depends on your point of view. Perhaps you should have a look at the print outs.'

He jumps at the idea. 'I'd love to. How about right away?'

'That would suit me fine. See you shortly.'

As John walks through the corridors he's puzzled. The news is either good or bad. As simple as that. He knocks on Winter's door, which is opened by the head of department. 'Please come in. We'll go to the inner office. It's quieter and we won't be disturbed there.'

The office at the back of the department is bright and pleasant although packed tight with papers and books. A familiar sight.

'Please sit and make yourself comfortable. How about coffee?'

'Fine. Thank you.'

John is impatient. Why the formalities, making sure he's comfortable and fussing about coffee? What's the news? Good or bad?

'Let me ask a direct question. Is the donor sample a good or bad match?'

Winter looks straight at him and hands over several sheets of printed material.

He is, as always, the voice of reason. 'John. Your sample is a perfect match. It's so close in most aspects it's hard to believe.'

John's face lights up.

'That's wonderful. At last we've come up with a positive finding for the unfortunate girl. It means we can proceed with transplantation. Isn't that correct?'

'That is correct.' Winter sounds testy. 'The results are amazing. There's really no other word. It's certainly good news for the patient. Does that answer your question?'

'Good news for the patient. That's what I meant.'

Winter looks at his hands trying to avoid eye contact. His concern becomes obvious as he skates around the issue. 'And is it good news for you?'

John begins to have doubts but doesn't know why. His answer is uncertain.

'It's unexpected. I didn't think things would turn out this way. Is it good news for me? It is good news for me. It means I can now help save someone's life.'

A reluctant smile dawns on Simon's face. 'You mean that John?

Have you considered the implications, pitfalls, complications and possible failures?'

John answers mildly. 'I should be in a better position than most.'

Winter is persistent. 'And you still wish to proceed?'

John senses caution, as if he's trying to tell him something but holding back. He moves uneasily in his chair.

'I get the feeling you're worried about something and you're not telling everything. Maybe you're too good a physician and being cautious with the whole truth.'

Winter replies gravely.

'There's some truth in that. Obviously I'm delighted for the patient. Now she'll have a fighting chance, whereas up to now the prognosis was bad. My only concern is for you. This is a new technique and we're improving all the time.'

Reason, frozen into calculation, now tells John he has no one to blame but himself. 'I see. But I think it's worth taking a chance.'

Simon sips thoughtfully at his coffee.

'Of course it is. I wouldn't express my caution so openly to a layperson, to someone I didn't know and that's quite an admission. But you--John--are a valued colleague, a respected physician and brilliant research worker. Your work, your health and your life are important to medical science and I'm speaking as a friend as well as a colleague.'

Winter waits in silence for a response. It comes slowly and in a considered way.

'You're too kind. And I appreciate what you say.'

Perhaps there's still another way. He offers an easy way out.

'We could wait and keep searching for another donor.'

'What's to be gained? Nothing except we'd be losing valuable time.'

'I can see you are determined to proceed.'

'Simon, give me twenty-four hours to come up with a final decision.'

'Of course. Let me know tomorrow and if it's still yes we'll set everything in motion. We'll send for the patient immediately. Treatment will take two weeks and even though you know this I have to warn you if you decide to withdraw at any time during these two weeks the patient is almost certainly going to die.'

'I realise that. I'll have to stay as healthy as possible up to the time of transfer.'

'You will be confined to barrier nursing for two days at least after harvesting of your marrow and you should take two weeks off work afterwards.'

John realises the implications of the procedure--things could be awkward.

'I know the registry requires that donor / recipient be confidential. But the Nolans must not be told who the donor is. That's the rule. Correct?'

'Correct. And they're very strict about it especially with regard to the patient.'

'Why so?'

'For two simple reasons. If everything goes all right an embarrassing situation could arise that could be unwelcome to the donor. But more importantly if things went wrong then we're into the blame game. And you know how much the legal profession feeds on that kind of situation. The registry has advised no contact for two years. That should give time for any emotional dust to settle and, hopefully, for the patient to be well on the way to recovery. One last thing, John, permission for recipient to contact donor should only be allowed if both parties agree to it.'

'The situation has been well thought out--for lay people. There's one snag as far as I'm concerned. The Nolans will know that I'm in charge of Annette's treatment here with my colleagues. If I have to disappear at the most crucial period and someone else takes over, the family are going to be upset. This happened before in Dublin and the child was put under the care of a not too kind colleague. I'm picking my words.'

'Don't worry John. From the start all of us will take part in her care and you can say that Dr. Winter, as head of haematology and the transplant unit, is in overall charge. For heavens sake don't say anything about disappearing for two weeks. Just let it happen. Maybe it won't even be noticed. If it is we'll think up some good excuse.'

'That's a relief. It would be embarrassing if no explanation were given. Perhaps I could get diplomatic 'flu or something.'

'Diplomatic 'flu would be appropriate. One last question. I've a lot of forms to fill in about reasons and medical history. You might help me with one. It is simply: "Why does the donor wish to proceed with the transplant even though it is completely confidential?"'
'Why was that question asked? It sounds a bit intrusive to me. There must be many reasons. A simple answer would be to help our fellow human beings. That's too wishy-washy, too vague. Not for me. It is a wish to pay something back for mistakes that I have made. Would that be enough?'

Simon smiles. 'More than enough. It's just a silly question thought up by some busybody who's too inquisitive for his or her own good.'

He stands up and holds out a hand. 'I think we've covered everything now. Have a final think about it tonight and let me know. After that there's no turning back.'

John leaves the office a lot wiser than an hour ago.   He needs more time.

There's a lot on his mind as he drives home that evening. He expected the decision to be straightforward--good match, good result for all concerned--and be redeemed back into the world of the living again, doing good and helping people. After the awakening with Simon Winter an unwelcome dilemma enters his mind and will not go away. His heart rings with fear, unexpected and unwanted. Years ago he learned when Linda was taken away for major surgery he was entirely alone. It's that feeling again.

When we are going through our deepest crises in life we usually experience them alone, in solitude. Maybe that's good. Whatever conclusion is reached it must come from inside. Still a crisis for him alone. He dares not telephone Karita. He knows the answer--self-preservation at all costs, forget about anyone else. He's the most important person to her and maybe he is and she's telling the truth. He's desperate to do the right thing, not least himself, not even Karita, and--by God--he tried against all odds to save poor Linda. And he had succeeded. But fate put paid to that. Fate had its own way with things. And there was no way one could influence it.

He pulls on his boots and decides on one of those walks along the country paths where only Nature talks eloquently without interference. The evening is getting dark and misty but he presses on. Normally he knows the way through the woods but a gathering mist adds to the confusion. He goes down a hill and stumbles over unfamiliar rocks and stones. He's lost and there's no one about. Where's he going? No matter, he'll move on until he finds the path again. An opening, a copse gives some degree of space and relief and he finds the path again. But his mind goes dark once more.

Suddenly he reaches the main road; the struggling through the forest has confused him but he's back on the main road again. Now which direction to go? Just walking and guessing would resolve nothing. He has to find the right direction, to make the right decision to get home. For a while he stands on the roadside in the mist and darkness. He does not know where he is. It's a strange sensation to be in, his heart beating.

He's alone and he's lost.

2 2

Shadows move in endless pursuit in the library of Kunsangen House, candles dance in drifting air and words chase one another across pages as a lone and graceful figure sits at a desk beside the French windows. Karita is engrossed as stories of courage valour pride conquest grief and sadness flow from her pen. The grief is real; she's going through it not just on the written page, but breathing, feeling and experiencing it.

She has spoken to John on the telephone. The decision has finally been made to proceed. He is the official donor and everything is ready. Her father, who'd always told the truth about everything, shares her concern and feels John should wait for another donor. John argued this had already taken up too much valuable time. Time spills a swifter sand each day echoed in his mind when, years ago, he was involved in trying to save Andrew Baker's life.

But Karita knows nothing of that. Maybe it is just as well because time did finally spill the last sands for him, unexpectedly, when he was well on the way to recovery. Chemotherapy was less successful then.

She stops work and wipes her eyes. She thought she'd found her prince and, as in her fiction, things would turn out. No ugly facts allowed to intrude. The decision is made and her intuition tells her he's probably already doomed. His decision though, not hers. He's willing to condemn himself to it, a commitment to a relationship with another human--to give precious life blood-forming tissue and lots of it.

Her father, who is aware how determined John can be, then advises her to enter a bond of trust and love with this brave man and ultimately with the unfortunate girl he's attempting to save--if the need arises. Yet in spite of all she cannot accept it. There is a numbness in her, a strangeness not experienced before. She had her own way at all times in life and even in her fiction she can influence the way things turn out--just as she wants them to do.

John advised her to stay away for at least two to three weeks. It would be less complicated and easier in a difficult situation. The unthinkable words--marriage or not--creep into her unsettled mind and the only answers are more tears on her cheeks.

The little cottage beside the harbour in Greystones and seashore is empty and locked up. It looks sad forlorn and neglected. The Nolans have left and Patsie lies pining away beside a warm fire in a kind neighbour's house.

2 3

John Nicholson is the first to meet the Nolan family when they arrive in the children's ward in Addenbrooke's. A special barrier nursing room is waiting for the patient and before settling in he invites them to his office to explain procedures.

He speaks directly to Annette. After all it's her life that's in the balance. They have found a close donor and they are now ready to get rid of the 'bad' cells in her body by X-rays and drugs. This will take two weeks and a donor will give new marrow fluid by a special technique--called transfer--to completely take over.

'And who is this wonderful person that's going to give me the transplant?'

'We can't tell you Annette. These are rules and there are reasons for sticking to them.'

'I see. But maybe some day I'll find out.'

'Perhaps in two years if both parties agree.'

Annette says weakly. 'That is if I'm alive in two years, Dr. Nicholson.'

John smiles confidently at her.

'Of course you will Annette. This technique has had great successes over the years. And you're going to be the next. Other arrangements have been made including accommodation for your mother nearby and your dad, if he wants it. But I believe he's to go away for a while. That's all right as long as mum will be with you.'

'And will you come and see me every day Dr. Nicholson? I do hope so. We all trust you so much especially after Professor Kennedy.'

'Of course I'll try. But you must remember the process in a team effort. There is Dr. Winter who will talk to you and the team of surgeons who'll actually operate. So there'll be new faces coming and going. Annette you're not to be frightened by anyone here. Everyone's kind and highly trained. This is probably one of the best units in the country.'

'I know. I'm so lucky. But I'm also terrified when the big treatment starts. I believe it can be exhausting and awful.'

Ruth holds her hand.

'Darling Annette. I'll be here all the time and so will Dr. Nicholson and all the others. Two weeks could be a short period. You'll see.'

Annette tries to see the reality of the ordeal. 'It could also be a lifetime.'

'It could,' John nods, 'but it won't. Now can I suggest you and mum and dad go to the room set aside and the special care nurse will explain everything to you.'

Annette walks straight over to John, holds out her hand and

takes his firmly.

'I believe everything you've said and I trust you completely with my life.'

'Thanks Annette. With luck we'll pull through. Get familiar with your new room.'

Next morning Dr. Winter visits the Nolans and spends time with them. He emphasises he is head of the transplant unit and will be directing procedures on a day-to-day basis. Others will have their roles to play including Dr. Nicholson but the treatment requires intricate teamwork and they must understand that. Of course they do! They will submit to what's required without question.

Day one of Annette's treatment is combined radiotherapy and chemotherapy. It makes her terribly sick. For this alone medication is required. John looks in on her in the evening, when through her misery she manages to smile and wants to touch his hand. It isn't possible because of nursing restrictions.

He then drives home in his red sports car in a strange state of mind. A fight for life has begun in earnest today and this will probably be the last battle the little girl will ever have to make. He has a secret admiration for this tempestuous family especially the father. Ruth is stoical and courageous and Annette is capable of much self-control even though her suffering must be unbearable. Over the next two weeks there's no doubt her endurance and tolerance will be put to extreme tests.

However stoicism doesn't end there. Dr. Winter allows John Nicholson's pioneering in vitro chemotherapy agents to be included in the protocol and, of course, John's marrow will be the replacement for Annette's. So he has a double interest in the outcome of this case of acute leukaemia in a patient in whom the prognosis some years ago would almost be a hundred per cent fatal.

Time at Addenbrooke's ticks away as routinely as ever; people come and go with fractures and complaints and many other problems and everything runs smoothly. And yet the following two weeks are a time of great tension for some in the little isolation ward in which a small underweight, yet beautiful, girl longs patiently for the sands of time to continue flowing and never to stop.

In this small corner of the children's department a degree of high drama is unfolding. As Annette continues with her treatment bigger doses of X-rays are applied. Her hair falls out and the drugs make her violently sick. She cannot eat or keep anything down. Ruth becomes increasingly agitated and at times fears the onslaught is rapidly killing her daughter. Witnessing the effects of this destruction terrifies her and she feels on the verge of a nervous breakdown.

In desperation she goes to see Dr. Nicholson one afternoon to vent her anger. He is not there. No one knows where he is. She breaks down completely. This couldn't happen at a worse time--at a time she needs him most. This is impossible. How could he do this? How cruel?

2 5

Annette's treatment is relentless. Her short life seems to be coming
to an end. She's going to die. Generalised pain absorbs all her attention and leaves her indifferent to the outside world. Consciousness
ebbs and flows as does light and darkness. Increasingly a silence
comes over her and she becomes less aware of surroundings. Her
mother is there but she has no energy to talk, she has no words to
say. Pain is gradually replaced by a lassitude, almost a paralysis,
and she has to be helped to move in bed. She hasn't the energy or
will to do anything. A void is lurking inside in the darkness tearing her apart and then there is silence--for a while. She tries not to
complain as she is vaguely aware of her mother's tears during lucid
intervals and then darkness comes again.

   Time is erratic, it races it drags and confuses and then disappears down strange tunnels. After moments of terrifying images
she emerges into the light again and sees familiar faces, her mother
and father. She tries to smile at them but cannot. She tries to lift a

hand but cannot. She smiles with her eyes and knows.

In some ways the trauma of treatment is worse for parents who witness the destruction, the gradual wilting away of their precious daughter. Ruth's despair is overwhelming as she struggles with simple things. She feels Annette's pain as her own; she shares her nightmares. At times she wanders about the wards and grounds of the hospital, staring at everything and seeing nothing. She rarely speaks to people now especially since Dr. Nicholson has disappeared and no one is able to say exactly why. Sister did hint that he had come down with a bad attack of influenza and would probably be back in a few days.

Because she rarely speaks she has no communication with the world. She finds it hard to think. A fierce tension consumes her like a prisoner. She becomes passive and quietly submits to everything that has to be done. Tom helps her and Annette even though words are almost useless. Towards the end of the two weeks Annette has drifted more and more out of life and the time for the operation arrives. Tom and Ruth now only have Annette's empty bed and time for company. Nothing more. Yet the experience of these weeks has changed him profoundly. He finds humanity alike everywhere. It is a strain and even an enlightenment. There are no straightforward answers to his questions anymore. He will have to go in a certain direction shortly, to find relief. He'll have to change. His previous ideals have become more difficult to maintain and he has to live in the real world. Not an ideal world. Circumstance has exerted a pressure as if a void occupied the centre of time. That has to go. He's to face reality. And live again.

2 6

Six weeks later three figures stand together in the main hallway of Addenbrooke's Hospital. Tom, Ruth and Annette Nolan all have their suitcases packed and are waiting patiently for someone. Gillian said he would be down in five minutes.

True to his word John Nicholson walks down the main stairs holding on to the rail for support and goes straight over to the Nolans.

It is time to say goodbye.

Annette is the first to respond. She rushes forward and completely uninhibited holds out both arms, reaches up and hugs him with all her might. She then kisses him on the cheek and whispers loudly.

'I owe my life to you Dr. Nicholson. I will never forget you for as long as I live. So thank you. Thank you. Thank you.'

Ruth is a little hesitant, as she feels ashamed of her behaviour during the crucial two weeks. That is all behind her now.

'Dr. Nicholson all I can say is thank you for your perseverance and dedication. We know without it Annette would not be alive today. You have given back to us the most beautiful gift in the world. You have given us back our family.'

Tom, who has been standing in the background, is last to step forward. All the old animosity is gone, all the aggression and anger. He glows compassion and gratitude to be given back, as he puts it, given back his own life--a life he can now feel proud to live.

He looks straight and hard at John, still holding his hand firmly.

'Dr. Nicholson. I want you to make us, the Nolan family, a firm promise. I want you to give the wonderful human being who was donor for our daughter a great big hug as I am going to do now. Will you promise that?'

'I promise,' John replies.

Tom Nolan gives John Nicholson a wonderfully tender and long hug of affection and gratitude as if in so doing he is trying to say, without words, that he already knows the hug has been delivered.

Back in the cottage on the A 10 on the way to Ely Karita Isselherg looks at her watch and mumbles.

'John will be home soon. I must light the candles for him.'

ISBN 1425177787-5